You
and
No Other

FRANCIS RAY

St. Martin's Paperbacks

YOU AND NO OTHER

Copyright © 2005 by Francis Ray.

Cover photo © Pure / Nonstock

ISBN: 0-312-98678-5
EAN: 80312-98678-0

Printed in the United States of America

St. Martin's Paperbacks edition / March 2005

St. Martin's Paperbacks are published by St. Martin's Press, 175 Fifth Avenue, New York, NY 10010.

10 9 8 7 6 5 4 3

To all my readers who have waited for Morgan Grayson's story. This one is for you.

Dear Readers:

I deeply appreciate your patience and support while you waited for *You and No Other* to continue the Graysons of New Mexico series. Your e-mails and letters made this possible. My thanks to you and to Monique Patterson, my editor at St. Martin's, who had the final call.

I trust that you will enjoy getting to know Morgan and Phoenix as well as being reacquainted with characters from *Until There Was You*. Believe me, I heard you loud and clear in your desire to know if Catherine would have a baby and what happened between Naomi and Richard. Please keep reading and you'll find out. Up next is Brandon's story, *Dreaming of You*.

Please visit my Web site to find my other titles and sign up for my mailing list. I look forward to seeing many of you when I go on tour this summer.

Have a wonderful life,
Francis Ray
P.O. Box 764423
Dallas, TX 75376

www.francisray.com
e-mail: francisray@aol.com

THE GRAYSONS OF NEW MEXICO—THE FALCONS OF TEXAS

Cousins by marriage—friends by choice
Bold men and women who risk it all for love

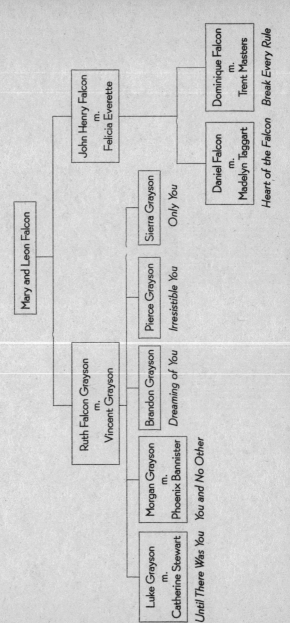

Mary and Leon Falcon

Ruth Falcon Grayson
m.
Vincent Grayson

John Henry Falcon
m.
Felicia Everette

Luke Grayson
m.
Catherine Stewart

Until There Was You

Morgan Grayson
m.
Phoenix Bannister

You and No Other

Brandon Grayson

Dreaming of You

Pierce Grayson

Irresistible You

Sierra Grayson

Only You

Daniel Falcon
m.
Madelyn Taggart

Heart of the Falcon

Dominique Falcon
m.
Trent Masters

Break Every Rule

You
and
No Other

Prologue

Ruth Grayson had made a mistake.

It was difficult for a mother to admit, but there it was, staring her in the face. Shelby Hendrix was gazing up at Morgan with what could only be described as rapt adoration as they made their way to the buffet table during the wedding reception of Ruth's oldest son, Luke, and his bride, Catherine. Shelby's reaction, pardon a mother for thinking so, was to be expected.

Morgan, her second child and son, was a handsome man. As always, he was dressed impeccably, but the black tailor-made Armani tuxedo he wore gave him a rakish, suave distinction that had woman after woman turning her head to get a second and often a third glance. And if a woman had the good fortune to catch his attention, he had a way of looking at her with those midnight black eyes of his that assured her she had his undivided attention.

Heady for any woman, but made more potent when it came from a man as commanding as Morgan. The look in turn could be awe inspiring, intimidating, or comforting, depending on his mood and the recipient. He was a lawyer after all and, from the way his private practice was thriving, an excellent one. But then, Morgan had always excelled at everything he did. He had a single-minded determination that refused to accept defeat.

Ruth sighed and shook her head, causing the wide brim of her sky blue straw hat to sway. She detested hats, but it had been necessary for the garden wedding. She lifted her hand to remove it, then felt a prickling sensation at the base of her neck. Even before she turned she knew who she'd see. Less than ten feet away was her sister-in-law, Felicia Falcon, staring at her with an understanding but adamant gaze.

The hat stayed.

Ruth withdrew her hand. Felicia's fashion sense was impeccable. She'd come from one of the wealthiest and most influential African-American families in Boston. Ruth's parents had been dirt-poor Native American Muscogee farmers from Oklahoma, but the two women were extremely close, that bond strengthened by the love of Felicia's husband and Ruth's brother, John Henry, and their children. Ruth didn't worry for a moment that her five children, Catherine, her new daughter-in-law, or her high-profile parents would disapprove of her being hatless, but there were over five hundred people in the ballroom of the Four Seasons Hotel in Beverly Hills to consider.

Her sigh came again, this time heavy and long-suffering as she waved away a tanned young man with a tray of sparkling mineral water and champagne. Her attention returned to her second born. You'd think with all the eligible women who had to be in a crowd this large Morgan would find one he was attracted to. But no, not him. Ruth barely refrained from gritting her teeth as she watched Morgan lead a smitten Shelby back to their table. Behind the polite gaze he was bestowing upon her was utter boredom. That wasn't what Ruth had hoped for when the two of them met earlier that evening.

Shelby was beautiful, sophisticated, and intelligent, and she had her own public relations firm in St. Louis. According to Shelby's mother, a soror of Ruth's, Shelby enjoyed the arts, the finer things in life, and had an eclectic taste in music just as Morgan did.

But the sparks weren't there between them. Ruth might have been a widow for twenty-five years, but she could still remember the wild leap of her heart, the giddy excitement, when she first met Vincent. You might fight the powerful attraction, the sensual pull, as she had done, but thank goodness her heart and Vincent's dogged determination had been stronger than her will. They had had ten wonderful years together before the Master of Breath and God took him. But the warm memories would remain forever.

With a sinking heart Ruth watched as Morgan, so like his father, turned his head and stared straight at her, a small knowing smile curving his lips. The smile grew as he tipped his dark head in silent acknowledgment of his winning this round. Even as annoyance swept through Ruth, she found herself smiling and conceding defeat. She had raised intelligent, quick-thinking children, and she couldn't help but be proud of them.

But Morgan should remember that he'd inherited his determination from her as well. Once she set her mind on something, she never backed off until it was completed to her satisfaction. She'd just have to adjust and reevaluate. She only had to glance across the room and see how happy Luke and Catherine were to strengthen her resolve. Luke wasn't happy at first, either, about her matchmaking. Now he couldn't stop smiling. He was so proud of Catherine and so much in love with her. Catherine felt the same about him. Their road to happiness hadn't been an easy one, but that only served to make them enjoy the results all the more.

All of her children deserved to be happily married. Since Morgan, Brandon, Pierce, and Sierra were still dragging their feet, it was her duty as their mother to correct the matter. Felicia had the good fortune to have her children, Daniel and Dominique, already blissfully wed. Ruth would see that hers found the same fulfillment.

Turning away from Morgan's pleased expression, Ruth began to circulate among the guests. Let him enjoy his victory tonight. His day was coming.

Morgan would be next to walk down the aisle. Not as the best man, but as the groom.

I

Morgan Grayson was in serious trouble.

Long, elegant fingers tapped out a synchronized beat on the steering wheel of his two-seater sports car as Aretha Franklin's unmistakable voice demanded respect. Morgan knew just how the lady felt.

Easing around the slow-moving Suburban, Morgan resisted the urge to press his foot down on the accelerator and take some of his growing frustrations out with a fast drive. The twisting roads beneath the Sangre de Cristo Mountains outside of Santa Fe were unforgiving when it came to fools and speeding vehicles. Morgan wasn't a fool, so he contented himself by increasing the volume of the CD and returned to pondering his problem.

His loving, stubborn, matchmaking mother.

Ruth Grayson had singled him out as the next one of her children to marry off. After she'd thrown Shelby in his path two weeks ago at Luke's wedding, Morgan had erroneously thought she'd need a little more time to regroup. After all, she had enlisted the help of her friends and associates from around the country in looking for a wife for Luke. Knowing she was too sensitive to thrust the same women at him anytime soon, Morgan thought he was safe. But she had out-witted him.

For him, she was staying local.

Last week, when he'd picked up his dry cleaning, he'd even heard there was a jackpot—a little some-thing so the lucky winner could have a blowout bache-lorette party. This morning he had stopped by his mother's house for breakfast and three of her single female colleagues from St. John's College, where she taught music in the graduate program, were there. You'd think she would be subtler or the women would have more pride. But no! They all acted as if this were some type of game. Unfortunately, he was the prize.

His mother had married off Luke, just as she pre-dicted. As the second born, Morgan was next. In the past he had always been pleased that he was next in line. No longer. Brandon, Pierce, and Sierra were con-stantly urging him to hold out. *Demanding* might be a more apt word. His younger brothers and sister didn't have to worry. He had no intention of getting married.

He was happy for Luke, and Catherine was a fan-tastic woman, but marriage wasn't in his plans. His law practice was his mistress and he liked it that way. The woman hadn't been born who would make him even think about getting serious. But his mother wasn't listening to him.

His fingers flexed on the steering wheel as he

wondered how Luke had coped, but since he and Catherine had been holed up in his mountain cabin since they returned a few days ago from their honeymoon in Bali, Morgan couldn't ask him. Probably just as well, Morgan thought as he came over a rise and saw the black iron gate of the Hendersons' ranch that signaled he was almost at his destination. Luke was an unwanted reminder that their mother had been right in her choice for her firstborn.

Slowing down, Morgan turned into the paved driveway and saw the white stucco ranch house at the end of the winding mile-long road. The red tiled roof gleamed in the bright morning sunlight. The aspen leaves were thick and shimmering with life, the air scented with the last, lingering scents of wildflowers. It was a beautiful fall day. Too bad he couldn't enjoy it.

Stopping in the circular driveway in front of the heavily carved red double doors, he cut the motor. The BMW roadster purred to a polite silence. He smiled. He'd always been a sucker for cars. He enjoyed the finer things in life and worked long, demanding hours in a job he loved to afford them. With his thriving law practice, his life was perfect in every way but one. His mother.

Thrusting his mother's matchmaking schemes from his mind, Morgan picked up the hand-stitched leather attaché case from the seat beside him and got out. He had business to take care of. Besides, he could handle any woman she pushed in his path.

Closing the door, he started up the walkway lined with purple sage. The neigh of a horse followed by the throaty laughter of a woman caused him to pause and turn toward the sound. He was just in time to see an elegantly shaped woman take a huge roan stallion smoothly over one six-foot rail, then another. Since Morgan had a fondness for women *and* horses, he watched the riveting combination of grace and beauty.

The woman's long legs were encased in tan jodhpurs pressed tightly against the animal's gleaming flanks as she guided him over another obstacle. It took strength, skill, and control to handle such a big, powerful animal and make it appear effortless. Morgan idly wondered if the woman was that controlled in bed or was as wild and as tantalizing as her laughter had been.

"Excuse me, sir. May I help you?"

The heavily accented voice effectively ended Morgan's speculations and his idle thought of finding out. Pleasure never outweighed business. Pushing the woman from his mind, he turned.

"Yes. I'm Morgan Grayson. I'm here to see Mr. Duval. He's expecting me."

The dark, austere face of the elderly servant dressed in unrelieved black became no less stern at Morgan's announcement. His closely cropped head of gray hair inclined slightly. "Yes, Mr. Grayson. Mr. Duval is expecting you. This way, please."

Morgan followed the man, his gait slow and deliberate, inside the rambling one-story ranch house. The interior was cool, the furniture sleek and ultramodern. Morgan knew the couple who owned the house but seldom lived there. They preferred the Mediterranean this time of year and saw the house as a tax write-off. Thanks to the investment advice of Morgan's brother Pierce, they were able to enjoy their retirement in style.

Crossing the slate gray carpeted floor, the servant knocked briefly on the heavily carved mahogany door. "Mr. Duval. Mr. Grayson is here."

"Send him in," commanded a curt male voice.

"Yes, sir." Standing to the side of the door he opened, the servant closed it as soon as Morgan walked through. Morgan saw Andre Duval turn from looking out the window, then take a seat behind his desk. Not by word or look did he acknowledge Morgan. Thankful that his business with Duval would be brief, Morgan crossed the polished oak floor and extended his hand.

"Good afternoon, Mr. Duval. It's a pleasure to meet you." He didn't even wince at the lie.

Duval ignored the hand and stared unflinchingly back at Morgan. "You're late."

Morgan's own eyes narrowed. He'd heard that Duval, a renowned sculptor, was temperamental. Apparently he was also rude. Slowly Morgan twisted the hand he had extended and glanced at the face of the eighteen-karat Rolex on his wrist. "I'm seven and a half minutes early."

"Where are the papers I'm to sign?"

Not even by a flicker of his thick lashes did Morgan show his irritation. If Duval were his client, he'd walk. He wasn't. He was the client of the Lawson & Lawson law firm in Boston. Kenneth Lawson, the senior partner, had been Morgan's mentor as well as his professor when he attended Harvard. He was now a good friend. Morgan respected and liked the crafty Lawson too much to disappoint him. His firm would get a sizable commission once Duval signed the contract to have *Courage,* the best of his earlier works, reproduced for limited editions. Besides, a lawyer learned early to deal with unpleasant people and unavoidable situations.

"May I?" Morgan asked, lifting the briefcase over the highly polished surface of the immaculate desk.

The affirmative nod from Duval was also curt.

Placing the case on the desk, Morgan opened it and handed copies of the two contracts to Duval. A black-gloved right hand emerged from beneath the desk, took the papers, and laid them carelessly aside. Cold brown eyes never left Morgan.

"You can leave now."

Morgan snapped his briefcase shut with a distinctive click. "If you have any questions I'd be happy to answer them. I understand you were expected to sign today and I could overnight them to Mr. Lawson."

"You understood wrong." Duval stood. His left hand was already in the coat pocket of his loosely constructed black jacket. He slipped his right into the other pocket. "Good-bye."

Morgan knew when he had been dismissed. He pulled a card from inside the jacket of his wheat-colored suit and placed it in the middle of the desk. "In case you need to reach me. Good-bye." Lifting the briefcase off the desk, he turned to leave.

A brief knock sounded on the door before it swung open. Bubbling laughter preceded the striking young woman into the study. "Andre—" She stopped her headlong dash, her smoky gray eyes widening on seeing Morgan. For a long moment she simply stared.

Morgan was doing the same. She was even more exquisite up close. "Hello."

"Hello," she murmured a bit breathlessly, then turned to Andre. "I'm sorry. I came in the back from the stable. I didn't know you had a guest."

"No matter, my dear. Mr. Grayson was just leaving."

Morgan noted Duval's voice had lost its sharpness and now almost crooned. Morgan could well understand why. If the woman's whiskey voice didn't get you, the smoky gray eyes and pouting lips would. She had the kind of face that a man would go to his grave remembering and a lush, curvaceous body created to satisfy any fantasy.

She flushed beneath her golden skin at Morgan's open appraisal. All that sex appeal and she could still blush. Innocence and carnality, an alluring and dangerous combination. Was she La Flame, the mysterious woman reported to be the inspiration and reason for Duval's sculptured pieces to have regained their fire and vitality after a seven-year absence from the art world? It would certainly explain his rush to get rid of Morgan.

Duval had an unimpeded view of the front of the house and the stable from the window in his study. It was safe to assume he had seen Morgan watching the vibrant young woman and hadn't approved.

Morgan smiled. Living on the edge kept a man sharp. "Mr. Duval, I didn't know you had a daughter."

"She's not," Andre snapped.

A smile tugging the corners of her enticing mouth, the woman came farther into the room. "I think Mr. Grayson is teasing, Andre."

"Phoenix, Morgan Grayson," Andre introduced them, obviously annoyed at having to do so.

"Hello, Mr. Grayson."

Morgan's large hand closed over the small, delicate one she extended and he noted the slight roughness of her palms. The unexpected contrast pleased him almost as much as the slight leap in her pulse at the base of her throat, the widening of her beautiful eyes. "Hello, Phoenix."

Moistening her lips, she withdrew her hand. He'd bet the farm that she wasn't the nervous type. Interesting. "Would you like something to drink?" she asked, her voice a fraction huskier than it had been.

Very interesting. "No—"

"Thank you, dear, but Mr. Grayson was just leaving," Andre interrupted. "Besides, you need to change after riding."

Embarrassment replaced the warmth in her face. Her hand fluttered across the front of her wrinkled white blouse, then down the side of her dusty jodhpurs. "Please excuse my appearance. I was so excited about Crimson settling in so well, I didn't think."

Morgan's own smile increased to put her at ease. Twin dimples he had always detested winked. "No apology needed. It was a pleasure watching you ride."

The corners of her very tempting mouth curved upward again. "Crimson did all the work."

"Since I ride, I know better."

"Phoenix," Andre called, his voice tight. "You really need to change out of those clothes, and don't forget to remind Cleo that we won't be dining in tonight."

Her eyes flashed; her body tensed. Morgan had seen the same thing happen when his sister, Sierra, became angry. The quiet before the storm. Morgan waited for Phoenix to tell the bossy Duval to take a flying leap.

Instead, in the next breath, she seemed to retreat before Morgan's eyes, leaving only the facade and none of the brilliance of the vivacious woman who had entered the room. It was as if a shade had been placed over a bright flame. Again Morgan wondered what the relationship between the two was.

"Of course, Andre. Good-bye, Mr. Grayson."

"Good-bye, Phoenix," he said, unable to keep the disappointment out of his voice that she was leaving and that she hadn't stood up to Duval. The door closed softly behind her.

"I'll show you out." Coming from around the desk, Andre led the way out of his study. As soon as they emerged, the same servant Morgan had seen earlier appeared. The elderly man reached the front door seconds before Duval stepped onto the terrazzo entryway. Despite the man's stiff left leg, Andre had not slowed in his haste to rid himself of Morgan.

Hands stuffed into the pockets of his jacket, Andre stood to the side as Morgan passed. "I'll mail the contracts directly back to Kenneth. There is no need to trouble you driving all the way back out here."

Morgan stopped in the middle of the stone walkway and turned. Duval wouldn't care if Morgan slow-roasted on a spit. They both knew it. He wondered why Duval even bothered to lie and then caught a movement . . . a flash of white behind him. *Phoenix*.

Inclining his head in acknowledgment, Morgan opened the car door, tossed his briefcase onto the passenger seat, then got in. Driving away, he again wondered exactly what the relationship was between Duval and Phoenix. Neither gave out signals of their being lovers, but that didn't mean they hadn't been intimate.

Morgan might not like the snobbish man, but he was well respected and wielded a great deal of influence in the art world. Certain women were attracted to that type of man. But for some odd reason Morgan didn't think Phoenix was that kind of woman. In his profession he had learned to read people quickly and accurately. Users weren't guileless and they certainly didn't blush.

Flipping on the signal, Morgan pulled onto the highway and headed back toward Santa Fe. He didn't like puzzles. He liked even less the pompous way Duval had treated Phoenix. Before the roadster had gone another mile Morgan knew he was going to find out exactly what was going on between the two.

"I thought I'd find you in here."

Phoenix turned from slipping on her smock to see

Andre enter the studio. Bright sunlight streamed through the three floor-to-ceiling windows behind her. The rays weren't kind to Andre. They sought out every line in his sixty-five-year-old face and delineated his thin frame. Unbidden came the contrasting and very vivid image of Morgan Grayson's muscular body.

The moment she'd seen Andre's visitor, she had been captivated by the intensity of his gaze, the raw masculinity his expensive suit couldn't hide. There had been something untamed and noble about him. Instinctively she'd known he'd make a good friend or a dangerous enemy.

"You aren't annoyed with me, are you?" Andre persisted.

She took her time buttoning the faded smock. They both knew it wouldn't matter if she were, just as they both knew he wasn't going to change. He was an artistic genius with the temperament to match. He could be rude, harsh, insensitive, but she never forgot he had saved her when no one else had cared.

She took a seat at the stool in front of the workbench. "Why were you so abrupt with him?"

"He was sizing you up."

Phoenix blinked, then laughed despite the sudden pounding of her heart. "He was doing no such thing."

"You always think the best of people," Andre sneered down his nose. "You believed the same of Paul Jovan."

Phoenix's entire body stiffened.

"I'm sorry you made it necessary to remind you of the incident," Andre said, his black-gloved hand sweeping over her hair. "Your naïveté and beauty attract the wrong type of men. I'm the only man you can trust. Remember that." Without another word Andre left the studio. There was no need for him to remain. He had accomplished what he intended.

Phoenix removed the cloth from the bust, lifted a pick, and began to delicately remove the excess clay. She couldn't argue even if she wanted to. Andre was right. He was the only man . . . including her father . . . who had ever wanted her for herself. It would be foolish, not to mention dangerous, for her to forget again.

2

"Morgan, I'm glad you're back. I just hung up from speaking with Mr. Lawson. He wants you to call him as soon as you arrived. He said it was urgent," Florine informed him, the usually calm and unflappable expression of his longtime secretary replaced by one of concern.

Morgan's brows knitted. Florine wasn't given to overreacting. That was one of the many reasons he'd hired her four years ago when he went into private practice. In her midfifties, she was intelligent, efficient, and had an uncanny ability to read people and situations correctly. The frown on her face wasn't comforting.

"I'll make the call myself." Morgan entered his spacious corner office on the fourth and top floor of the seventy-year-old office building in the heart of Santa Fe and went straight to a hard-carved oak desk that was nearly as old as the building. Placing his attaché case on the hardwood surface, he picked up the phone to punch in Kenneth Lawson's number in

Boston. What bothered Morgan was why Kenneth hadn't told Florine the reason for the call and why he hadn't attempted to call Morgan on his cell.

"Hello," answered a crisp male voice on the first ring. Despite living in Boston for thirty years after his graduation from Harvard, Kenneth still maintained his Philadelphia accent.

"Morning, Kenneth," Morgan said, taking a seat in the plush executive chair behind his desk. "What's up?"

"What happened at Duval's place?"

Still unsure as to what was so urgent about the situation, Morgan gave his old law professor the information as succinctly as possible. "Despite your indication that he was ready to sign the contracts, he had me leave them to look over. He intends to mail them directly back to you."

"I don't mean about the contracts. I mean between you and Phoenix."

"Phoenix?" Morgan repeated, not liking the way the conversation was going. "Suppose you tell me what you're talking about."

Kenneth didn't waste time. "I just got off the phone with Andre Duval not three minutes ago. He called to tell me you were late for your appointment, then instead of coming in you started toward the stable to watch Phoenix until a servant stopped you. Then later when she came into the study and you two were introduced, you flirted with her. In his words, you were incompetent and grossly unprofessional in the way you conducted yourself."

Morgan had long since gone from a simmer to a boil by the time Kenneth finished. "Do you believe him?"

"Andre is an important client who carries a lot of weight with a lot of other important clients."

"Do you believe him?"

"I've seen Phoenix," Kenneth answered, then went on to say, "but I trained you."

Morgan almost relaxed. "Thanks, but how about dropping the other shoe?"

"You were always sharp," Kenneth said. "Duval doesn't want you to come out to his place anymore. If you do, he'll find another firm to represent him."

"Son of a—"

"It's that beautiful face of yours," Kenneth interrupted. "Duval was practically foaming at the mouth when he called. I should have remembered how possessive he is of her and had you send a clerk."

Morgan's insides tightened. "They're involved."

Kenneth sighed. "No one knows for sure. If they are, they aren't talking. Duval can be vindictive to anyone who crosses or displeases him."

Morgan's thoughts immediately went to Phoenix and how she had knuckled under to Duval, how the light had gone out of her beautiful eyes.

Kenneth continued by saying, "When he returned from his self-imposed sabbatical from Europe she was with him. She was introduced as his protégée/assistant."

"She sculpts?" Morgan asked, remembering the unexpected calluses on her otherwise delicate hands.

"She's never shown anything. But Andre has sponsored a newcomer in another art form," Kenneth told him. "The man's work didn't show much promise when it was shown here."

Morgan tsked. "You don't think Duval would let anyone show him up, do you?"

"Point taken, which leads me back to the original problem."

It was his call. Kenneth was a good enough friend and a sharp enough judge of character to let Morgan make the decision for himself. None of the Graysons pushed worth a damn.

He could go back out there and teach Duval about the truth and jeopardize a sizable commission, or shrug it off. He realized the only reason he hesitated was Phoenix.

Unconsciously his hand tightened on the phone. "I'll have a clerk call and see when it would be convenient to pick up the contracts, then overnight them to you. If that would meet with Mr. Duval's approval?"

"It will. I know your decision wasn't easy. Betty thought you'd ram the contract down Duval's throat."

Betty, a diminutive redhead who made men quake in their shoes when she was presiding in criminal court, was Kenneth's wife of forty-odd years. She didn't take guff from anyone. "I admit the thought briefly came to me."

Kenneth, who unlike his wife was always diplomatic, grunted. "I'm glad to see you've mellowed. Duval is not a man to cross."

Once again, Morgan thought of Phoenix. "Someone should teach him better manners."

Panic entered Kenneth's voice. "I hope you're not considering taking on the job. Duval can make a bitter enemy."

"The same thing has been said about me," Morgan returned idly.

A long-suffering sigh drifted through the phone. "Just be careful. You don't want to do anything that might jeopardize your flourishing law practice."

Anger harshened Morgan's face. "If he comes after me again, I won't be so accommodating."

"Morgan, just think before you act," Kenneth advised. "Your character has to be exemplary if you plan to run for city council. One out of six people in Santa Fe has ties in some way to the art community. You don't want to piss Duval off."

"If I have to slink on my belly to be a city councilman, I'll pass." Too agitated to sit any longer, Morgan pushed to his feet and strode to the windows to look down at the narrow, busy street. "But set your mind at ease. It will be my pleasure to stay as far away from Duval as possible."

"What about Phoenix?" Kenneth asked.

A quick thump of Morgan's heart told him that would be harder.

"Morgan?"

Morgan turned away from the window. His gaze caught a flash of light off the glass étagère across the room. It was filled with plaques and accolades for his work with teenagers at risk, especially young drug offenders. There were still so many more he needed to help. One way were to put away the sleaze who preyed on the weakness and insecurities of children. He had goals and plans. Nothing could interfere. "The same goes."

"I feel much better now. You had me worried for a moment there," Kenneth told him.

I'm glad someone feels better, Morgan thought. He felt like kicking something, preferably Duval's skinny behind. He chose to sit behind his desk instead. "For what it's worth, I'm aware that you made the call for my benefit. I'm sorry you got caught in the middle."

"Goes with the territory," Kenneth said mildly. "Since you're a patron of the arts you're bound to run into him or Phoenix."

"I can handle it," Morgan said without a moment's hesitation.

"Good. That's what I wanted to hear. We'll talk soon. Give my and Betty's best to your mother. Bye."

"Bye, Kenneth." Morgan hung up the phone and opened his attaché case. How difficult could it be to treat Duval and Phoenix as nothing more than casual business acquaintances?

Morgan believed his statement all through getting dressed the next night for the open reception for Andre Duval's work. April through November was the prime season for gallery openings in Santa Fe, but they were held year-round. The city claimed over two hundred galleries, a number of them serious art spaces that could hold their own anywhere in the country.

The City Different, as some referred to Santa Fe, had been on an upward gallery swing since the early 1980s. Morgan and his mother were on the city's arts council. He saw no reason to let his aversion to Duval interfere with his responsibility. He'd make his appearance known, then leave. There would probably be so many people hovering around Andre that he wouldn't notice Morgan.

An hour later Morgan found he was right about one thing: a throng of people surrounded Duval as soon as he and Phoenix arrived fashionably late at his own opening at Persians, a unique art gallery with a mixture of mediums. However, Morgan was dead wrong in his estimation of handling Phoenix. He felt the punch to the gut as soon as she walked in. The sparkling cider he'd been drinking certainly hadn't done it.

She was exquisite. Regal and breathtaking in a figure-hugging red gown. The material looped around her slim neck before spiraling downward to crisscross her high, firm breasts, then swirl to the back. He'd seen women wearing more provocative gowns, but none had made his hands itch or another part of his body harden.

As though she wasn't aware of the furor she created in him and probably every other male in the crowded room, she stood perfectly poised by Andre's side, a warm smile on her face as Andre held court. As the crowd ebbed and flowed, Morgan noted that Andre kept a proprietary gloved hand on her bare arm.

"They say Duval has his hands insured for ten

million dollars by Lloyd's of London," whispered Howard Askew, a banker and fellow patron of the arts.

"The way he's holding on to his protégée, I'd say they're worth every penny," came the envious comment of Wallace Huey, a middle-aged real-estate investor.

"Excuse me," Morgan said; he didn't want to hear any more. He crossed the polished sheen of the hardwood floor to the other side of the gallery intending to circle the crowd and leave. But somehow he found himself in an unobtrusive corner of the hexagonal gallery, watching Phoenix.

"You might want to wipe the drool off your chin before Mama sees you."

Morgan slowly turned to see his sister, her heart-shaped face staring up at him with open annoyance. "Hello, Sierra. I didn't expect to see you here tonight."

"You might want to do so something about the lust in your eyes as well."

"Is that a new dress? Valentino, perhaps?"

Sierra's satiny black brows arched higher over intelligent jet-black eyes. "All right, have it your way, but I'm watching you."

Casually Morgan sipped his drink. "Boring, don't you think?"

"Hardly, after what I just saw." She crossed her bare arms over her chest. "After Luke we're not taking any chances."

Morgan frowned. "You can't be serious. I'm not seeing anyone, let alone thinking about getting married."

"As I recall, that was the same thing Luke said, and we all know what happened to him," Sierra said, letting her arms fall to her sides.

"He tripped over his big mouth," answered another male voice. "Drink?"

"Thanks." Sierra lifted a fluted glass. A wine charm with the letter *n* indicating nonalcoholic jangled from the stem. She smiled over the rim of the glass at her brother who had just served her. "Don't you look nice in your tux?"

Brandon frowned and glanced down from his considerable height of six-foot-plus to the white dinner jacket and the polished red and black cowboy boots peeking from beneath the cuffless black slacks, then at his immaculately groomed brother and equally flawless sister. "Don't start."

Morgan eyed his brother suspiciously. He might own the catering business that was hired for tonight's events, but he usually stayed in the kitchen. "What are you doing out here?"

"For a smart man, that's a dumb question," Brandon said without heat; then he offered two passing ladies a drink. Both chose champagne.

Morgan waited until the women moved on. "What's dumb is the two of you watching me." He glanced around the milling crowd of people, refusing to let his gaze linger on Duval and Phoenix, who were finally circulating. "Should I expect Pierce to show up?"

"Pierce is on a hot date." Brandon sighed wistfully. "He has a smile a mile wide by now."

"At least he has more sense than to watch me."

Sierra shook her head, causing her lustrous waist-length black hair to shimmer in the light. "The only reason he isn't here is because he figures if you and Brandon fail, he needs to have some memories stored up."

"That's ridiculous." Morgan set his glass back on the silver tray with a decided click.

"That's planning," Brandon corrected, a twinkle in his black eyes. "You know how Pierce always likes to be prepared for any eventuality."

"I'm not getting married," Morgan gritted out.

Sierra didn't look convinced.

Brandon held the tray out to a passing woman in a low-cut gown. She accepted the champagne and returned Brandon's interested smile before moving on. He turned back to Morgan. "Luke said the same thing, and look at him."

"He and Catherine have been back from their honeymoon for four days and they've only called Mama. I went by the cabin this morning to take them some food but left it on the porch when no one came to the door after I knocked." Sierra wrinkled her pretty nose. "I know they were inside because Hero was in the yard. When I was halfway back to town, Catherine called me on my cell to thank me. Then she started laughing. Luke came on, said, 'Thanks,' and hung up."

Hero was the wild wolf hybrid that Catherine had befriended despite Luke's strenuous objection. After the animal had protected Catherine, Luke had changed his mind. Part wolf, part dog, Hero didn't let anyone except family get within a hundred feet of the cabin. That included Richard Youngblood, the veterinarian who had removed a bullet from Hero, and Naomi Reese, a homeless woman Catherine befriended who later became Richard's receptionist, before she was hired as a kindergarten teacher for the school district.

"I thought Luke and Catherine planned to rejoin the world tonight for the opening," Morgan finally said.

"Apparently they found something better to do with their time," Sierra said. Both she and Brandon stared at Morgan, daring him to be the next Grayson to get married.

"You have *nothing* to worry about," Morgan said. Since they didn't look convinced and he was tired of discussing marriage, he chose to do what he did best in the courtroom: attack. "The fit of that dinner jacket is disgraceful."

Brandon shrugged his wide shoulders. The jacket lapels shifted and remained loose. "Can't be helped. Straight off the rental rack. I had to fill in for a sick waiter."

Before Brandon had finished, Morgan was straightening his brother's crooked black bow tie. "If you're going to stay in catering, you might as well have a dinner jacket tailor-made and keep it at your office. You, of all people, know how important presentation is." Satisfied with the tie at least, Morgan stepped back. "I'll have Florine call my tailor and get you an appointment on Monday."

Brandon's eyes widened. A panicky look crossed his handsome golden-brown face. "Now wait a minute. There's no need to go that far."

"There is every reason if you expect to be successful," Morgan told him.

Brandon shook his head. The thick black hair secured at the base of his neck with an inch-wide silver band studded with turquoise swayed in response. "All of us can't be clothes hounds the way you two and Pierce are."

"That's *clotheshorse*," Sierra corrected, smiling sweetly.

"Whatever," Brandon said, dismissing Morgan's idea completely. "From now on, I'll always have a backup." He tugged the tie, completely destroying the perfect knot while ignoring Morgan's narrowed gaze. "I'd better see about the food. Now that Duval is here, we can start serving the appetizers. He's getting beluga caviar and vintage champagne now and at the private after-reception party."

"Figures," Morgan muttered as Brandon walked away.

"I'd better find my date," Sierra said, glancing around the crowded room.

"Anyone I know?" Morgan asked mildly. Too mildly.

Sierra merely lifted a delicate brow.

He hadn't thought he'd get an answer that easily. Sierra was too independent and too headstrong for her own good, which led her to believe she could take care of herself in any situation. Morgan playfully flicked a long finger across her dainty nose. "Lighten up. I know you can handle yourself. We taught you. But indulge your big brother."

Her face softened. "Jim Carlson, president of Agamo. If his credit card company decides to relocate here from Phoenix, I want to be his exclusive realtor for finding the site for his office building and homes for his three hundred–plus employees. If he does, I'll be one step closer to opening my own agency."

"You'll get him," Morgan said with complete confidence. "You're the best there is."

A wide grin split Sierra's face. "Thanks. I'd better get going." She took a couple of steps, then turned back. "Morgan, watch yourself."

He didn't understand the depth of concern he saw in her eyes. "Sierra, I told you you have nothing to worry about."

She didn't appear convinced. "I saw you watching that woman with Duval. There was more than lust in your eyes. There was something much more dangerous for a man like you."

Only his years of training as a lawyer kept Morgan from showing his surprise. He didn't let people read him so easily, in or out of the courtroom. He didn't try to evade. This time he wanted an answer. Of all of them, Sierra was the most perceptive and sensitive. "What do you think you saw?"

"I'm not sure, but you always have fought for the underdog, and although Phoenix doesn't fit the mode or act that way from the little I saw while I watched her watching you and vice versa, I got the sense that she was unhappy being an ornament on Duval's arm," Sierra finished.

"Then she should do something about it." He'd think about Phoenix watching him later.

"Her problem. Not yours," Sierra told him. "You may have an image of being unbendable, but I'm aware of what a pushover you can be."

"You promised you'd never mention that again."

She chuckled. "I didn't mention what. I'd better go, but remember, watch yourself."

Sierra had barely left before Jim Carlson approached her. The Arizona businessman was only a few inches taller than Sierra's petite five-foot-three. Slim and prematurely balding at forty, he was generally a nice guy. Nodding in Morgan's direction, he took Sierra by the arm and led her away. Since the man's hand wasn't anyplace else that might get him into trouble, Morgan's concern eased.

Morgan glanced at his watch. Eight-thirteen. He'd finish his obligatory tour of the art on display, then go home . . . alone. He worked his shoulders, then started across the room. Perhaps that was his problem. He'd been sleeping single for the past several months.

First he'd been busy with a couple of cases; then, after his mother had gotten it into her head to marry her children off one by one, every woman he'd asked out seemed to think she might be the one. He'd stopped dating and spent more time as a board member of the Southwestern Association for Indian Arts as they prepared for the annual Indian Market in a couple of weeks, and with the kids at Second Chance, a program for teenagers recovering from drug addiction.

You couldn't be self-centered or remain unmoved when you stared into the eyes of kids who had been to hell and were slowly making their way back. They'd thought drugs would be the answer to their problems or, like his best friend, Gene Bates, thought they'd experiment once and be able to walk away. Gene had been so very wrong. His life had spiraled out of control and nothing anyone said or did helped him regain the control he traded to show himself impervious to drugs.

Six months later, a week from what would have been his high school graduation as salutatorian, he was flying high on crack and drove his Jeep off the side of the mountain going ninety miles an hour. His life had ended and Morgan's crusade had begun.

Morgan had mourned the senseless loss and promised himself then that he wouldn't stop trying to help young people find their way back. He could forgive them, even understand their reason: it was the drug dealers, the pushers who preyed on their weakness, who were responsible. Tougher laws were needed.

Morgan wasn't sure if going into politics was the answer. He just knew he'd never stop trying to help. If he could save one person it would be worth it.

Deep in thought, he stopped in front of the first of three oversize paintings by Duval's protégé, Raymond Scott. This one was titled *Midnight*. Morgan barely kept from grimacing. The moonlight-draped forest scene lacked imagination and depth, and the scale was off.

"Breathtaking, isn't it?" commented the man who joined him. "Are you interested in it for your collection?"

If Morgan hadn't learned to think before he spoke, he might have said not while he was sane. As it was, he slanted his head to see a lanky black man in his late twenties in a black suit that could have come off the same rack as Brandon's jacket. At least his red silk tie was straight.

"I'm sorry. I thought I knew everyone who worked here," Morgan returned.

The man grinned self-consciously and extended his hand. "I'm the artist, Raymond Scott."

Morgan understood the man's eagerness to sell. His work languished while Duval's had sold out all three shows before he came to Santa Fe. "Morgan Grayson, just browsing." The handshake was brief and limp.

Disappointment pulled the corners of Raymond's mouth down. "If the price is the problem, I'm sure we can negotiate."

"It's not." Morgan had never liked pressure sales tactics.

"Perhaps you'll like the others. I'll let you continue. Good-bye."

"Good-bye." Morgan moved to the next picture, and the next. They were as uninspiring as the first one. It was as Morgan had thought. Duval wouldn't want anyone to show him up. Scott probably thought Duval was being magnanimous. Another person duped by Duval.

Morgan's mind leaped to Phoenix, and he firmly pulled back. If she wanted to let Duval run her life it was no concern of his.

Doing his best to make himself accept his declaration, Morgan started toward Duval's exhibit on the other side of the gallery. Unlike the scene surrounding Scott's work, people were waiting in line to get a closer look at the seven bronzes Duval had on display.

Finally the two couples in front of him moved and Morgan was able to see the statue, a nude woman reclining, her face and one arm lifted skyward. The nude was powerful in an eloquent yet simple way that Morgan would have sworn Duval wouldn't have had a clue how to create.

Morgan moved on, finding each piece more moving than the one before. He found himself almost impatient to view the last bronze on a platform raised to eye-level. He immediately understood why it was last. It was simply stunning.

He stared as if mesmerized at the small bronze statue of a woman, her back arched, one arm curved gracefully over her head, the other slender arm around the neck of a man bending over her, their bodies distinct but blended. It was bold and sensual and Morgan felt the intensity of the piece in the tingling down his spine. He wanted it for his collection as he had never wanted another piece.

His questing hand was already reaching out to touch the figures when he remembered who the creator was. His gaze flickered to the gold plate at the base of the bronze. *Everlasting*. Andre Duval. Morgan snorted.

"You don't like it?"

Morgan slowly turned his head to see Phoenix, her brow bunched, her sensually full lower lip caught between her beautiful white teeth. The woman sent a punch straight to his gut. For the space of two heartbeats he forgot about his mother's matchmaking, his promise to Kenneth. All Morgan could remember was that he wanted this woman with an intensity that was becoming more and more difficult to ignore.

Casually he slipped his hand into his pocket. What he really wanted to do was slip it around her slim neck and bring her mouth to his. He could almost taste the sweet fire and passion.

"You don't like it?" she repeated.

Morgan clamped down on his unexpected desire for Phoenix and tried to concentrate on the question. As much as he might have wanted to say otherwise, his innate honesty and the obvious distress in her beautiful smoky gray eyes pulled the truth from him. "It's the best piece of the show."

Her face glowed and for the briefest of time Morgan thought of acting out his earlier thoughts. "Thank you."

Her blind devotion to Duval irritated him and quenched his desire. "If Duval wasn't such a manipulative snob, I might buy the piece for my collection."

Surprise widened her eyes. She had thought from the first that Morgan was different from most people she had met and she had been right. He wouldn't yield or bend. What must it feel like to have such strength, such courage? "People usually go along with Andre."

"Does that include you?" Morgan asked, his deep black eyes watching her closely as he waited for her answer.

Her smile wavered. "Yes."

"I see. Good night."

Phoenix watched Morgan move easily through the crowd. Many of the women there watched him just as she did. He opened the leaded glass door to the gallery and left without once looking back. A deep sadness washed over her.

Concerned that Andre might see the unmistakable longing in her eyes, she turned back to the statue, but she still saw Morgan, the wide breadth of his shoulders, the strikingly handsome face that clearly noted his Indian blood. His ancestors had been warriors, intelligent and resourceful men who fought and died for the People.

She sensed Morgan could be just as fierce and dedicated. He had a way of moving and speaking that denoted supreme self-confidence.

A quality she lacked.

Reaching out her slender hand, she traced the figure of the man. What must it feel like to be loved so deeply, completely, by such a magnificent man? Helplessly her gaze returned to the door.

She was afraid she'd never know.

3

Phoenix had been to numerous private receptions in the seven years she had lived with Andre as his assistant. Whether in Europe or in America, there were always people attending who wanted to see and be seen as well as those who truly appreciated and loved art. The middle-aged man with a wife half his age and size who had purchased *Everlasting* and boasted he didn't know a thing about art but figured it was a good investment was one of the former. Morgan would have valued the piece for itself.

Phoenix rubbed the dull thudding in her temple. Why did she continue to think about him? Perhaps she was tired. She'd like nothing better than to go home and crawl into bed. But that wouldn't happen until Andre was ready. Since he was surrounded by admirers and people from the arts council, she knew it wouldn't be anytime soon.

She wasn't blind to Andre's faults. He enjoyed the

spotlight. There was no way he was leaving when he was holding court.

Standing on the fringe of the group was Raymond Scott. As usual, he wasn't smiling or being included in the conversation. She didn't understand why he put himself through it again and again. But then, his association with Andre was just as puzzling and had come as a complete shock to her.

She'd never heard Raymond's name mentioned while she and Andre lived abroad. They'd only been in the States a week before Andre began receiving calls from Raymond.

At first Andre had refused to speak with him, but a few days later she'd come back from a walk to see a jubilant Raymond leaving Andre's hotel room in Boston. Moments later when she'd seen Andre he'd been moody and impossible to get along with.

She'd attributed Andre's behavior to the pressure of having his first show in seven years a few days later. The revival of his career, and his financial security, hinged on the success of the opening. Seeing Raymond's work on display along with Andre's the night of the opening had shocked and hurt her when Andre had repeatedly told her that she wasn't ready.

Then she'd caught Andre's smug expression when all his bronzes had sold and people barely glanced at Raymond's paintings. Whatever Andre's reason for letting Raymond show with him, it wasn't kindness.

Phoenix came out of her musings to see Raymond, apparently tired of being excluded, accept a glass of champagne from a passing waiter and start toward her.

Since he knew she'd seen him, Phoenix was trapped into waiting for him. Raymond wasn't a pleasant man, and as his paintings went overlooked and remained unsold show after show, he became more difficult to be around.

"Who were you looking for?" he asked when he stopped in front of her.

Phoenix realized she had been scanning the crowd for Morgan. Again. "I was admiring the room." To prove her statement, she glanced around the spacious great room with two immense wrought-iron chandeliers and heavy carved furniture. The stone fireplace was big enough for five men to stand in shoulder-to-shoulder.

Raymond finished his champagne, his narrowed gaze still on her. "Duval wouldn't like it if you don't devote all of your time to him."

Phoenix couldn't tell if he meant the words as a threat or had simply made a statement. "You needn't concern yourself about my life."

"*Rellenos*?" asked the waiter, a twinkle in his black eyes.

"No, thank you," Phoenix told him. She remembered the tall, strikingly handsome man from the opening. He had been talking with Morgan.

Raymond took two. "Just looking out for your best interest. Never can tell when something unexpected might happen." He took a large bite of the skewered food, blinked. His mouth gaped. His eyes watered as he stared at the batter-fried green chile pepper oozing with cheese in his hand.

"I'll get you some . . ." Phoenix's voice trailed off as Raymond rushed toward the nearest waiter serving beverages.

"Guess he doesn't like my cooking," commented the waiter.

Phoenix couldn't help but notice he didn't look the least bit disturbed. "You're the chef?"

"Chef and owner of The Red Cactus, where you'll find the freshest and best food in Santa Fe," he told her. "Brandon Grayson. Drop in and the meal is on me."

"Thank you," Phoenix said, but he was already moving away. She saw Andre coming toward her and thought it best that Brandon had left. She probably shouldn't ask if he was related to Morgan Grayson.

"Why was Scott racing to the champagne like an idiot and making a spectacle of himself?" Andre asked, his mouth tight.

"He bit into a chile pepper," Phoenix explained.

"He's been here long enough to know they put chile in everything. That's why I had my food specially prepared," Andre quipped. "At least it was edible."

She didn't bother to comment that the arts council wasn't about to cater to Raymond the way they did to Andre and her. She knew she was included because people weren't quite sure of their relationship. "The smoked salmon was heavenly."

"I've had better." Andre held out his arm. "Let's go. I've said my good-byes. I've wasted enough of my time."

Phoenix didn't say anything about his callous remark. She'd long since found it did no good. The more you did for Andre, the more he expected. No, demanded.

The arts council would soon learn as she had that their generosity, which far surpassed any sponsorship thus far, would be pushed to the limits. She took his arm and wondered how much longer she could live with a man who was so self-centered.

Outside, the limousine and driver provided for them waited. The uniformed driver opened the back door and Phoenix climbed inside. Andre was about to follow when Raymond rushed out of the two-story hacienda.

"Wait, Andre. I need to talk with you."

Andre stiffened, his nostrils flaring in annoyance. "I'm extremely tired. You can call me tomorrow. Good night." He climbed inside and the driver shut the door.

Through the back window Phoenix saw Raymond, still on the sidewalk watching the car speed away. Whatever reason Andre allowed Raymond to show his work, it wasn't because he wanted to help struggling artists as he'd told the newspaper. If she didn't know better, she'd think he did it to humiliate the man.

Andre was silent on the way home. Phoenix didn't try to initiate conversation. When Andre was in one of his moods it was best to take cover. She planned to do so as soon as she arrived home.

She practically leaped out of the big black Lincoln once the driver opened the door. Ben, as usual, was waiting for them. "Good evening, Mr. Duval. Miss Phoenix."

"Good evening, Ben. Good night, Andre," she said, heading for her room.

"Phoenix, I wish to speak with you," Andre called.

There was just enough displeasure in his voice to make her dread the coming conversation. Slowly she turned to see Andre's rigid posture and Ben quietly leaving the room. "Can't this wait until morning? I'm tired."

"I don't want you to have any contact with Morgan Grayson," Andre ordered.

Phoenix had suspected he had seen her watching Morgan. He'd joined her moments after Morgan left. His mouth had been as pinched with disapproval then as it was now. He had stayed by her side until they left for the private reception.

"Why? It's obvious he has no interest in me." She tried to keep her voice light, her expression uncaring.

The sneer in Andre's voice told her she hadn't succeeded with either. "You are so naive. Nothing but a baby chick with a sly drooling fox at your door, and you'd open it."

She couldn't reconcile the picture Andre painted of Morgan. A stalking panther perhaps. There was nothing sly about Morgan.

"Are you listening to me?" Andre snapped.

"Yes." Aware that her attention had shifted, she accepted Andre's harshness, but her nails bit into her hands. It was becoming more and more difficult to excuse his rudeness and her own cowardice. She owed him her life but not her self-respect. "I was thinking of a piece I wanted to do."

"I told you, you're not ready." Stalking across the room to the built-in bar, he reached for the square decanter, only to knock the bottle over. "Damn."

Phoenix quickly went to help. Righting the decanter, she uncapped it, poured him a measure of whiskey, and handed him the squat glass. "Are they bothering you?"

He downed the drink before speaking. "Would you care?"

Instantly she felt contrite. No matter what, she mustn't forget where she'd be if not for Andre. Gently she placed her hands over his black-gloved ones. "You know I do. Not just because of what you've done for me, but because the world deserves to see your great art."

Tension seemed to seep out of him. Pleasure spread over his thin face. "All the pieces sold tonight, as they have at each showing."

Phoenix's mind wandered to the obnoxious man who'd bought *Everlasting*. His eyes had held none of the appreciation that Morgan's had held. The man had shown very little respect for the statue that had taken days to create. Morgan's hands would have been reverent instead of indifferent. But would he touch a woman he desired the same way? She flushed and quickly shook the unwelcome thought away.

"Raymond didn't sell any of his paintings," she finally said. "He's becoming difficult to be around at times."

Andre watched her closely. "Has he said anything to offend you?"

"No," she quickly said. Raymond had enough problems. "I feel sorry for him."

Andre shrugged his narrow shoulders beneath his expensive black tuxedo jacket and moved away from the bar. "It happens."

Troubled, Phoenix followed. "But he hasn't sold any in four shows. The art critics were brutal in Chicago, and those in Boston and Philadelphia weren't much better." She wanted to add that she agreed with them, but she didn't.

Andre stopped in the hallway leading to the master suite on the other side of the house. "You're too soft-hearted. A little humiliation is good for the soul."

Phoenix bit her lip. Andre could be so cold and sanctimonious at times. She often wondered why he had saved her.

"Go to bed, Phoenix, and get some sleep. I have an idea for a new bronze, but I want to sleep on it before I start," he said. "I want the other finished pieces sent to the foundry to be cast and our schedule checked for the next show in Seattle. It has to be spectacular. It has to be another triumph." His eyes shimmered with zeal. "The show is in two months."

"Can I show my work as well?" she asked before she could stop herself.

Irritation thinned his mouth. "I'll tell you when you're ready. You don't want to suffer the humiliation that Scott has, do you?"

"No," she quickly answered. She couldn't take that kind of rejection. . . . She'd been rejected too many times in the past.

Andre came back and placed his gloved hand on her arm. "It's for your own benefit. We'll talk about it again after the next show. I promise."

"Really?" He'd never promised before.

"I'm a man of my word. Remember?"

She remembered all too well what would have happened to her if he hadn't been. "Thank you."

He patted her on the shoulder. "Go to bed. We have a lot of work to do tomorrow."

"Good night," Phoenix said.

Once in her room and in bed she was too restless to sleep. A pair of black eyes kept intruding. Getting out of bed, she pulled on a snug pair of jeans and a faded cotton blouse and went to the studio. Once inside, she went to the workbench on the far side of the well-lit room and knelt to retrieve a mound of clay. Then she began to work.

For now, this was all that mattered. To let herself think otherwise was to be hurt again. She had suffered enough.

Morgan woke in a foul mood and it didn't get any better as the day progressed. His mother visiting him late that afternoon at his office didn't help. Always casually dressed, she wore a broomstick skirt, a light blue blouse, and a denim vest. Her long black hair was twisted into looped plaits and fell just below her shoulders.

"Hello, Morgan."

From behind his desk he leaned over in his chair to peer behind her. "Should I expect a woman to suddenly pop up behind you?"

Instead of answering, she rounded his desk and took his face in her hands. "Didn't get much sleep last night?"

"I wonder why."

One eyebrow lifted.

Morgan felt about two years old. No wonder his mother got away with trying to run their lives. None of them could stand to displease her. How could they when she had always put their welfare above her own? "Mama, can't you just be happy that I'm happy?"

She smiled and kissed both his cheeks before sitting on the edge of his desk. Ruth Grayson was a striking woman. Sixty-two years old, she looked fifty and had flawless golden-bronze skin, high cheekbones, and beautiful black eyes that she'd passed on to all of her children.

She'd kept the same trim figure she had at twenty. Good genes and good living, she always said. "You'd be happier with a wife."

Morgan picked up the case file. "*You'd* be happier. I'd be miserable."

"Luke isn't."

Even with his considerable talent as a lawyer, Morgan couldn't argue with the truth. "I'm not Luke."

Her soft hand rested on his shoulder. "I know that

better than anyone. You feel things deeper than he does. You hurt more. Luke is the protector. You're the defender."

He glanced up. She'd told him the same thing when he was a child. She'd known before he had that he would be a lawyer. She knew all of her children so well. That's why they were in so much trouble. "Can't you wait a year or two?"

She came off the desk with a lithe movement. "I'm not getting any younger."

Morgan tossed the folder aside. His mother hadn't made it a secret that she wanted grandchildren before she was too old to play with them. It had come as a shock to them that Luke's wife, Catherine, couldn't have any children. She'd tried to run away from Luke because of it. But Luke wasn't the type of man to let the woman he loved get away. He'd gone after her and brought her back. He loved her irrevocably, completely. She loved him the same way.

"Can't you be satisfied with your success with Luke and Catherine?"

"I won't be satisfied until all my children are happily married, just like Daniel and Dominique," she said, determination in every fiber of her body.

Morgan would have banged his head against the desk if he hadn't had monumental discipline. Daniel Falcon had a reputation for being heartless in business and with women, but he'd caved like a marshmallow when Madelyn Taggart walked, rather ran, into his life. "Daniel started this," he growled.

Laughing, his mother picked up the folder Morgan

had tossed, straightened the papers inside, then placed it directly in front of him. "Don't be too harsh on your cousin. It takes a smart man to know when the right woman walks into his life. Besides, without his financial support, the arts council wouldn't have been able to score such a coup and bring Andre Duval here. We were competing with several cities. I just hate that I had a faculty meeting last night and missed his opening."

"Some coup, and you didn't miss much," Morgan snorted. "He had stipulations a mile long before accepting, everything from housing to food. The man is an egotistical jerk."

"But an artistic genius," Ruth reminded her son. "I received a call from the president of the arts council this morning saying that every one of Duval's sculptures sold. Art critics from around the country were there. Samuel was very pleased and thankful."

Morgan briefly regretted the loss of *Everlasting*, then moved on. Regrets were not a part of his life. "The one meeting I've missed of the arts council in three years, and look what happened."

Placing both hands on the desk, his mother stared at him. "You aren't usually this hung up on things. Is there something about Duval you're not telling me?"

Morgan jerked upright. How could he have forgotten his mother's sixth sense where her children were concerned? "He just gets to me."

"But, dear, you work with lawyers."

She said it so deadpan that Morgan blinked, then laughed. She laughed with him.

"Now, that's more like it. I'd better let you work." She started for the door. "I'm cooking fajitas with fresh tortillas tonight."

His mother was a fantastic cook—Brandon had learned from her before going on to culinary school—but the draw of her cooking was outweighed by the prospect of facing a wannabe bride. "No, thank you."

"Will you come if I promise not to have a woman hiding in the closet?" she asked, her lips twitching.

"There are a lot of other places in your house to hide," he commented. They'd moved her out of her smaller house several years ago and had a custom single-story ranch house built on an acre lot in a gated subdivision. He and Luke had liked the area so much, they'd built there as well. However, since Catherine had come into his life, Luke had stayed with her at the cabin he jointly owned with Daniel in the Sangre de Cristo Mountains.

"The only women there will be me and your sister, if she can make it. See you at six." She opened the door and closed it behind her.

A frown on his face, Morgan reared back in his chair. It wasn't like his mother to give up or give time-outs. It wasn't in her nature. She'd taught them to be the same way.

So what was she up to?

Morgan picked up the folder and opened it. Worrying about it certainly wouldn't give him the answer; he just had to be ready. But at least he had a reprieve for today. He just wished thoughts of Phoenix would grant him the same favor.

Every time he closed his eyes last night she'd been there, one moment laughing, the next staring at him with a mute plea in her beautiful sad eyes. He tried to tell himself that she was an adult and could take care of herself, but he couldn't quite manage to make himself believe it.

She obviously wasn't cruel the way Duval was. Just as obviously she was included in the people Duval lashed out at.

So what made her stay?

Repositioning his body more comfortably in his chair, Morgan realized he wasn't going to find out, no matter how badly he wanted to. She was off-limits. One thing he could do was take to task the person who had started his mother on a crusade to get her children married. Picking up the phone, he punched in Daniel Falcon's private cell number, the quickest and surest way to catch up with him.

"Daniel Falcon," came the laughing answer.

Morgan's annoyance increased. More fodder for his mother. "Couldn't you be a little less happy all the time?"

"Nope. Little Daniel and I are getting ready to go see his mother."

Morgan leaned back in his chair. He would never have thought a tough businessman like Daniel would give up many of his business interests to stay at home and care for Little Daniel while his wife worked as a production engineer for a petroleum company in Houston. Just the kind of thing Morgan's mother would adore. "You're the reason Mama started her wild scheme to get us all married in the first place."

"Luke wasn't complaining at his wedding," came Daniel's amused reply.

"I admit Mama picked a winner for Luke, *but* the rest of us don't want to get married," he said with heat.

"I didn't, either, until I fell in love with Madelyn," Daniel said. "Believe me, I'm thankful that she loves me, too. Every time I think of how close I came to losing her and Little Daniel I get chills."

Morgan had heard the story of the lengths Daniel had gone to to prove his love after Madelyn refused to marry him. "Marriage isn't for everyone. You said that yourself once."

"Again, that was before Madelyn. Look, I hate to cut this short, but we have a plane to catch. Madelyn had to go out on-site in the Gulf of Mexico, and she's spending the night in Port Arthur. We're going to surprise her."

Morgan rolled his eyes. "Little Daniel is racking up more miles than a seasoned flier. I don't suppose it occurred to you to stay at home and wait for her to come back like most husbands?"

"Maybe they have more patience than I do or maybe they aren't married to a woman like Madelyn. Besides, we all sleep better when we're under the same roof."

More likely the women weren't married to multimillionaires who had their own private jet at their disposal. However, Madelyn's brothers, Kane and Matt Taggart, weren't as wealthy as Daniel, but as far as

Morgan knew, they had never spent the night apart from their wives. Neither had Daniel's sister, Dominique, and her husband, Trent. "I guess when you're in love it is tough being apart."

Laughter drifted through the phone. "Glad to hear you finally admit it. Maybe when it's your time, I won't tease you so much."

"I am *not* getting married." He was tired of repeating himself.

"I believe we all said the same thing," Daniel replied with humor.

Daniel, Dominique, and Luke had all fought against falling in love. Matt had fought just as hard, but he'd walk barefoot through hell with a smile on his face for his wife, Shannon, and their daughter. At family get-togethers all of them were bubbling over with happiness and love.

Morgan sighed. He was happy for them; he just wasn't ready to join them. "Give Madelyn my best and have a safe trip."

"Thanks, and as hard as it may be to imagine now, when you do meet her, you won't be able to imagine how you could have lived without her. Just ask Luke."

"I can't. He's holed up in the cabin with Catherine," Morgan told him.

"My point exactly. When you aren't with the woman you love, you're thinking about her. When you are with her, you don't want to think of the time when you aren't."

Morgan thought of his inability to get Phoenix out of his mind. He scowled. "Go catch your plane."

"We're going. But speaking from personal experience, love has a way of sneaking up on you. Fighting it is a useless waste of time."

"I'm not falling in love."

"I believe we all said that, too. Little Daniel is anxious to see his mother and so am I. Bye."

Morgan hung up the phone in disgust. Daniel certainly wasn't any help. What did he know? He was a financial wizard, not an expert on love or relationships. Morgan could take Phoenix or leave her. The only reason he kept thinking about her was because she was such a dichotomy. As soon as he figured out who the real Phoenix was, he'd move on, just as he always had.

Assured he had everything figured out to his satisfaction, he picked up his folder and settled down to work.

Phoenix was in the stable brushing down Crimson when Ben found her early Wednesday morning. She'd taken the stallion out for a ride before dawn. With just the two of them racing the wind she could almost believe that her life was about to turn around. She just had to keep that belief when she was back at the house.

Hearing a noise, she straightened and glanced over Crimson's broad back toward the barn's entrance to see Ben, Andre's valet and butler, in his perennial black suit, crisp white shirt, and tie, entering the barn. Her heart went out to him at his slow but dignified steps.

One of the few times he had left Andre's side, Ben had been injured in an automobile accident in his hometown in Jamaica. The broken leg hadn't healed properly. No amount of physical therapy would help. It was heartrending to see him walk now and remember the long, smooth strides of before. "Good morning, Ben."

"Good morning, Miss Phoenix."

A smile touched her lips. She'd long since given up trying to have him or his wife, Cleo, the cook and housekeeper, call her by only her first name. She'd finally understood they did it out of respect and love. She loved them as well.

She probably wouldn't have survived those first lonely months if not for their quiet support. Andre had cared enough to help her, but he hadn't hidden his impatience for her to stop crying over what couldn't be changed and move on.

"There was no need to come get me for breakfast," she told Ben, a teasing smile on her face. He and Cleo always worried about her not eating enough. She often lost track of time when she was working. "I'm almost finished brushing down Crimson."

"Mr. Duval would like to see you immediately."

A slither of unease went through her. Andre never left his room until after ten. She tried to remember if she'd been too tired when she finally finished the piece last night to hide it properly. Andre wouldn't like it if she were working on her own pieces instead of doing the work he'd assigned to her.

And there was no way to tell from his message. No matter how displeased Andre might be with her, Ben always phrased Andre's requests politely.

"He received a call from Dr. Johansson," Ben went on to explain when she remained silent.

She felt ashamed at the rush of relief she felt. At least one of her secrets was safe. "What's the matter?" She walked around the stallion to the stall's half door where Ben stood waiting. Andre hadn't been feeling well the last few days and all of them had felt the bite of his tongue.

"He wants Mr. Duval back there as soon as possible."

Switzerland.

Unlatching the stall's door, Phoenix placed the brush on a small bench beside it and took off running, trying to think of some reason that would let her stay. She didn't want to leave. Not now. The thought that she was reluctant to leave because of Morgan Grayson popped into her mind. She firmly dismissed the idea. She only wanted to stay and finish her bronzes.

She didn't slow down until she was standing at Andre's open bedroom door. On his bed were two designer suitcases. One was already packed. Standing in front of the cheval mirror, Andre studied himself.

Phoenix knocked on the open door before speaking. "Did Dr. Johansson say how long he thinks you'll have to stay this time?"

The frown that crossed Duval's austere face

showed his displeasure at being questioned. "No," Andre answered, running a black-gloved hand across the lapels of the tan silk sports jacket.

"The preliminary work has been going so well," she commented, coming farther into the spacious room that commanded a spectacular view of the rugged Rocky Mountains.

"I've pushed myself to make sure of that. After my triumph in Seattle the price of my work will double for the following show in New York." His hard gaze met hers in the mirror. "I'll finish up there if necessary."

Her mind fumbled for words and found none. She nodded and accepted what she couldn't change. "I'll go pack."

"Unnecessary." He finally turned and looked at her directly.

Her start of surprise was immediate. "I'm staying?"

He crossed until he was less than a foot away. "I want you here to personally receive the shipments from me, be my go-between with the final papers for *Courage,* and field any calls from galleries or the media."

Fear and a wild elation swept through Phoenix. Since she was nineteen she'd never been away from Andre for more than a few days, and always where she could come at a moment's notice if he wanted. "Of course."

He picked up his camel-colored cashmere overcoat and draped it expertly over his arm just as Ben knocked respectfully on the door. "Shall I finish packing, Mr. Duval?"

"Yes," Andre replied. "You and Cleo packed?"

"She's finishing up now." Moving with as much dignity and quickness as his stiff leg would allow, Ben went to the closet and removed three of Andre's tailored suits.

Andre watched him for an assessing moment before turning his attention back to Phoenix. "Phoenix, you'll take us to the airport. A private jet will be there within the hour to take us to New York and from there to Switzerland."

They had always lived and traveled well, but not that well. "A private jet?"

Andre's thin nose tilted. "Seems you were correct in choosing to go with the arts council of Santa Fe. Their well-known association with Felicia Falcon, an art patron herself, and her son, Daniel Falcon, the multimillionaire of Falcon Industries, is paying off."

He chuckled smugly. "Luckily, I thought to use that connection and called the arts council president and told him of my need to get to New York as soon as possible, but I was having difficulty getting my entire staff on the same flight. I mentioned that I would appreciate any assistance he might give me. Fifteen minutes after I hung up he called back to say that Falcon was sending one of his jets."

Phoenix couldn't gloat along with Andre. With each passing day he seemed to grow more callous. Or maybe she was becoming less tolerant as he used people for his own benefit.

She'd chosen Santa Fe for the selfish reason that she had fallen in love with the mountains and the vastness of the area on the video they sent. She'd also loved that it was an art haven. The added benefit that she could stable a horse there made it perfect. "That was very generous of Mr. Falcon."

"I deserve the best, and after a couple of more shows I'll have it," Andre told her. "The icing on the cake will be all the accolades I'll receive when I show in New York after Seattle. Following on the heels of my triumph in Seattle, it will place me at the pinnacle of my career and permanently place me as the premiere sculptor in the world."

The snap of the lock on the Vuitton luggage was loud in the room. "Ready, sir."

"Carry them out to the car," Andre instructed. Then he turned to speak to Phoenix. "Hurry and change."

"All right." She turned to go but glanced back over her shoulder when she felt the soft, supple leather of his gloved hand on her upper forearm. "Was there something else?"

"I don't want you seeing Morgan Grayson while I'm gone."

Phoenix's gaze flickered to Ben, who was locking the second suitcase. Although he and Cleo were privy to everything that went on in the house, Phoenix didn't like discussing her personal life in front of them. "I already told you that he's not interested in me." Why did just saying the words make her chest feel tight?

Andre's fingers tightened. "That man wants you."

Phoenix's heart pounded. "Y-you're mistaken."

The older man's face harshened. "I'm not. I forbid you to see him or contact him in any way."

She opened her mouth to promise but found herself saying, "I've always done as you requested," instead.

"Good." He withdrew his hand. "Go get dressed. I want to leave in fifteen minutes."

Phoenix hurried away before Andre realized she hadn't promised. No matter what Andre said, there was something about Morgan Grayson that intrigued and drew her. If the opportunity to get to know such a fascinating man better presented itself, she was taking it.

Andre had literally saved her life, but he had also shaped it for his own benefit. It was about time she started taking some of her life back.

"Mr. Duval had nothing but praise for the way the arts council has made his stay here so enjoyable. Our timely intervention with him regarding his air travel today set us apart from his other host cities."

Morgan couldn't believe his ears as he sat at the oblong table in the conference room of the Santa Fe arts council with his mother and the other members, all intelligent men and women. At least he had thought so until Samuel Haskell, the president, began talking.

Morgan gazed at his mother. Although she wore her usual serene expression, he wasn't fooled. She was probably doing handsprings in her mind. For a woman who usually was a good judge of character, she had on blinders where Duval was concerned.

"Mr. Duval was so appreciative for our assistance that he called personally to thank us before he boarded the jet," Samuel practically gushed. A small, bearded man in his early sixties, as president of the council he was the only full-time employee. He lived and breathed art and was usually levelheaded, but that quality seemed to have gone out the widow when Duval appeared. *Everlasting* attested to Duval's talent, but he was also a pain.

"Ruth, the council owes you and Mr. Falcon a debt of gratitude," Samuel continued jovially. "Please convey our thanks to him."

Morgan's mother nodded. "We believe in leaving a legacy behind for our children and our children's children. That is all the thanks either of us needs."

Applause erupted around the table. Morgan found himself applauding with the rest of the council members. His mother wasn't shoveling horse apples. Too many of the contributions on both sides of their families, Native American and African-American, had been lost through ignorance, neglect, or pure meanness. He just wished Andre Duval wasn't one of the people whose work was being celebrated.

"I'm still getting calls from reporters and art critics around the country, especially since Mr. Duval will be here working on the pieces for his next two shows." Haskell looked fondly at Ruth Grayson again. "We have another Grayson, Sierra, to thank for Mr. Duval's satisfaction with the house."

More applause. This time Morgan was less enthusiastic. Much as he admired his sister, he was still perturbed by Duval's snow job. Why should he want to leave when he was receiving free rent, food, and an arts council ready to jump at his every whim?

"Ms. Bannister, his assistant, called me this afternoon to tell me that he and his staff had arrived safely in New York."

"He took his staff with him?" Morgan blurted. All eyes converged on him. The only pair he was concerned about was his mother's. She hadn't mentioned Phoenix, so perhaps she didn't know of the rumors circulating about her relationship with Duval or that she was young, stunningly beautiful, and single. *And pigs flew.*

"That was the reason Daniel sent his jet, Morgan," his mother explained. "Mr. Duval was unable to get his staff reservations on the same flight."

Her speaking to him dictated that he turn to her. He kept his expression dispassionate when he did. "Did anyone think of asking why he just didn't have them take another flight?"

The council members traded questioning glances. He had them now.

"Because he's always accompanied by his staff," his mother answered. "You can't expect a man of Mr. Duval's stature and temperament to collect his own luggage or be bothered by obtaining transportation. And what about when he arrives at his final destination? His staff is imperative to make his life seamless. His mind must be clear of the tedious details of life to enable him to create."

"Exactly," Samuel quickly interjected, although moments before he'd looked as baffled as the rest of the council.

Morgan's mother bestowed a sweetly innocent smile on Morgan. He grunted and settled back in his chair. His mother had been around her sister-in-law, Felicia Falcon, too much. His aunt, like Sierra, had a way with people. They bent over backward to accommodate Felicia. She might be beautiful and appear fragile, but she was as tenacious as his mother in going after what she wanted.

There wasn't a pretentious bone in his aunt's body, but she enjoyed the benefits of her wealthy and influential upbringing to the fullest. Morgan knew of only one person, her husband, John Henry, who had ever said no to her or tried to dissuade her from what she wanted. She loved him unconditionally. They lived happily on their working ranch in Oklahoma.

"I think it's wonderful that Morgan is concerned about the financial interest of the council," Alecia Stephens said from beside him, a flirtatious smile on her face, not an auburn hair out of place, her hand on his arm.

Since Alecia was one of the few women whom his mother hadn't paraded before him, Morgan gave her back a smile with interest. They'd graduated from high school together. Back then, she hadn't given him a second look. Lately that's all she'd been doing. She was a pretty, rich widow looking for a second husband to spoil her as much as her deceased husband

and her parents had. Until tonight, Morgan had taken a wide berth around her.

"Thanks, Alecia. Nice of you to notice."

"I noticed all right," she whispered suggestively.

Her hand dropped from his arm and then Morgan felt a small, knowing hand on his thigh, heading toward dangerous territory. Since it wasn't the first time this had happened to him, he didn't start, but it was definitely the first time it had happened with his mother looking on disapprovingly.

Casually he reached under the table and removed Alecia's hand. This time the look he sent her said, *Behave or else*.

Morgan felt his mother's gaze on him and refused to look. Women were certainly messing up his life. Despite his best efforts, he couldn't help missing a woman he had no right to miss. Mentally he added another item to his growing list of reasons to dislike Duval.

He had taken Phoenix away from Morgan.

He barely knew Phoenix. It shouldn't matter that she was gone, especially since he wasn't supposed to contact her, but he couldn't seem to help himself.

"Well, if there is nothing further, I think we can adjourn the meeting early tonight," Samuel said, grinning for all he was worth.

"Morgan, there's some business I'd like to discuss with you. Can you follow me home?" Alecia asked, her voice a suggestive purr.

The type of business she wanted to conduct was

clearly written in her hot gaze and would be conducted between the sheets—if they managed to get that far. But Morgan had never substituted one woman for another and it was Phoenix who was firmly in his thoughts. "I'm afraid I have another engagement." He came to his feet. "I'll have my secretary call you tomorrow and set up an appointment."

Alecia's seductive smile dimmed. Her lips pressed tight in annoyance, she stood as well. "On second thought, I've changed my mind. Good night."

"Night." Morgan tipped his dark head.

"Wise decision," his mother said when Alecia had walked away. "She's not the one for you."

"What do you mean?" Morgan asked, although he already knew the answer.

His mother gently patted his cheek. "It will all be revealed in time. Good night."

Morgan stared after his mother as she left with the others. The hunt had begun again and he was the prey.

4

Be careful what you wish for. Phoenix had heard Cleo repeat the old adage many times but had never paid it much attention or thought it would have anything to do with her . . . until she had wandered the four-thousand-square-foot home by herself for two days.

Sighing, she covered up the project she had been working on for the past two hours. Instead of creating, she was simply shifting clay. Her gaze drifted to the three windows and the beautiful mountains in the distance. Instead of inspiring her as they usually did, they made the loneliness more intense.

She had wanted the freedom to create, to be her own boss. Now that she had it, she was lonelier than she had been in a long time. In the past forty-eight hours she'd learned she didn't deal well without people around, nor did she sleep well.

The first day hadn't been so difficult, but since then she'd found herself spending more time in the stable with Crimson or out riding him to keep from being by herself. She'd even taken to doing the sketches in the stable. Her work was suffering. She couldn't afford the waste of time. Creating bronzes was a time-consuming multistep process.

Unlike some people thought, sculptures were not created directly from bronze. Hers and Andre's were created by the "lost wax process," as had been done for thousands of years by their African ancestors. After the original was sculpted from clay, a mold was cast by the foundry and used for making a wax duplicate.

Molten wax was then poured into the mold, sloshed around, poured back out, and allowed to cool. The process was repeated until a layer of wax one-fourth to three-eighths of an inch thick was built up inside the mold.

Afterward, the sculptor would go over the wax duplicate and then the final bronze to ensure no detail was lost in the transition. A sculpture was made three times to get a finished, permanent bronze. She had yet to finish the first step.

Finally accepting that she wouldn't be able to work on her own projects, she came off the stool and headed for Andre's study. There were eight finished pieces that were ready to be sent to the foundry. The wax work could take hours or days, depending on the quality of the mold and how complex the sculpture was. There mustn't be any slipups for the coming shows or Andre would have her head.

He called every night around nine. He always said it was to ensure himself she was doing all right and was safely in for the night. They both knew it was to reassure himself that she wasn't out with Morgan.

Fat chance, she thought with a wry twist of her mouth. He'd practically run from her. She wished she knew what had caused the change in him from their first meeting. Perhaps Andre was right; she had very little experience with men. However, Morgan looked and acted as if he knew all there was to know about women.

Sitting behind his desk, she reached for Andre's Rolodex to get the number, but her hand paused as she saw the signed contracts for *Courage*. A clerk from Morgan's office had called last week wanting to know when the papers would be ready. Phoenix supposed that because of Andre's unexpected trip he had forgotten to call her and ask her to pick them up.

An idea forming in her head, she picked up the contracts. Andre had said he wanted her to see that everything went well. That couldn't happen if Morgan's firm didn't have the contracts to forward. She could drive into town faster than the mail or courier service could pick up and deliver them. Pleased with her reasoning, she pulled the Rolodex to her. First the foundry, then she was getting dressed and going into town.

Phoenix didn't have any difficulty finding Morgan's office building in the Plaza, the heart of the shopping district and downtown. After being in so many cities where skyscrapers were the norm, it was refreshing to see many of the buildings no higher than five stories. Even with the crowds and the busy traffic, the city still possessed a charm all its own. She felt she could easily live here and be happy. She'd never felt that way about any other place.

When she saw a woman and a small child of about four holding hands and laughing together, a deep sadness struck. If only . . .

Biting her lip, Phoenix looked away. There was no sense living in the past or thinking of what might have been. In that at least, Andre was right. Now and the future were what mattered. She had to focus on the upcoming shows and snap out of her gloomy mood. But first, she had to deliver the contracts to Morgan.

Instead of moving forward, she clutched the manila envelope closer to her chest, stepping aside as a chattering group of women passed. She stared at the entrance to Morgan's office building and chewed on her lower lip. He hadn't been too pleased to see her the last time. Why risk rejection? Perhaps she should just find a post office and mail them. But that would be the coward's way. She had done that too much in the past.

Lowering the envelope, she glanced down at her white blouse and black gabardine slacks to check her appearance, then shoved the thick strap of her hobo handbag over her shoulder and started toward the recessed doorway. It was time she took control of her life.

She was a few feet away from the three steps leading into the office building when Morgan came out the door. Both came to an abrupt halt and stared. It was a toss-up as to who was more surprised.

"Phoenix?"

Her throat dried. Her heart thudded. He affected her as no other man ever had. It wasn't just the beautiful face or the muscular build; it was something else she was still trying to figure out. "Good morning, Morgan. I . . . er . . ." She couldn't finish. His face wore that same look of disapproval it had the night of the art show.

"So Duval is back?" he asked tightly.

She briefly wondered why he had taken such a dislike to Andre, then answered his question. "No. I didn't go with him."

Morgan frowned, then briefly took her arm and pulled her closer to the building out of people's way. "I understood he took his staff with him."

"Except me. I found these on his desk." She thrust the manila envelope toward him. "Andre must have forgotten to call your clerk back and tell her they were signed."

He accepted the papers, still staring at her. "Thank you."

She wished she knew how to make him smile at her the way he had when they first met. "You're welcome. It gave me a chance to get out of the house and be around people."

"You're there by yourself?"

She smiled shyly. "Crimson is there."

Morgan thought he should probably move on, but

his feet apparently didn't agree. "What do you plan to do now that you've delivered the contracts?"

She shrugged self-consciously. "I hadn't thought past dropping off the papers."

Morgan came to a quick decision. Staying away from her didn't mean being rude. Obviously she was lonely. "How about having lunch with me?"

Her smile lit up her face. "I'd love to."

Morgan's breath caught. Phoenix could present a problem if he wasn't careful. But he was always careful.

He took her by the arm and they started down the street. "What do you like? Santa Fe has everything, but don't be surprised if most of it, even the Chinese food, has chile peppers in it."

"I know, but it's all right. I like spicy food."

He wondered what else she liked. He'd like to nibble on her ear and other parts of her. He cleared his throat. "So where do you want to eat?"

She stared up at him, her expression thoughtful, as if she'd never had the privilege before. "Well, there is one place."

"Name it," he said, inordinately pleased that he could grant her her wish.

"The Red Cactus. The food at the private reception for the art show was wonderful. I briefly met the owner, Brandon Grayson," she said, then sent him a puzzled look. "Are you related to him by any chance?"

"My younger brother."

Her eyes widened in surprise; then she smiled. "I'm certainly glad I said only good things about the food."

Morgan brushed a strand of her hair behind her ear. Her skin was soft as the finest silk. "Somehow I think you only have good things to say about people."

Her breath seemed to snag. "I-I try."

Her reaction to his touch went straight through him. He shoved his hand in his pocket. She was off-limits. He was just being nice. Nothing more.

One thing for sure was that if he took Phoenix to The Red Cactus, Brandon would tell Sierra and Pierce. And after Sierra's warning the other night, Morgan didn't want her camped on his doorstep when he arrived home tonight. "Brandon's restaurant is usually crowded for lunch. How about we go someplace quieter?"

"All right. Since you know the city, I'll let you decide."

"I know just the place."

Morgan took her to the Mexican Grill just off the Plaza. He knew the hostess. Morgan had helped her brother, a young man who was heading for college and a better life until drugs had sidetracked him. He'd been arrested for possession of marijuana. With Morgan's help he had his life back, but no NBA team would take him after his conviction. But he had a good job and he and his wife were expecting their first baby in a few months.

After giving Morgan and Phoenix their menus, the hostess left. A server appeared, bringing two bowls of salsa swimming with red and green chile peppers and salty hot corn chips.

Phoenix bowed her head, said her blessing, then double-dipped a chip. Her eyes closed. Morgan was about to signal a waiter for milk to quench the fire, when she moaned in pleasure.

His body hardened as he imagined drawing similar sounds from her body. Suddenly he was the one in need of something to quench his own fire.

Opening her eyes, she reached for another chip. "You're not eating?"

"Watching you is more enjoyable," he said.

She blinked those big expressive eyes of hers at him and appeared at a loss for what to say. A woman unused to taking compliments with aplomb was not what he would have expected from *La Flame*. Neither had he expected her to be so down-to-earth. Once again, Morgan had the feeling she hadn't socialized much, at least doing the everyday things.

"Please continue," he said, and reached for his napkin. While placing it in his lap, he said his grace. He didn't want to embarrass her. Apparently, Duval was a man who didn't thank *anyone*.

Lifting his head, he dunked a chip. "The restaurant probably can't compare to some of the places you've eaten."

"Nope. This is better."

Morgan started to ask her in what way, but she was studying the menu. "I can guarantee everything is good," he said.

The menu lowered enough for him to see amusement in her eyes. "And hot."

"That, too."

Down went her head again. "I think I'll go for the blue corn enchiladas and a half order of chicken fajitas."

"Sounds good," Morgan said, and placed his menu aside. "Where did you learn to eat chile like a pro?"

"All over," she said just as the waitress appeared to take their orders. "I'll have iced tea."

"I'll get those drinks right out to you." Gathering the menus, the slender woman in a red blouse and black slacks left.

Phoenix picked up another chip, dunked, then propped one arm on the small wooden table and stared at him. "Is it just the two of you?"

"Hardly. I'm the second of five."

She straightened. "Five. It must have been wonderful growing up with so many to play with."

"And get into arguments with," Morgan said without heat.

"You would have been the peacemaker," Phoenix said as the waitress set their drinks on the table, then withdrew.

"Only if Luke wasn't there," Morgan said, trying to figure out how she'd known he was the peacemaker.

"Luke? Is he the oldest? Does he live here?"

If anyone else had asked Morgan all those personal questions, he might have balked. The thought didn't enter his mind with Phoenix. It was as if she was starved for knowledge and friendship. All through the meal he found himself relating tales of his family— and enjoying it as much as she seemed to.

"You have a wonderful family, Morgan."

"When they're minding their own business," he growled, pushing away his empty plate.

She briefly touched his hand. "From what you've told me about them, it's because they love you. Always remember that." She picked up her oversize purse and stood. "Thank you for a wonderful dining experience. I'd better get home."

Morgan placed some bills on the table, then came to his feet and took her arm. "The ranch is pretty isolated. You ever consider staying in town until Duval returns?"

"I wouldn't want to leave Crimson." She extended her hand when they were on the sidewalk. "I know you must be busy. Thank you again for making my day so enjoyable."

As Morgan's fingers closed around hers, he felt her hand jerk. He didn't want to let it go or for her to leave. "I'll walk you to your car."

A small tongue rimmed her lips. "You must be busy."

"I have time." He curved his arm around her waist to settle the matter and bring her closer. "Besides, I need the exercise after that meal."

She grimaced. "Don't remind me. I may need to forgo riding Crimson if I keep eating like this."

Lucky horse, Morgan thought, and clamped his

teeth shut to keep the words from spilling out. "That would be a shame for both of you."

She looked at him oddly, as if she didn't know how to reply. "There's a candy store across the street. Since we've already committed gluttony, what do you say we stop in there and get pralines for dessert? My treat."

He'd wager her lips would taste as sweet and be as addictive as any confection ever made. But because of Duval's lies Morgan would never find out. Only strict self-discipline kept the scowl from his face. "I'd say you've got yourself a deal."

After they left the candy shop Morgan saw Phoenix safely to her car, then went directly to his office. "Please hold all calls, Florine," he said, then entered his office and placed his attaché case on his desk. When he messed up, he *really* messed up.

He'd seen no fewer than three of his mother's close friends on the way back from lunch with Phoenix. Two had passed in their cars while he and Phoenix waited for the traffic light to change; the other one had been in the candy store. He and Phoenix hadn't been able to get their candy fast enough to prevent an introduction.

Morgan grimaced when he recalled how Mrs. Day had made it a point to tell Phoenix what a wonderful young man he was. The way the older woman gushed, he wouldn't have been surprised if a halo had appeared over his head. It hadn't done any good to skip having lunch at The Red Cactus; before the day was over his family would know that he'd taken Phoenix to lunch.

Sighing, Morgan took a seat behind his desk; what was done was done. Although he'd enjoyed being with Phoenix, he realized that he had done most of the talking. He hadn't learned anything about her, which was odd.

Most people revealed some tidbit about themselves in the course of a conversation. From Phoenix there had been nothing. He recalled she had kept the conversation flowing. As soon as he answered one question or finished telling her about his family, she'd ask another question. If he hadn't been so concerned with seeing that she enjoyed her lunch, he might have caught on sooner.

The average person wasn't so noncommunicative about herself or as skilled in obtaining information without sharing any—unless she had something to hide. But what?

Deep in thought, he rubbed his hand behind his neck. There was obviously more going on with Phoenix than he had originally thought. Did he want to bother ferreting out the truths she concealed or keep walking?

As a lawyer, he'd long since learned the meaning behind opening Pandora's box. Truth, like lies, often had repercussions. Ultimately, he had to weigh whether Phoenix would be better off with her secrets.

Perhaps a better question, he mused as he picked

up his day planner, was why he couldn't stop thinking
about her.

Morgan was running late. Clients and paperwork had
kept him in his office until seven that evening, the
same time he was supposed to be at a meeting with
several teenagers and the director of Second Chance.
He wheeled his roadster into a parking spot between a
battered, dented Ford and a new Jeep. Both cars be-
longed to two of the kids in the program. Drugs cut
across all socioeconomic status and races. They were
an impartial killer of dreams, and too often of lives.

Getting out, Morgan sprinted toward the brightly
painted adobe building nestled in the shade of several
mature trees. The teenagers who came to the center
had wanted to leave their mark on it to say that it was
theirs, and he'd let them. The kaleidoscope of colors
made him wince every time he saw the broad sweep
of magenta, orange, pink, and the numerous other
colors that each teenager who entered the center
painted to put his or her stamp on the building—thus
taking ownership of the program and control of their
lives.

Pushing open the thick wooden door, Morgan
waved to Thelma, the receptionist, and went straight
to the meeting room. "Hi, sorry I'm late."

Every one of the six people crowded into the small
room turned to him. A chorus of, "Hi, Mr. G.," greeted
him as he squeezed his way into the small space left
and took his seat in a folding chair. It was a world

away from the plush offices of the arts council or the recently dedicated SWAIA building.

"Good evening, Morgan," said Marie Bates, the director of the center. Slender, with soft curls framing her round face, she doled out love and discipline in equal measures. As a former high school counselor, she had firsthand knowledge of how drugs devastated lives. Gene had been her oldest son. She was just as determined as Morgan to save others from the same horrible fate. "Actually, we're just getting started planning the party."

"Great, then I didn't miss much," Morgan said, loosening his tie.

Erica, a slender, dark-eyed beauty who had begun sniffing glue when she was seven, then went on to use the harder stuff before cleaning up nine months ago, grinned and glanced around the table. Morgan didn't have to see Mrs. Bates's lips twitch to know what she was about to say.

"We were about to get to refreshments," Erica said, her pencil poised over her spiral notebook. "Any suggestions?"

Morgan chuckled. He'd offered to bring the food for their first get-together, and with few exceptions, he still did. "Let me check with Brandon's schedule."

Cheers went up around the room. Erica pushed her long auburn hair behind her shoulder and scribbled in her notebook. "Brandon won't let us down. What about decorations?"

"Pink balloons and streamers hanging from the ceiling," offered Cicely, her eyes sparking as much as the five gold earrings of varied sizes in the lobe of each ear. But it was a natural high and not from cocaine. "I just love pink."

"So we noticed," quipped James, who had been hooked on speed.

Cicely looked up at him through a sweep of eyelashes. "What else did you notice, James?"

James grinned and gave Cicely a thorough onceover. "You fill out that pink T real good."

"You two can flirt on your own time," Mrs. Bates told them. "What about a decorating committee?"

"The others said they'd help," Erica informed them. "Do you think your brother would give up some munchies for that?"

"He'll have enough to do preparing the food for the party. Why don't I just bring chips, salsa, and soft drinks?" His thoughts went to Phoenix and her undisguised delight while eating. "I'll also see if I can invite someone to help decorate as well."

"A babe?" Rob, the newest member of the group, asked. Slouched down in his chair, he wore dark shades, oversize jeans, and a black jacket. Morgan wasn't worried that Rob's eyes were hidden; his hands were steady and at rest on top of the battered table.

"A lady," Morgan corrected.

Rob straightened and placed his arms on the table, then lifted his glasses to reveal startling blue eyes. "If you need any pointers, I'm your man."

Morgan didn't doubt it. Rob was a good-looking kid with just enough edge to make him appealing to females. "I'll take that under advisement."

"From what I hear, Mr. G. could give us pointers," Noble informed them, his hair in neat microtwists, his words precise and clear, unlike the night several months ago when he had been arrested for being intoxicated. It hadn't been the first time he'd been drunk, but it had been the last.

"I don't think—" Morgan began.

"Gossip. Give," Cicely said, popping her bubble gum.

"Let's not," Morgan said firmly.

"Mr. G., all I was going to say is that these two women today at the video shop where I work think you're hot," Noble informed him, smiling that he'd been able to say what he wanted. "And that's not the first time. But your brothers get their props, too."

"Noble," Morgan said firmly.

Holding up his hands innocently, the teenager settled back in his chair.

Thankfully Mrs. Bates got them back on track. "I can pick up the decorations tomorrow. Any volunteers to go with me?"

The girls' hands went up.

"Wonderful. If you'll be here at noon, we can all go in my car."

"Refreshments, decorations, and decorating committee are taken care of. How about music?" Mrs. Bates asked, her question assured to get the kids' attention off Morgan.

He might have been grateful for her intervention if he hadn't known whatever music they chose would be blasting from the biggest speaker they could find. His ears would still be ringing hours later.

Less than thirty minutes later they were almost ready to go. "We can meet here Wednesday night and start on the streamers and wire flowers. Don't be late," Mrs. Bates told them.

Assuring her they would be on time both days, they gathered their things.

"Wait a minute, young ladies. The fellows and I will walk you to your car after I speak with Mrs. Bates." Crime was just as rampant there as in any metropolitan city.

"We got it, Mr. G.," James said, slinging his arm around Cicely's shoulder.

She giggled up at him and they left the room, their heads close together, the other kids following close behind.

Shaking her head, Mrs. Bates stared after them. "Well, I think you and I will have to have another talk about responsible sex soon."

"Looks that way." A couple of the other girls in the program were already parents. "You want me to wait and walk you out?"

"No, thank you. Herb is picking me up and we'll see that Thelma gets home all right."

Herb was her husband and a good man. Thank God they had two other children they'd never had a moment's problem with. "I'll be on my way then. Good night."

"Night, Morgan."

Morgan left the center and saw the kids still in the parking lot, laughing and talking. Just kids having fun and living. He planned to do everything in his power to keep them that way.

Three late-model cars were in Morgan's driveway when he arrived home later that night. The owners of those cars watched him from their seats on the padded iron benches on either side of his front door on the wide front porch.

Seeing them, he almost turned the car around, then decided against postponing the inevitable. They'd track him down sooner or later. Activating the garage door, he drove inside, then went into the single-level Mediterranean-style house he'd helped design and opened the one-hundred-year-old oak door.

Sierra, Brandon, and Pierce were waiting for him. From the dusty pink Ralph Lauren suit Sierra wore with matching bag and shoes, she had probably come directly from showing one of her million-dollar listings, which wasn't difficult with the escalating price of real estate in Santa Fe. Pierce wore one of the three-piece pin-striped suits he favored. Brandon, as usual, was in blue jeans and his red cactus boots.

None looked happy.

"Come on in, but let me get a drink before you start in on me." Turning, Morgan crossed the terrazzo floor of the art-filled entry and continued to the stainless-steel kitchen whose appliances he seldom used. Removing a glass from the cabinet, he opened the built-in refrigerator and took out a slender pitcher of cranberry-colored liquid. "Anyone else?"

Sierra, always the most impatient of his siblings, spoke first. "How could you? After I told you to be careful?"

Morgan calmly replaced the pitcher, then sipped his cranberry tea. "What did I do?"

Sierra's small hands rested on her hips. "It's all over town that you were hugging and laughing with that woman."

Somehow he didn't like Phoenix being referred to as "that woman." "If you mean Phoenix Bannister, I was not hugging her. Opal Day is nearsighted and refuses to wear her glasses and you know it."

"Does the same go for Paula Howard and Eva Rutley?" Pierce asked quietly from beside his sister.

Pierce was a financial adviser and as such never rushed into things before he saw a clear way out. He was a thinker, a planner, and always fair. "I had my hand around her waist in broad daylight."

"But where was your mind?" Sierra asked.

"That," Morgan set his glass aside, "is none of your business."

"I'm too young to get married," Brandon groaned.

If Morgan hadn't loved them so much he would have tossed them all out. "How many times have you put your hand on a woman's waist or had a man put his hand on your waist? I don't see any of you married."

"There's women and there's *women*," Brandon said. "I saw Phoenix in that red dress. She's gorgeous."

Morgan's eyes narrowed.

"Hate I missed that," Pierce said.

"You've got a woman," Brandon reminded him.

Pierce shrugged his shoulders and reached into the cabinet for a glass. "I'm thinking of moving on. Tell me more about Phoenix."

Pierce ignored Morgan's stare just like Brandon did.

"Will you stop being men!" Sierra snapped. "I'm not about to give up my life to pick up after some man."

"Sierra," Pierce said calmly as he filled his glass. "Most likely the man would be picking up after you. You're as messy as Brandon."

"Not in the kitchen," Brandon pointed out proudly.

"That's the one room in her condo that's spotless, because she can't cook," Morgan threw in.

Sierra stuck up her nose. "I can cook. I simply choose not to. I'm certainly not going to work all day, then come home to cook for some man."

"Then, as I see it, the three of you have nothing to worry about. I'm not going to cut myself off from women because Mama wants me to get married." Folding his arms, Morgan leaned against the counter. "I don't see any of you giving up dating."

"We're not the next in line," Pierce said.

"So that means that if, by some astronomical twist of fate, I, then Brandon, get married, you're going to give up dating?" Morgan already knew the answer.

Pierce looked stunned. He changed women faster than their cousin-in-law Matt Taggart had when he was single. "I don't think there is any need to do anything that drastic."

"I rest my case." Morgan picked up his tea.

"I don't know." Shaking his head, Brandon opened the side-by-side refrigerator and began sifting through the contents. "I need to think."

Since Brandon thought better when his hands were busy, Morgan left his brother alone. Brandon was an excellent chef and he was well acquainted with Morgan's kitchen. Morgan might not cook, but his housekeeper did, and she always kept the refrigerator well stocked.

Brandon continued talking as he pulled out several giant green chile peppers, shrimp, and cheddar cheese. "Mama has her mind set on us getting married for our own good." He obtained a bowl from beneath the cabinet and mixed the cheese, shrimp, and a few other ingredients, then stuffed them into the washed peppers. "She loves us enough to see this through."

There was total silence. Screwing up her face, Sierra poured a glass of cranberry tea for her and one for Brandon. "That's why it's so important for Morgan to remain strong. If he falters, there will be no stopping her."

Morgan found the deep fryer Brandon would need, filled it with canola oil, then pulled four plates from the cabinet and placed them on the table. "I'm not going to turn into a monk over this."

Tableware in his hand, Pierce cringed. "Will you please stop making those statements?"

Sierra found the black damask napkins and gave Brandon a chile pepper–shaped serving dish for the *chile rellenos*. "Perhaps we did overreact. I just know Mama has heard by now."

"Mama picked out Catherine for Luke. She wouldn't have chosen Phoenix," Morgan told them.

"Why?" they all asked.

Morgan didn't like repeating that the association between her and Duval was murky. He liked thinking about it even less. "I have my reasons."

"You plan to see her again?" Pierce asked. Brandon turned from watching the food sizzling in the oil.

"I haven't decided yet."

Sierra looked relieved.

Pierce smiled like a hungry cat in front of an open birdcage door. "Then I just might—"

"No." One word. Flat. Inflexible. Morgan didn't care that they were all staring at him as if he'd gone round the bend. They might fight, but never with one another and never over a woman.

"Well, that certainly puts a cap on things." Pierce took the serving dish from the black granite counter and placed it on the hand-carved table. "Let's eat. Seems I have some living to do before it's my turn."

Morgan wrinkled his mouth, seated Sierra, then took his own seat. "Just because I don't want you seeing her doesn't mean anything."

"Luke acted just that possessive when he thought I was trying to come on to Catherine," Brandon reminded them, then said grace for all of them and stabbed a chile pepper. "At the rate we're falling, I'll be married by this time next year."

"I am *not* getting married," Morgan gritted out.

"There's only one way to ensure that that doesn't happen," Sierra said, spearing her own food. "At least not with Phoenix."

"And that would be?" Brandon asked.

His sister stared straight at Morgan. "Morgan already knows. He can't see her again. Ever."

5

Never see her again.

Those words played over and over in Morgan's head. They were there when he went to sleep at night and waiting for him when he woke the next morning.

He wasn't sure if it was the stubborn side of him that didn't like people warning him off or his own need to see her. There was one way to find out.

He was going to see Phoenix Bannister.

Morgan was not a man to second-guess himself, so once he made the decision he drove out to Duval's place Saturday morning. He'd find out if his gut settled when he saw her, heard her voice. He admitted to himself as he parked in front of the house that he also wanted to make sure she was all right. Duval should have left one of his staff with her, but he was too selfish. He'd rather have them cater to him than see that Phoenix was safe.

Getting out of the car, Morgan went to the front door and rang the doorbell. When there was no answer after a few minutes, he started toward the stable. The door behind him suddenly opened.

He turned around. Phoenix stood in the door, a surprised but pleased smile on her beautiful face. The tension that had stayed with him the past couple of days disappeared. "Good morning."

"Good morning, Morgan. Please come on in." She stepped back and closed the door when he was inside. "Excuse my appearance. I saw you through the curtain and was afraid you'd leave if I took time to change."

She looked adorably sexy in an oversize gray sweatshirt and jeans. Her feet were bare. Her toenails were painted siren red. "I'm glad you didn't."

She blushed. "Please have a seat. Would you like some coffee?"

What he'd like was to kiss her until they were both breathless, then start all over again. "If you don't mind."

"I'll be back in a minute."

"I'll go with you."

Her head tilted as if trying to figure out why he was here, but she was too polite to ask. "Of course."

Morgan followed her through the house to the kitchen and took a seat at the island. He noticed her hand trembled as she picked up the carafe. Good. "I take it black. No sugar. How are things going?"

"Much better, thanks." She set a delicate cup and saucer in front of him.

"You joining me?" he questioned, lifting the cup.

She hesitated, then poured another cup and sat next to him. "The contracts all right?"

Morgan sipped the rich Colombian blend. "Yes. I sent them off the same day you gave them to me. That's not why I'm here."

"Oh." Her cup rattled in the saucer. "Was there something else you needed?"

A smile touched his lips. "That's not a question a beautiful woman asks a man, especially when they're alone."

She looked nonplussed, then laughed, but it was shaky. "I'm not beautiful."

"Yes, you are." Two fingers gently brushed her cheek. "You have the most incredible skin."

Looking a bit dazed, she lifted her hand to touch the exact spot he had. Her reaction made what he had to say next easier. "I need to ask you a question. A very personal one. You can tell me to mind my own business, but I have to know."

Wariness entered her eyes. "What?"

Hearing the uncertainty in her voice, Morgan was no longer so sure, but he had no intention of leaving without the answer. "Are you and Duval romantically involved?"

The relief in her face and voice was immediate. "No."

"Have you ever been?"

"No."

"Have dinner with me tonight?" His hand covered hers, felt the warmth, the slight tremor. "We can go to The Red Cactus."

Shyly she smiled at him. "I'd like that. Is eight all right?"

"Perfect." Still holding her hand, he stood and went to the front door. "Thanks for not dashing the coffee in my face."

"Thank you for asking me and not listening to rumors," she said quietly.

It was on the tip of his tongue to ask her why, if she knew about the rumors, she fed into them by dressing the way she did and living with the man; then he remembered a lesson his mother had taught them as children: "You can't stop people from saying bad things about you; all you can do is live your life."

"See you at eight," Morgan said.

Phoenix watched Morgan drive away. *A date*. Morgan had asked her out. She didn't go inside until his car disappeared. She hadn't realized how much she wanted him to ask her until now.

Grinning, she ran to her closet to find something to wear. Whatever it was, it wouldn't be red. She was reaching for a teal blue sheath when the doorbell rang. She spun around, smiling and anticipating seeing Morgan again.

She opened the door. The smile disappeared on seeing her visitor. "Raymond. I thought you had returned to New York."

"As you can see, I didn't. I need to see Duval."

"He's gone."

Surprise widened his eyes. "Where? When?"

"About five days ago. I can't tell you his location."

"Why the hell not?" he asked sharply.

Rudeness from Andre was difficult; from Raymond it was intolerable. "I can see you're upset, but don't take it out on me."

His eyes narrowed, but his tone softened. "When will he be back?"

"I don't know. He's doing research for his next pieces," she repeated the lie she'd always told when Duval was away.

"He wouldn't leave you alone," Raymond said suspiciously.

"He calls every night. If you'd like to leave a message, I'd be happy to give it to him."

"Yeah, tell him to call me. I'm staying at the same hotel here in Santa Fe." He started to leave, then looked back. "I'll be back in the morning."

"There's no need—"

"There's every need."

Frowning, she closed the door. She'd never understood the relationship between Andre and Raymond. Sometimes they talked as if they were friends; other times it appeared as though they couldn't stand each other.

Their problem. Her problem was finding a dress to wear. Morgan had called her beautiful. She didn't think so, but she was going to do her best to dazzle him. At least her possible romantic liaison with Andre was cleared up between them.

She wasn't ignorant about what people said about her relationship with Andre. Some had even said it to her face. Andre hadn't understood how deeply the talk had embarrassed and hurt her. His concern had been in creating the image he needed.

Deciding on the teal blue sheath with a bolero jacket, she went to wash her hair. This would be her first date in over a year. She just hoped it didn't end the way the last one had . . . with her in tears.

Morgan was almost back in town when he slipped on his cell phone headset and punched in Kenneth's home phone number. Using a cell phone without a headset was illegal in Santa Fe.

The phone was picked up on the fifth ring. "Hello."

"Morning, Kenneth. I'm sorry, but I can no longer represent Duval for you," Morgan told him as he eased around a slow-moving van.

"Might I ask why?"

Kenneth was taking it better than Morgan expected. Kenneth might try to be diplomatic, but when it was warranted, he could shred a man to ribbons. "Conflict of interest. I have a date with Phoenix tonight. The first of many, I hope."

"Wasn't it a little over a week ago that you told me it wouldn't be difficult to stay away from this particular young lady?"

"I was wrong." Morgan flicked on his signal to pass a horse trailer.

"Ah," Kenneth said, then, "However, I was not wrong in my estimation of Duval's reaction to your being anywhere near her. Have you considered the repercussions?"

"In a word, no," Morgan said. "Phoenix is a grown woman and if she isn't saying no, then I couldn't care less what Duval thinks or does."

"Morgan," Kenneth said quietly. "Do you know what this means?"

Morgan's hands flexed on the steering wheel. "I'm sorry if I didn't justify your faith in me."

"You should be. If you had lasted just one more day I would have won."

"What?" His hand pressed against the earpiece.

"The bet with Betty," Kenneth said, then went on to explain. "We both agreed that you wouldn't be able to stomach Duval's high-handed behavior for very long. I thought you'd last at least ten days before you put him in his place." Kenneth's heavy sigh drifted through the receiver. "Now, I'll have to attend the opera tonight. You know how much I hate the opera."

Morgan smiled. He and Betty had become good friends as well, because he had been her escort to the opera when he lived in Boston. Kenneth preferred his easy chair and a good murder mystery to relax. "Then I take it you're not upset."

"I never would let a client dictate to me how to run my firm. I'll call Duval and ask if he wants us to finish or if he wants me to refer him to another firm."

"He's out of town and I'm not sure when he'll return." Morgan eased to a stop at the signal light just inside Santa Fe's city limits.

"I see. You never were one to waste time."

He'd wasted too much time, in his estimation. "Thanks for understanding."

"You just watch yourself."

"Don't worry about me. I've got it covered. Bye." Feeling freer than he had in days, Morgan eased off the brakes. He had one more stop before he went home.

Morgan decided to look for Sierra at her office first. He hit pay dirt when he saw her jazzy red BMW Sports Activity Vehicle in the parking space for Top Realtor. Sierra had held the title for the past two years. As Luke was fond of saying, Sierra could sell a lean-to on the side of a cliff.

Intensely competitive, she was prone to let her quick temper get the best of her. Her saving grace was that she loved her family unconditionally and would go down fighting for any of them, even if she had to fight against them. She wasn't going to be pleased that he was taking Phoenix out.

Inside the one-story building, he nodded to the receptionist and continued to Sierra's office in the back and knocked.

"Come in."

He did as requested. Sierra was sitting behind her cluttered desk with the cordless white phone in one hand and the other hand poised over the keyboard as she studied the monitor on her computer.

"Mrs. Jones, you can take a virtual tour of the three homes, any of which I think would be ideal for you and your husband." She motioned for him to come closer.

"If you'd like to drive out and look at them or other homes by the Internet or in person, please contact me. I'm here to serve you and make sure you get exactly what you're looking for and what you deserve. You have my number. Good-bye."

Replacing the receiver, she leaned back in her chair. "You've never visited me with your lawyer face on before. I guess I don't have to think too long to figure out the reason."

"I enjoy being with her. Nothing more, nothing less." He leaned against the side of Sierra's desk and stared down at her. "I came because I don't want you making more out of it than it is. I certainly can't be expected to not date indefinitely."

"All right, Morgan." Sierra rocked forward in her chair. "I guess it was a bit drastic to expect you to cut women out of your life. Brandon and Pierce would have had a stroke."

"I'm taking her to The Red Cactus for dinner tonight. Why don't you stop by and meet her? I think you two could be friends."

"I just might do that."

Phoenix was dressed and ready to go by 7:30, which left her plenty of time to brood and worry whether she looked all right, what Andre's reaction would be if he found out, and about her pitiful record with men. She hoped to circumvent Andre by having the calls to the house transferred to her cell phone. She planned

to excuse herself around nine and wait in the ladies'
room for his call.

She didn't see it as cowardice so much as wanting
to keep peace. She owed Andre a great deal and re-
grettably, she had trusted the wrong men too many
times, starting with Royce when she was a sophomore
in college. He'd captivated her with his good looks
and smooth charm, then betrayed her in the worst possible way. She hadn't minded leaving the heartache
behind and going with Andre to Europe. It had taken
her two years to go out on a date, and again she had
chosen wrong.

Colin Cook, her English riding instructor, had been
older, and looking back, she could see that she had
sought to substitute him for her father. He had thought
she was a way to Andre's money. Determined not to be
used again, she had thrown herself into her sculpting.

Italy was a beautiful country and increasingly
lonely with only contemporaries of Andre for company. She'd yearned for someone her own age to
share the experience with.

Her prayer seemed to have been answered when
she'd met Paolo at a gallery opening she was attending with Andre. Paolo had been suave and attentive
and offered to show her sights in his country that few
tourists were privileged to see. She'd happily accepted his offer.

They were on their second date when Paolo asked
her to put in a good word for him with Andre. Paolo
wanted to study under him. He had actually tried to

convince her that they could spend more time together if he became Andre's pupil. She'd left him at the olive vineyard and hadn't looked back.

Royce's betrayal had devastated her. Colin's had made her doubt her judgment. Paolo's had made her angry. That dating disaster had happened a year ago.

What was there about her that men wanted to use her instead of love her? Or had she simply chosen unscrupulous men?

The chime of the doorbell interrupted her thoughts. She glanced at the thin gold watch on her wrist. Seven forty-five. With Morgan she might have difficulty keeping a straight thought in her head, but his honesty and integrity had never been in question. Taking a deep breath, she went to open the door.

For a long moment, Morgan simply stared. She took his breath away and made him wish they were going to bed instead of out to dinner. "You're more beautiful each time I see you."

The reverence in his deep voice and strikingly handsome face made Phoenix feel almost lightheaded. But there was another emotion in his black eyes that made her tingle all over. "Thank you. I'll get my purse." Picking up the small alligator clutch that exactly matched her dress, she turned and caught him looking at her legs with open appreciation. She quickly recalled that she'd worn pants or a long dress the other times they'd been together.

"Perhaps I shouldn't take you to The Red Cactus," he said when she joined him.

"Why?" She closed the door behind her, expecting Morgan to step back.

Instead he reached around her and checked to ensure that the door was locked, bringing the tempting heat and hardness of his muscled body closer to hers. "Brandon likes to flirt and you're too much of a temptation for him to pass up the opportunity."

Her gaze flickered to his mouth, then quickly away. She moistened her lips. "He probably won't even notice me. Shall we go?"

Morgan knew differently. There was a sensual allure about Phoenix that made a man itch. "There's just one thing I have to do first."

Somehow she knew he was going to kiss her. Her fingernails bit into the bag as his dark head lowered until his lips, warm and gentle, brushed against hers, then settled. She sighed into his mouth, her body leaning against him, her arms going around his neck as if she had done so a thousand times.

Pleasure spiraled through her as his tongue swept the moist interior of her mouth with a greedy thoroughness that caused her to whimper and cling tighter. Slowly he eased back.

"You're as potent as I'd thought you'd be." He brushed his knuckles against her cheek because he couldn't help touching her. He wanted to feel the silky softness of her skin, feel the slight tremor she was helpless to control. He'd never been the possessive or the jealous type, but he was honest enough to admit the kiss had been to stake his claim as much as it had been for pleasure. "You have your key?"

"Y-yes," she managed, hoping her legs didn't give out on her on the way to the car.

"Then let's go."

The Red Cactus, housed in an 1867 Territorial-style adobe house, had a long line waiting as usual. People spilled out from the two red double doors onto the sidewalk. Those who couldn't be seated inside were happily dining outside on the patio even with the temperature dropping from a high that day of eighty-three degrees to a brisk fifty-eight.

Phoenix's shoulders slumped in disappointment on seeing the line. "I know some men don't like to wait, but maybe the line will move fast."

"It usually does, but that won't be our problem." He urged her forward when she would have stopped behind the last couple. "The family table is always available."

Phoenix stared up at him. "Always?"

"Always," he repeated, and ushered her inside the brightly lit restaurant. Indian corn and chile ristras dangled from the walls.

"Good evening, Mr. Grayson. Welcome back," the hostess greeted him, and picked up two red menus in the shape of a red cactus. The menu cactus had a red Stetson tilted to one side and a black bandanna around its spiny neck. "Your table is ready. Marlive will show you the way."

"Follow me, please." Marlive, wearing an off-the-shoulder white blouse and short black skirt identical to that of the hostess, started through the open restaurant with a tiled floor and earth-toned walls.

"Your table." She indicated the large booth near the back with a small Reserved sign on top of the scarred wood, then waited until Morgan seated Phoenix and slid into the bench facing her. "Can I get your drink orders?" Marlive asked, handing them their menus.

"Sweetened iced tea, please."

"My usual, Marlive. Thanks."

"Be right out."

Phoenix smiled across the table at him. "Do you always get this great service?"

Before he could answer, their drinks, salsa, and hot chips arrived. "Anything else, Morgan?" asked a lanky young man in the requisite white shirt and black pants.

"No, thanks, Peter."

Another young woman with a head of red curls served Phoenix her tea and Morgan raspberry lemonade. "Hi, Morgan, miss. You ready to order or do you need a few minutes?"

"Phoenix?" Morgan asked.

"I must be in restaurant heaven," she said impishly, then opened the menu. "Any recommendations? I haven't eaten since breakfast."

"Everything's good. We offer a mixture of Hispanic, Anglo, and American Indian dishes," the waitress said, then laughed. "I've had to increase my exercise program by fifteen minutes a day. I'm a sucker for Brandon's specially fried catfish."

Phoenix handed her the menu. "I'll have the catfish, Cathy."

The waitress glanced down at her name tag. "Good choice. Baked potato or French fries?"

"French fries. If I'm going to clog my arteries I might as well do the job right."

Cathy turned to Morgan. "What about you? Or do I have to ask?"

"Prime rib. Rare."

The waitress took the menu with a smile. "Be right out."

"Something tells me you've ordered that a time or two." Phoenix folded her arms on the table.

"I like beef, and Brandon's is the best."

"I'd say from the size of this crowd a lot of people agree with you." She glanced around the room, then picked up a chip. "I don't see chips and salsa at all the tables."

"I ordered it before we got here."

She sent him a pleased smile. "That was very thoughtful of you. Thank you." She dipped and munched. "Mmmm. Delicious. How was your day?"

He wasn't prepared for the question. He didn't think a date had ever asked. "Busy. Yours?"

"The same. I finally stopped around six. The foundry delivered two of Andre's pieces that I had to carefully check over; then I had to make several calls finalizing the details for his Seattle show and the one following in New York. Both are extremely important in cementing his reputation as a genius and undisputed master of his craft."

Morgan made a face. "He'll be impossible to be around after that."

Since Phoenix agreed with him, she couldn't think of anything to say. She was glad to see their food arrive.

"Here you are." Another waitress set a heaping platter of batter-fried catfish fillets, apple cider coleslaw, and a mound of French fries in front of Phoenix.

"I'll never eat all this, but I'm going to give it a try." She took a bite of the crispy deep-fried fish, savored the taste. "Delicious. No wonder everyone was talking about this place. This is marvelous."

"Thank you, Phoenix."

She glanced up to see the handsome young man who had served her at the gallery standing next to her. This time she wasn't distracted with thoughts of Morgan and easily noticed the strong jaw, jet-black hair, and devilish black eyes so much like Morgan's. "Thank you, although my scale might not."

"You look fine to me," he said, moving closer and eyeing her with undisguised male admiration.

"Brandon," Morgan said quietly.

Brandon twisted his head without moving his body. "Yes, Morgan?" he answered innocently.

"Isn't there something in the kitchen you should be doing?"

"Probably, but I'm enjoying what I'm doing now." He sat down beside Phoenix. "Being the owner does give me some privileges."

Morgan gritted his teeth so hard, his jaw ached. "Will you cut it out?"

"Did you hear a buzzing noise, Phoenix?"

She glanced between the two brothers and burst out laughing. "You must have given your mother a terrible time."

"They did. I didn't." A broad-shouldered, handsome man extended his manicured hand. "Pierce Grayson, and you must be Phoenix."

Phoenix placed her hand in his, then glanced from one brother to the other. "You're magnificent," she said, then put her hand over her mouth.

"Please don't make their heads bigger than they already are," said a strikingly beautiful woman with lustrous black waist-length hair that fell in a wavy profusion down her slim back. She sat beside Morgan.

"You have to be Sierra." Phoenix smiled across the table at the other woman. "Thank you again for finding such a perfect place. Crimson loves it, too."

"Your thoroughbred?" Sierra asked.

"Yes. I owe you another debt for recommending the stable to rent a horse. One of the many things I'll miss when I leave is Crimson and riding daily. I wish I could buy him, but Andre's schedule is too hectic. This is the longest we've stayed in one place since we arrived from Italy two months ago."

Sierra dipped a chip. "Perhaps I could come out sometime and see him. The horse, that is?"

Phoenix's lips twitched. "I'd like that. I'll fix lunch."

"I'd like to come." Pierce dipped his chip and crunched. "I admire horses as well."

"You're welcome anytime," Phoenix said. "Although I'm not anywhere near as good a cook as Brandon."

Brandon stuck out his chest beneath his spotless chef's jacket. "Very few people are."

Sierra rolled her eyes. "Please. He won't be able to get his head through the door."

"Leave Phoenix alone," Brandon said. "She knows an artistic genius in the kitchen when she meets one."

"Phoenix, it's getting rather noisy in here," Pierce said. "There's a little spot near here that is quieter and has a dance floor."

Morgan had had enough. "If the three of you don't take off in exactly ten seconds, I won't be responsible for my actions."

"You invited me, remember?" Sierra eyed Phoenix's French fries. "I know we've just met, but I'm starving and Brandon's shirking his duty. Can I have a fry?"

Phoenix shoved her plate toward her. "Please. Help yourself."

Brandon immediately stood up. "Why didn't you say something? I'll bring you a chicken Caesar right out."

As soon as he moved, Pierce took his seat. "Now, about that dancing?"

Phoenix looked at him, then at the fuming Morgan. "Thank you, but I think dating one Grayson is all I can handle."

Pierce sighed dramatically. "Win some, lose some." He picked up a chip. "Sierra, you're going to share your salad with me?"

"I'll think about it if you'll go add a couple of beef enchiladas and a diet cola?" Sierra said.

"Done." Pierce looked over and said loudly enough

for Morgan to hear, "Don't let him take my seat."

He hadn't gone three steps before Morgan said, "Sierra, please trade places with Phoenix."

Sierra looked at her brother, then rose. "If this costs me my enchiladas you're in trouble."

Phoenix scooted out of the booth and took Sierra's seat, then started to push the plate toward Sierra. She shook her head. "I'll wait for my salad. Please eat or Brandon will act huffy."

Pierce returned and stared from Morgan to Phoenix. "Lawyers are tricksters."

Morgan smiled. "Thank you."

Phoenix picked up her fork and glanced at Morgan. "Thank you for the best date I've ever had."

Morgan, who had been annoyed with his family, didn't know quite what to say. "They're certifiable."

"And they love you. You're very fortunate." Her hand tightened on her fork, she lowered her head but made no attempt to eat.

Morgan, Pierce, and Sierra shared a look. There had been an open longing in Phoenix's voice, a hurt. He wanted to ask about her family but decided erasing that haunted look on her face took precedence over anything. "Who did the exercise today, you or Crimson?"

Her head lifted. A small smile played around her lips. "Crimson."

"Why don't I come out tomorrow afternoon with my horse, and we can exercise them and each other?" Morgan said.

Phoenix blinked. There was a strangled noise from

across the table and a clearing of throat from Pierce.
Morgan backpedaled. "We could ride and walk the
horses afterward."

"Of . . . of course."

"Here you are." Brandon set the large Caesar salad
loaded with croutons and grilled chicken breast on
the table along with three plates and six steaming enchiladas; then he promptly sat down by Phoenix and
began to dish up the food. "Phoenix, I was thinking,
why can't I be the Grayson you're going out with?"

"Because she's already dating me."

Brandon handed Sierra her plate, then that of
Pierce, who had sat down beside her; then he prepared his own. "You don't have to get hostile."

"I'm not hostile; I'm merely stating a fact."

"Lawyers are like that," Phoenix said with a straight
face.

They traded looks, then all laughed, including
Morgan.

"I had a wonderful time, Morgan," Phoenix said as
she opened the door to her house.

"Despite my sister and brothers?" Morgan quipped,
closing the door behind him.

The corners of her mouth tilted upward. "They
certainly aren't dull."

"Enough about them." His hands settled on her
waist, which they could almost span. "I'll see you
around one. In the meantime . . ." His head lowered,
his mouth settled on hers. He could spend hours just

kissing her, learning the taste of her, listening to the little moans she kept making. He was learning something else: he was greedy where Phoenix was concerned.

The long, lingering kiss made her toes tingle, her blood sing, and her body hum. Her fingers stroked the back of his neck even as his hand made a restless sweep of the curve of her back. Much too soon he lifted his head.

"Good night. Lock up tight and don't forget to set the alarm," Morgan said, his voice deep.

"I won't." He had the most sensual mouth. She wondered what he'd do if she brushed her lips against his.

As if he'd read her thoughts, he kissed her softly; then he was gone.

Already missing him, Phoenix closed the door, then started for the window to watch him leave. It didn't surprise her how much she had wanted him to stay. From the last smoldering look in Morgan's eyes he had felt the same way. The knowledge was both scary and exhilarating. The strident blast of the telephone pulled her up short. She whirled and stared at the ringing phone on the side table. *Andre.*

Excuses ran through her mind, but she discarded each one. She was a grown woman. She picked up the phone. "Hello."

"Where have you been?"

Her hand tightened on the receiver. "Out to dinner. I just returned."

"At least I know it wasn't with Morgan Grayson. He's removed himself from my case. He saved me the trouble of having to fire him."

"He's not your lawyer anymore?" she said, genuinely baffled.

"Isn't that what I just said?" Andre snapped. "It's for the best. Lawyers are inquisitive and nosy. We wouldn't want him learning too much about your past, would we?"

The wonderful food Phoenix had eaten settled heavily in her stomach. Morgan's profession suddenly didn't sound so laughable anymore.

Andre continued as if he hadn't expected an answer, but there was a buoyancy in his voice that hadn't been there before. "I should be home in a couple of weeks at the most. I expect you to have completed everything by then."

"The foundry delivered *Timeless* and *Forever* today. The other pieces will be ready in a couple of weeks. They're beautiful." It had been her idea to give his work one-word titles that people could equate with love. She might not have inspired it in many people, but she yearned for it and she knew others did as well. Andre had accepted her idea because he thought it would add to the rumors of *La Flame*.

"Excellent. I can always count on you, can't I, Phoenix?"

She accepted the rare praise but understood it was also his way of keeping her in line. "Yes, Andre. By the way, Raymond came by to see you."

There was a long pause before he asked, "What did he want?"

She took a seat on the arm of the chair. "Just said he wanted to talk with you. He was surprised to learn you weren't here. He said he'd return in the morning to see if I had given you the message."

"You didn't tell him how to locate me, did you?" he asked.

If she hadn't known better, she would have thought she heard fear in his voice. "You know I wouldn't do that," she reassured him. "He's staying at the same hotel in Santa Fe. I have the number, if you'd like."

"Give it to me."

Phoenix repeated the phone number. "Is everything all right?"

"Couldn't be better," Andre said, but he didn't sound happy. "Good night, dear. Sleep well."

Very much aware that she would do anything but, she murmured, "Good night." Her life had taken another turn, and as usual, it wasn't for the best.

6

"Why didn't you mention last night that you had removed yourself as Andre's lawyer?" Phoenix asked the second she opened the door the next afternoon.

Morgan hadn't expected her to throw herself in his arms, but he certainly hadn't expected to see the wary look in her eyes he saw now. "You mind if I come in?"

Her face heated. She stepped back. "I'm sorry."

"Don't be." Taking her hand in his, he shoved the door closed with the other. "And the reason is this." He bent forward, capturing her lips. He felt her resistance and moved closer, determined to break down any barriers she might have. He never wanted to see doubt in her eyes again when she looked at him. When he lifted his head their breathing was labored and she stood easily in his arms. "Conflict of interest."

"Weren't you getting a commission?" she asked, her voice husky and breathless.

"Integrity, not money, governs my decisions." His

hand followed the curve of her cheek. "Besides, some things are without price."

"Morgan." She whispered his name like a prayer.

He couldn't resist claiming her mouth again. This time she was with him from the beginning, burning in his arms. She tasted like forbidden promises on a stormy night, hot and sexy. It was much harder to pull back the second time. "I think we'd better go riding."

She bobbed her head in agreement. "Crimson is ready except for the saddle."

Catching her hand in his, he opened the front door. "Let's go and you can meet Lady."

Trying to calm her racing heart and catch her breath, Phoenix followed him out of the house to the one-horse trailer behind a red Dodge Ram truck. A mare lifted her blazed head and nickered as they neared. Her black coat glistened.

"Do you stable her?"

"Yes, at a friend's place. Richard Youngblood is a veterinarian, one of the best in the country," Morgan explained. "He has a ranch five miles out of town with the top private stable in the state."

The animal turned intelligent brown eyes on Morgan as they neared. Another female who adored him.

"She's beautiful. I can see where she gets her name."

Morgan released Phoenix's hand and opened the back of the horse trailer. "You wouldn't know or suspect it now, but she wasn't much to look at as a foal and didn't get much better when she was a yearling."

"Did you know she'd turn out so well?"

Morgan finished backing out the animal before speaking. "I've always been taught to look beneath the surface. The owner asked for one hundred dollars as a joke. He thought I was crazy for wanting to buy her." Retrieving the blanket and saddle, he tossed them on the horse's back.

Phoenix patted the horse's long, sleek neck. "I bet he's sorry now."

"A couple of months ago he offered fifty thousand. Her sire has sired two Kentucky Derby winners."

"Not a lot of people would have turned down that kind of offer," she said, knowing that Andre wouldn't. Money meant more to him than anything or anyone.

"I've never been bothered by what other people would or wouldn't do." He slipped the bit into the horse's mouth. "I have enough trouble keeping up with my own life."

Phoenix studied him. In her world, his sense of self was almost unheard of. People too often judged their own success or lack thereof by what others thought of them. "It must be wonderful to be that self-assured."

"My mother taught all of us to be that way."

A shadow crossed her face. "Come on; let's go get Crimson."

Taking her hand, he fell into step beside her. "What about *your* parents?"

Her hand jerked in his. "My mother died when I was nine. I think the polite term for the relationship between my father and me is *estranged*."

Morgan's arm circled her shoulder and drew her closer. "He's missing knowing a hell of a woman."

She shrugged. "It doesn't matter."

The quick way she spoke told him that it did. He gave her Lady's reins as they entered the barn. "I'll saddle Crimson."

She reached out to stop him. "I can do it. Sometimes he gets cranky with strangers."

Morgan sent her an easy smile. "Animals and I understand each other." Picking up the saddle blanket, he opened the stall's door and went inside. Immediately the animal's head jerked up. His ears half-flattened.

"Morgan," Phoenix said, a note of warning in her voice. "Please, let me."

"It's all right," he said, moving slowly toward the watchful stallion, murmuring soft words over and over in a ceaseless current of sound until Crimson's ears came up and he bumped Morgan with his head. Morgan laughed. "You know I'm your friend, don't you, big fellow?"

"How did you do that? The reason the stable owner let him stay indefinitely was because Crimson had given him so much trouble. A stable hand, a man, abused him."

A muscle leaped in Morgan's jaw. He easily picked up the saddle. "Some people are born mean and stupid." Tightening the cinch, he opened the door and exchanged reins with her. "You need a leg up?"

Still a bit fascinated by what she'd just seen, she gathered the reins, stepped into the stirrup, and swung easily up into the saddle. It had taken the male stable hand thirty minutes to put a bridle on Crimson.

Morgan handled people and animals with equal ease. "I can manage."

Nodding, Morgan mounted in one lithe movement. "Any place particular you want to ride?"

"The stream in the meadow," she said, walking the horse outside to the bright afternoon. "It's about a mile west of here."

"Lead on."

Her eyes twinkled. "You think you can keep up if I give Crimson a good run?"

He grinned. "Why don't we find out?"

Before the words were out of his mouth, Crimson went from a sedate walk to a gallop. Morgan admired the alluring sight of woman and horse in perfect sync, then took off after them.

Phoenix looked back and was unsurprised to see Morgan gaining on her. The sight of him took her breath away. If she'd ever seen anyone as handsome she didn't remember when. The beauty and strength were in every line of his muscular body and stamped with indelible courage.

Laughing more freely than she had in years, she turned her attention to the race. They finished in a dead heat several feet from the rushing mountain-fed stream.

Drawing back on Crimson's reins, Phoenix nimbly jumped off, her landing softened by the thick grass beneath her boots. "Since my feet hit the ground first, I win."

Morgan eyed her, then dismounted. "I don't remember that being a condition for winning."

"I just made it up," she said with a broad grin.

He shook his head. "Come on; let's walk the horses and cool them down." He glanced around. "It's beautiful here. The stream is as clear as glass. I'd forgotten."

"You know the owners?" she asked.

"Yes. Pierce has been their financial adviser for the past four years," Morgan told her.

"He's certainly done well for them." Phoenix bent and picked a wildflower. "Is Pierce taking on any more clients?"

Morgan sent her a curious frown. "You want to invest?"

Stopping by the edge of the stream, she tossed the flower and watched the swift current carry it away. "I have a little money, but I need more."

"Mind if I ask why?"

She shrugged. "Every woman needs a little nest egg."

He watched her closely. It was more than that, but he wouldn't push. At least not now. "Pierce is good at what he does, but he'd be the first to use caution in any type of investment."

"I'll keep that in mind." Closing her eyes, she held her face up to the sun. "If I had a place like this, I'd never leave."

Once again Morgan heard the longing in her voice. "Sierra would be happy to help you look."

Opening her eyes, Phoenix swung toward him. This time he couldn't tell if it was weariness or fear in her eyes. "I can't stay here."

He'd known that, but somehow it didn't help the

knot untwist in his gut. "Yes, you could. Duval could get another assistant."

She turned away from him and looked at the rushing stream. "When he goes, I'll go with him."

Her refusal to even fight for what she wanted angered him. "What kind of hold does he have on you?"

This time he was sure he saw fear in her eyes when she faced him. "W-what do you mean?"

"You dislike the way Duval treats you. I saw it." Morgan came to stand beside her. "If you're afraid of not finding employment, I'll help you. You don't have to stay with him."

"Yes, I do."

"Why? Are you in love with him?"

She looked stunned rather than offended. "I owe Andre more than I can ever pay."

"I can't imagine Duval doing anything for anyone unless he thought he'd get something out of it."

"Andre has helped countless artists. I'm sorry if you don't see it that way."

Morgan was afraid the argument would escalate, so he decided to let it drop. "We're never going to agree on Duval, but there's one thing we don't have to argue about." His lips descended to meet hers. His mouth devoured her, worshiped her. With a little whimper, Phoenix, her mouth as bold as his, kissed him back.

Somehow they were on the grass, his body over hers. Her body aligned with his perfectly, as if she had been made just for him. Through their clothes he felt the heat of her body, the brush of her hard nipples against his chest. There was no way he could keep his body from hardening or her from realizing he wanted her.

There was as much wonder in her eyes as there was passion. And despite the caution he had glimpsed earlier in her beautiful eyes, she lay easily in his arms. Desire for her racked his body, but the trust in her eyes helped him keep the need in check. "You're exquisite."

Closing her eyes, Phoenix tucked her head into his shoulder. He kissed her ear, her cheek. The shy Phoenix was as alluring as the sultry lady in red. He wanted her but sensed it was too soon. Bounding up, he pulled her to her feet. "Let's walk."

It was late that afternoon when they arrived back at the house. Phoenix had never enjoyed a day more or wanted one to end less. "Thank you," she said, walking with Morgan to his trailer.

"Thank *you*," he replied. "It isn't often I get a chance to relax these days."

"Why?" she asked without thinking.

"You ask more questions than I do."

She flushed. "I didn't mean to pry."

Stopping at the back of the trailer, he led the horse inside and closed the door. "You're not. I've been busy with my practice, the board of the Southwestern Association for Indian Arts, and working with Second Chance."

Her brow knit. She'd heard of SWAIA but not the other organization. "Second Chance?"

"Outreach center for troubled teens," he explained. "Some of their parents are supportive, but others are ready to kick them out."

She knew only too well. Her father certainly hadn't stood by her when she'd gotten into trouble. "I'm glad they have you."

"If I can save one—"

"You will. You're too strong not to," she said quietly.

The back of his knuckles stroked her cheek in a familiar gesture of affection. "We're decorating the center for a dance Saturday night. We need all the help we can get," he told her. "Since I'm in charge of bringing refreshments, I can guarantee you'll be able to have all the salsa, chips, and drinks you want."

She didn't even think of saying no. "Tell me when and where and I'll be there."

"I'll pick you up."

She was already shaking her head. "From the way it sounds, you'll be busy. Just tell me the time and place, and I'll get there on my own."

Figuring that she wouldn't change her mind, he did as requested. "See you Wednesday night around six-thirty."

Phoenix stepped back and watched him drive away, already looking forward to seeing him again. Turning, she slowly entered the house.

The next couple of days passed slowly for Phoenix. She accepted that it was because she wanted to see Morgan. Dangerous, but she didn't seem to be able to help herself. Nothing could come of their association, but that didn't stop her from thinking about him. What sane woman wouldn't?

His strength of character was as much a part of him as his handsome face and muscular body. Kind, gentle, caring, he appealed to her on every level. Not even Andre's nightly reminder when he called of how fortunate it was for her that Morgan was out of her life swayed her.

She pulled into the parking lot of the center on Wednesday night with a bemused look on her face. Morgan had called twice in the last hour to make sure she hadn't changed her mind. That kind of attention from a man like Morgan was heady and exhilarating. She couldn't wait to see him.

Getting out, she slung the wide strap of her hobo bag over her shoulder. The myriad of colors on the adobe building made her think of Raymond. He hadn't returned or called. When she asked Andre if they'd spoken he'd said yes, then quickly changed the subject and asked about preparations for the Seattle opening.

Sadness slowed her steps. They'd be leaving in a few weeks. She'd never see Morgan again. Not even the prospect of finally showing her own work could bring a smile back to her lips. It hardly seemed fair that she was so close to realizing one dream and losing another—that of finding an honest man she could care about and who cared about her, only her.

Her feet were practically dragging as she passed the

side of the building. A whimpering sound pulled her up short. She paused, glancing around the well-lit parking lot. Only the leaves in the trees moved. Thinking she must be hearing things, she started walking again, then heard the sound once more. Her grip tightened on the wide strap of her purse.

She peered into the thick darkness on the side of the one-story building bordered by a cluster of mature trees. Unlike the front of the building and the other side, the security light on that corner of the low building was out.

"Is anyone there?" she asked, inching farther into the shadows. The lights on the poles in the parking lot weren't strong enough to penetrate the darkness shrouded by dense trees. "Hello. Is anyone there?"

"Phoenix."

She jumped and whirled, her hand going to her chest, then sagged in relief when she saw Morgan. "Y-you scared me."

"Sorry." He stepped closer. "I was on my way to my car to get the rest of the food when I saw you. What are you doing?"

She debated only a moment before telling him. Perhaps he wouldn't think staying by herself had made her jump at nothing. "I thought I heard a sound back there." She nodded down the side of the building.

"Sound? What kind of sound?"

A bit embarrassed, she shoved her hand through her hair. "Like a child or a young woman whimpering. I heard it twice."

Morgan tensed as his gaze swept the parking lot, then upward to the unlit security bulb. A curse hissed between his teeth. Shoving Phoenix behind him, he screwed the bulb back in.

Light illuminated the darkness. Phoenix gasped. Twenty feet away a huge man, his face twisted in a snarl, stood behind a young girl with his large hand clamped over her mouth. Morgan took off like a bullet. When he had almost reached them, the man shoved the crying young girl into Morgan's arms and ran toward the opening where Phoenix stood.

As he barreled down on her she didn't think, she just stepped to one side, lifted the heavy handbag she carried, and swung it with all her might at his face.

The man howled, cursed, then went to his knees holding his face.

Morgan was there seconds after the man hit the ground. Jerking him to his feet, Morgan sent a powerful fist to his chin. This time when the assailant went down, he stayed there.

Phoenix gathered the sobbing teenager into her arms. "You're safe. He can't hurt you."

Unclipping his cell phone, Morgan came back to them, his eyes cold, his face hard. "You all right, Cicely?"

The young girl nodded, then gulped.

"This is Morgan Grayson. Snake Redden attacked a young woman at the center." Morgan stared coldly at the unconscious man on the ground. "Don't worry; he'll be here when you get here."

"Snake wanted me to start using again. When I told him no he said he was going to fix me and drug me in there." Cicely's voice quivered as she glanced over her shoulder where she'd been held. "I saw a girl he used his fists on. That big ring he wears sliced her skin like butter." She shuddered. "She's scarred for life."

"Don't think about it." Morgan gently drew her into his arms. Snake outweighed her by a hundred pounds or more. She would have been defenseless against him. "Just don't think about it."

Cicely directed her gaze toward Phoenix, her head still on Morgan's chest. "I prayed someone would come. If you hadn't—"

Phoenix touched the young girl's arm, felt her tremble. Or was it her own trembling? "You're safe."

She sniffed. "Because of you and Mr. G."

In the distance Phoenix heard a police siren. The sound made her shiver even more. She wrapped her arms around her chest, her hands rubbing her arms.

"Phoenix, you all right?" Morgan asked.

No. "Yes."

Two police cars pulled into the parking lot with sirens wailing, lights flashing. Four officers jumped out of the police cars. Two went to Snake, who had started to rouse.

The door of the center opened and people piled out and rushed over to them. The second policeman tried to keep the group back, but his orders and out-stretched arms were ignored. He caught two teenage girls in his arms, but the rest simply went around him.

Seeing Snake in handcuffs and Cicely in Morgan's arms, the group quieted.

"Does she need to go to the hospital?" The fourth police officer kept his attention on Morgan.

"No," Morgan gritted out.

The officer nodded in understanding. "She'll have to come down and make a statement. You call her parents?"

"Mr. G. knows they're in Europe on vacation. They won't come back just for me," she told him matter-of-factly. "Our housekeeper, Maria, is in charge of things until they get back at the end of next week."

The officer rubbed the back of his neck. "We need to reach them."

"I'll take care of it, Dakota, and bring her down in the morning to make her statement."

"Since you put him down, Morgan, you need to be there anyway."

Morgan's attention switched to Phoenix. "Phoenix helped."

Phoenix had an urge to step into the shadows when the large police officer turned his attention on her. "I didn't do anything," she said.

"Yes, you did. She hit him with her purse," Cicely related. "He dropped like a stone. Wish I could have hit him," she said, staring at the police car Snake was being held in.

"Anyone else in on taking Snake down?" the sergeant asked. When no answer came, he tipped his Stetson. "See you all in the morning."

Phoenix felt her throat tighten. She didn't want to

go. She never wanted to be inside a police station again.

The next morning Phoenix stood outside the police station in a near panic. She didn't want to go in there. Her hand clamped and unclamped around the strap of her shoulder bag as she worried her bottom lip between her teeth.

Even in the cool morning breeze, she felt a trickle of perspiration roll down her spine. She hadn't slept at all. Fear wouldn't let her.

She rubbed her sweaty palm against the leg of her black slacks. Everything she had worked so hard for could be ruined. She didn't regret helping Cicely; she just wished there had been some way to keep her name out of it. Even as the thought crossed her mind, she knew it was wishful thinking. How could she explain her reluctance and not have anyone become suspicious?

The last thing she wanted was for the police to do a background check and tell Morgan what they'd learned. Even as terrified as she had been last night, she had noticed that he and the police sergeant were on a first-name basis. If the police checked on her . . . The muscles in her stomach clenched as dread rolled through her.

But she couldn't stand outside the police station all day, either. She had already called enough attention to herself. More than one policeman and a few civilians had asked if she was all right. The lie that she was

didn't come any easier than when she had lied to
Morgan last night. Or when he had called this morning to check on her.

On a trembling sigh, she made herself enter the
building and go to the information desk. Her mouth
was so dry she had to twice repeat the reason that she
was there before the officer on duty understood and
pointed her down the hall.

"Thank you," she said out of habit. She had gone
only a short distance before she saw a pretty young
woman in a pink T-shirt, jeans, and pink-tipped hair
walking toward her. It wasn't until she came to a halt
in front of Phoenix that she recognized the smiling
young woman as Cicely.

"Hi, Phoenix," she greeted her, a wide smile on her
face. "Morgan is making his statement now. He told
me to look out for you."

Phoenix couldn't get over the transformation. "You
look wonderful."

The teenager grinned. "Better than Snake. Bet he
won't try to mess with us women again."

The reference caused Phoenix's stomach to do a
flip-flop. "Have you given your statement yet?"

"Sure did. Mr. G. went with me." Taking Phoenix's
arm, she started toward a wooden bench in the hallway. "I live in a gated community, but Mr. G. talked
Security into letting my friends hang out with me, got
my counselor out to the house, and called my parents.
He was there with me all the way, just like he always
told us he'd be there for us."

"I'm glad you had him to help you," Phoenix said as she joined Cicely on the bench. She knew firsthand how important it was to have someone you could count on and the disastrous consequences when you didn't.

A look of wonder on her pretty face, Cicely stopped popping gum. "You should have heard him tear into my parents. I think they might be coming back early." There was awe and hope in equal measures in her voice.

"Morgan thinks a lot of you and the other teenagers at Second Chance."

"He's pretty cool." Cicely propped one pink tennis shoe on the bench and wrapped her arm around her knee. "He doesn't talk down to us or get on us about what we wear. If we get into trouble, he always asks us what went down. He doesn't automatically think we did it, like our parents do. You know what I mean?"

Phoenix knew exactly what she meant. Her father hadn't believed her. Only Andre. "That unshakable faith means a great deal."

"We'd do anything for Mr. G." Cicely learned over and whispered, "You don't have to worry about what happened getting out. He explained everything."

"What?"

Cicely winked and straightened. "We got your back. Is that the bag? I may get me one. It would be so cool."

Phoenix didn't understand a thing the teenager was saying. "What did Morgan explain?"

"Everything." The teenager came to her feet. There's Mr. G. and I see Maria coming. Gotta run. See you at the dance." With a wave, she ran to meet a middle-aged woman and then was gone.

Confused, Phoenix stood and waited for Morgan to join her. Even with her nerves on edge, she couldn't help but admire the easy way he moved, the broad width of his shoulders. He was a commanding figure. He'd protect those he cared about. They were blessed to have him.

Morgan's first thought when he saw Phoenix was that she was still upset by last night. She had a death grip on the big purse and looked ready to keel over. He captured her free hand in his, felt the dampness, felt her tremble. "Good morning. Everything is going to be all right. Don't worry."

"Good morning." She swallowed. "I'm not worried."

A lie, but he'd let it pass. He pulled her to one side. "If you're concerned about Duval getting upset, don't be."

Her hand jerked in his. "Cicely mentioned you talked to the kids last night about me. What was she talking about?"

So that was it. "I asked them not to tell anyone that you helped. I explained to them that if there is any retaliation, I don't want it on you."

Terror leaped in her eyes. She stepped closer. "You think he or his friends might try to hurt you?"

Her concern touched him, but he didn't want her worried. That was what he was trying to avoid. "People like Snake have no loyal friends, especially when there's trouble. I'm not worried. Our statements are mere formalities. He's going to be tried for drug trafficking."

"I don't understand."

"They found a large amount of cocaine and other drugs in Snake's car last night. Enough so his lawyer can't claim he had them for personal use. He's been convicted twice before for dealing. He's looking at a life sentence this time."

Morgan's face harshened. "Dealers deserve a permanent place in hell, but I'll take what I can get. He's caused a lot of pain and grief. This time he won't be able to lie his way out of it and claim the drugs were planted. His fingerprints were all over the containers with the drugs in them. Cicely and the other kids who are trying to get their lives straight won't have to worry about him anymore. Because he's a flight risk, he'll be denied bond."

At least Morgan and Cicely were safe. "I almost didn't recognize Cicely. She really bounced back."

Morgan nodded. "She's a fighter. Her counselor said Cicely's ability to stand up to Snake despite her fear went a long way in helping her see she has control over her life."

For a split second there was a longing in Phoenix's dark eyes; then it was gone. "You must have things to do. I'll wait until they call me."

"We'll wait together." His arm curved around her waist, drawing her to him.

She wished she was strong enough to say she'd be fine by herself, but she'd lied enough. "I'd like that."

After she'd given her statement, Phoenix turned down Morgan's offer to take her to lunch and returned to the house. She needed to be alone, to think. The incident with Snake brought up too many painful memories of the past. A past she had to keep hidden from Morgan at all costs.

When Morgan called later that afternoon to ask her to dinner she told him she was tired. The next day when he called again she said she was waiting for a shipment. She was surprised when he called the following day. He was a man who didn't give up easily. At another time in her life she would have admired his tenacity, but not when it presented such a great risk.

Andre had been right. Her association with Morgan was dangerous. If her heart paid the price, it was better than the alternative. She did her best not to think about Morgan or dwell on what might have been. Sometimes she was successful; other times she was not.

In the studio Friday afternoon, she sat in front of her latest creation, her hands shaping the clay into the figure of a little girl playing hide-and-seek with her mother. If nothing else, the past few days had helped to crystallize the image that had been circling in her head since she saw the woman with the child the day she went to visit Morgan.

Creating the piece had also helped ease the pain of the loss of her own mother and the disinterest of her father. Andre might have been right about something else as well. She had to accept what couldn't be changed and go on. For some, life was a constant battle; unfortunately, she was among that number. She had a chance to change that.

Phoenix's hands delicately smoothed over the features of the child. She wanted this finished when Andre returned. He'd see that she was ready.

Phoenix heard the phone and ignored it just as she had the doorbell. She wasn't expecting anyone. The foundry wouldn't deliver the cast pieces back for another week.

The chime of the doorbell came again. Her fingers stilled. Maybe it was Morgan. She was tempted to go.

That was the problem. Morgan tempted her too much. Becoming involved with a man when you knew it wouldn't last was foolish and counterproductive, especially considering the dire consequences.

She couldn't let anything interfere with her art. She used her thumb to shape the eye sockets of the one-third-life-size happy child peeking from behind a tree, an impish smile on her face. Phoenix wanted people to be able to feel the joy and love of life when they looked at *Innocent*. If she couldn't have it, at least she could give it to others.

The phone and the doorbell sounded at the same time. Her fingers jerked, stilled. Her eyes closed, her head fell forward.

Why wouldn't he let her go? Perhaps for the same reason thoughts of him were never far from her mind.

Covering up the work-in-progress to keep it dust-free, she came off the stool. She didn't plan to be gone long, but habits die hard. After cleaning her hands, she went to the front door and opened it, ready to quickly send Morgan on his way.

Surprise widened her eyes when she saw Cicely, a huge gift basket in her hands, and a good-looking, well-dressed young couple standing directly behind her who, from the resemblance, had to be her parents.

"Hello, Cicely." Phoenix nodded to the couple behind her.

"Hi, Phoenix," Cicely greeted her, with a wide grin, handing her the basket filled with an assortment of chocolates and cookies. "A little thank-you from me and my parents." She smiled up at them. "They came back just like they said."

Morgan had to be pleased. "Won't you come in?" Phoenix asked, stepping to the side.

"No, thank you." The slender man in his late thirties in a tailored suit curved his arm around his daughter's thin shoulders and extended his hand. "Timothy Jenkins, and this is my wife, Wanda. We can't thank you enough."

Wanda, in an ecru Dior suit, ran her fingers through her daughter's pink-tipped hair. "The incident scared us, but not as much as Cicely thinking we wouldn't come home when Morgan called."

"Morgan believes in the kids," Phoenix told them.

"We found out just how much when he contacted us," Cicely's father said in a way that made Phoenix think Morgan must have given it to him pretty straight about taking more responsibility for Cicely. She wished someone had been there to talk to her father on her behalf.

"I'm glad we have this second chance." He gave her his card. "If there is ever anything we can do, call. Day or night."

Setting the basket aside, Phoenix accepted the card. "I'm just glad Cicely is all right."

"Bye, Phoenix," Cicely said. "I'll see you at the dance tonight."

Phoenix's curling fist crushed the card. "I'm not going."

Cicely twirled back around sharply. "But you have to! Mr. G. expects you. Although we're keeping it on the quiet side, *all* the guys there that night are expecting you."

"I'm sorry." Phoenix hated to see the disappointment in the young girl's face, but there was no other way. "I have a lot of work to do."

"I'll help you finish," Cicely quickly offered. "You *have* to be there. I didn't go back to help with the decorations. I haven't been back since that night. It would help if I knew you were coming."

Emotions swelled in Phoenix's throat. Too many people had turned their back on her for her to do the same to Cicely. "All right," she finally conceded.

"Yes!" Cicely screamed, giving Phoenix a big hug before stepping back. "Eight sharp."

Phoenix closed the door as they drove off, and wished she could close the door on her growing feelings for Morgan just as easily. She couldn't. Her heart had a will of its own. Tonight when she saw him she just had to be ready. She didn't doubt that if Morgan saw any weakness on her part, he'd take full advantage of the situation.

The problem was, she'd be fighting both of them.

7

Pink and white balloons bobbed on the ceiling amid pink crepe paper streamers in the game room of the youth center. Tables, chairs, and the television had been pushed back against the wall to leave room for the dancers, who took ample advantage and stayed on the floor or at the food station.

Morgan, in jeans, white shirt, and an apron, tried to keep up with the demand for the bite-size pizza, nachos, and quesadilla rolls Brandon had dropped by earlier along with chips and salsa and soft drinks. Morgan definitely needed another pair of hands. Mrs. Bates and the receptionist were circulating.

Morgan trusted his kids, but since the incident with Snake more and more teenagers had started coming to the center. Until he knew they were for real, he and Mrs. Bates were keeping a close eye on them.

He heard a squeal of delight and watched as Cicely and Erica pushed their way through the horde to Phoenix. He only glimpsed her for a moment before she was lost in a crowd of laughing teenagers. His disappointment was huge when he no longer saw her. He hadn't known he could miss a woman so much or be as aggravated by one.

"Mr. G., you all right?" asked Miguel, a regular at the center who had gotten mixed up with a gang before cleaning up his act.

"Yes. Sorry." Morgan handed the lanky youth the plate of nachos and reached for another plate, his mind refusing to relinquish Phoenix completely. Since the day at the police station she'd spoken to him only briefly and refused to go out with him. The lady was avoiding him and he didn't like it. Before the night was over, he was going to know why.

Morgan divided his time between feeding the bottomless pits called stomachs of the teenagers and watching Phoenix. He was glad he did, because he saw the furtive glances she kept throwing in his direction. She couldn't keep her eyes off him any more than he could keep his off her. The knowledge pleased him immensely.

Finally Cicely and Phoenix started in his direction. He made sure he kept his attention on preparing the plate of food and not on the sensually beautiful woman in a soft pink dress that showed off her great legs and figure. "Enjoy."

"Mr. G., look who's here," Cicely said, her speculative gaze darting between the two of them.

"Hello, Phoenix." He grabbed a paper bowl for the nachos and filled it with chips. "Glad you could come."

"Thank you." Moistening her lips, Phoenix looked around. "The turnout looks good."

"I think we reached capacity an hour ago." He ladled cheese sauce onto the chips. "We could sure use some help. Mrs. Bates is circulating."

Phoenix hesitated and he was sure she was going to say no. "What do you want me to do?"

Tell me why you've been avoiding me. "Come around here, put your purse under the table skirt, and start filling bowls."

"Catch you later," Cicely said. "Time to get down and boogie." The teenagers popped their fingers and bobbed their bodies to the beat of the music on the way to the dance floor.

Phoenix served the next person in line. "I didn't want to ask in front of Cicely, but is the noise level always this loud?"

"The music or the kids?" Morgan began putting canned soft drinks on the table.

"Both."

Morgan straightened and came back to stand beside her. He frowned as she took a small step away. "Yes. My in-law by marriage Kane Taggart and my cousin Daniel both work with young people and had warned me."

She turned with the ladle in her hand. "Daniel. Daniel Falcon? The man who helped Andre is your cousin?"

Morgan made a face, then took the plate out of her hand and gave it to the next person in line. "At the time I learned about Daniel's help I wasn't too happy about it, but now I'm glad Duval's gone. I might have missed the pleasure of getting to know you if he hadn't left." His eyes bored into hers. "I guess some things are just meant to be, no matter what."

Phoenix swallowed and turned back to serving food. Morgan decided to let it go. He had given her enough to think about. Besides, he had one more ace up his sleeve.

Mrs. Bates shooed them from behind the refreshment table an hour later. "You two have worked hard long enough. Time for some fun. The dance floor is waiting."

"I asked the DJ to play something slow," beamed Cicely, who, with a group of her friends, had just joined them.

With so many people watching them, Phoenix couldn't think of an excuse fast enough before Morgan asked, "Shall we?"

Taking a deep breath, she stilled herself against the touch of his hand on her bare arm as he led her to the empty dance floor. Either Vanessa Williams's "Saving the Best for Last" was not the teenagers' kind of song or they wanted Phoenix and Morgan to have the dance by themselves.

Phoenix felt a bit awkward being the center of attention until Morgan stopped and slowly drew her into his arms. Then everything except the man staring so intently down at her ceased to exist. The strength, the power, of his arms holding her so tenderly felt as wonderful as she remembered.

He gathered her to him as if she were the most precious thing on earth. She heard the music as if from a distance; her senses were too busy assimilating being held against the muscled warmth of his body, the ease and gentleness with which he held her, the clean male scent of him that made her want to sniff, then bite, the fast tempo of his heart that echoed her own excited beat.

"Holding you again is like being given a private glimpse of heaven."

Morgan's softly spoken words went straight to her heart. She lifted her head. If she gave even a hint that she felt the same way, there'd be no stopping him. He went after what he wanted. He probably didn't know any other way.

She placed her head back on his chest. His sigh drifted out to her, through her, as if she had breathed it. She'd never been so in tune with a man before, hadn't known it was possible.

"*Madame Butterfly* is at the opera house Sunday night. How about joining me? Afterward we could have a late supper."

He'd phrased it casually, but it was still a date. "The company that is reproducing *Courage* wants to do another piece. I'm going through Andre's work to help him decide which bronze we want to use. Then there's the launch party for the initial piece in Boston that I have to coordinate."

His finger lifted her chin so that they stared into

each other's eyes. "I'd just like to know, are you running from me or yourself?"

She glanced away. "I *am* busy."

"Never said you weren't." He drew her closer, fitting her effortlessly against him. "I might as well make this good if this is the last time."

Phoenix closed her eyes against the turmoil his announcement caused. It was for the best. She just wished she could totally convince herself.

Morgan spoke over her shoulder. "Play it again, Cicely."

Phoenix's head came up. The music had stopped. She quickly glanced around. Thank goodness they weren't the only couple still on the floor. Mrs. Bates and her husband and three other older couples were dancing. They all appeared to be having a good time. They each had found love with that special someone. She was afraid she was destined never to discover either. She didn't need a mirror to know her expression was sad and wistful.

The music started and he drew her into his arms again. "Care to tell me why you're so quiet?"

She stirred restlessly in his arms. "I'd rather not."

He lifted away from her. He wore a smile on his face that made her heart beat faster. "Refusing to divulge information is a direct challenge to a lawyer. I'd have to take extreme measures."

Unease rolled though her. "Like what?"

"I'll tell you tonight when I follow you home."

"That's not necessary," she quickly said.

"It is for me." The smile was gone and the intensity of his gaze made her body tingle.

Whether she wanted to or not. He was seeing her home. Then what?

A little over three hours later Phoenix's hands were trembling so badly she could hardly insert the key into the lock. Finally, she unlocked the door and faced Morgan. "Thank you for—" That was as far as she got before his mouth captured hers in a kiss that stole her breath and scattered her thoughts. Warmth and desire swept through her. She was powerless to keep from returning the kiss, from clinging to Morgan as if she never wanted to let him go.

"I won't ask you why you've been avoiding me because I have a feeling you won't tell me. All I ask is that you don't shut me out." He kissed her again. "I have season tickets to the opera, or we can stay here or go to my place."

She opened her mouth to object, and he kissed her once again, drugging her senses. "Which?"

Her breathing off-kilter, her heart racing, she managed to say, "The opera."

"I was hoping you'd pick my place," he teased. She blushed.

Laughing, he kissed her one more time as if he couldn't get enough of the taste of her. "Good night, and thanks for coming. It helped Cicely."

Since he was no longer kissing her, she could think

clearly. "She's a remarkable young woman. She'll make it."

"Now that she believes in herself," Morgan said easily. "You can tell a person something a million times, but until they experience it themselves, many won't believe you."

She straightened. "Walking by faith is never easy."

"No, but it beats living in fear."

He watched her glance away. He'd push later to find out what was bothering her. One victory at a time. He gently urged her inside. "I'll pick you up at seven."

Heads turned when they entered the opera house. A multitude of the town's leading citizens were there, many of them the same people who had been at Duval's opening. Phoenix might have on a long black evening gown instead of red, but there was no way they didn't still recognize her as *La Flame.* Speculation about her and Morgan would run rampant . . . and straight to his family.

For her part, Phoenix appeared unbothered by the turning heads and whispers. At least he thought so until he took her bare arm and felt her shiver. He leaned down to her ear. "It's me they're whispering about. Wondering how I got so lucky to have such a beautiful woman with me."

She sent him a look that warmed his heart. "I'd say I'm the lucky one to have such a gallant escort."

"Let's find our seats."

"Morgan, please wait a moment."

He turned to see Steven Cramer, a prosperous businessman and leader of the community. With him was Dan Rodgers, the outgoing congressman for Morgan's district.

"Good evening, Steve, Dan. I'd like you to meet Phoenix Bannister. Steve Cramer and Dan Rodgers."

Both men greeted her warmly, then gave their full attention to Morgan. "Have you thought any more about running for city councilman?"

"From there you could spring to Congress. You'd make a darn good congressman," Dan said before Morgan had a chance to say anything. "We need someone in my old position who cares about the little man when I retire in two years."

"Gentlemen, I told you I'd think about it and I will," Morgan said. "Tonight, however, I just want to enjoy the opera and a lovely lady's company."

Both men's attention switched to Phoenix. "The filing is not that far away. It would be a shame to miss the deadline."

"With your leadership skills you could galvanize the party into a cohesive force to be reckoned with. We could change some things," Dan hammered home.

Seeing they weren't going to leave, Morgan tried to explain his ambivalent feelings. "It's taken hard work to build up my practice. My clients and my staff depend on me. I have to make sure that this is what I want to do. No one can push me into it."

"Of course not," Rogers quickly said. "We just wanted you to know that you have our entire support. Your reputation is unquestionable and your work with troubled teenagers is commendable. As a congressman you could effect laws with stiffer penalties."

"That's the reason I decided to 'think' about running," Morgan informed them.

"Five minutes to curtain. Five minutes," announced the attendant.

"We really must take our seats. Good night, gentlemen." Morgan and Phoenix merged with the crowd.

Phoenix sat through the first half of the opera, her thoughts chaotic and desolate. It had happened again. The past was taking something else from her. She couldn't continue seeing Morgan. His association with her might jeopardize his chances if he decided to seek a political office.

She barely paid attention to what was happening onstage. She kept wondering why life continued to knock her down and why she even kept trying to get back up. Intermission couldn't come fast enough. As soon as the curtains closed on the first act, she turned to Morgan. "Do you mind taking me home? I have a headache."

"Of course not. Let's get your wrap." His immediate and deep concern made her feel worse.

In the lobby he handed the woman the check stub for·Phoenix's wrap, then draped the cashmere shawl tenderly around her bare shoulders. "Do you have something at home to take or do you want me to stop at the drugstore?"

She looked anywhere but at him. "There's no need to stop."

"Then let's go."

On the drive she leaned her head back against the seat and closed her eyes. She could feel him watching her. It was all she could do not to let the tears fall. It was so unfair. Her hands clamped in her lap, she remained quiet.

Pulling up in front of her house, he quickly came around the car and opened her door. "Do you get these often?"

"No." Head bowed, she opened her evening bag and took out the key. He took it from her trembling hand and opened the door. She stopped just inside the house. "I hope you don't mind my not inviting you in."

"Of course not, but I hate to leave you alone, and you not feeling well." His hand rested gently against the curve of her face. "Why don't you go lie down and let me get your medicine?"

"I'll be fine. Good night, Morgan."

He hesitated, studying her closely. "I don't like this, but I've learned how stubborn you can be. Go take your medicine and lie down. I'll call in the morning." Bending, he kissed her softly on the cheek. "Good night."

She closed the door before he was halfway down the walk. "Good-bye, Morgan."

Phoenix was in her studio when dawn broke. She had tossed and turned most of the night and had finally given up and gone into the studio and taken out fresh clay. Usually she worked from a sketch, but this time she didn't have to. The clay bent easily to her will.

Soon the rough outline of a man's face appeared. Even in the roughness she recognized the face as Morgan's.

She let her head fall forward. How long would she have to pay for something she hadn't done? There was no answer, just as there had been none seven years ago when she had been arrested, her life almost destroyed.

When her father had turned his back on her it shouldn't have surprised her. He hadn't been there for her since she was nine and her mother had died. He hadn't known what to do with Phoenix and even less how to cope with the loss of the woman he loved. His answer was to bury himself in work.

Phoenix looked down at the clay. Tears pricked her eyes. Her association with Morgan would destroy his aspirations for a political career if he continued to see her. Why ruin his chances when there was no hope for anything permanent between them?

A few weeks of bliss wouldn't make up for the hell she could put him through. She'd ceased believing in the forever kind of love a long time ago.

Reaching for a clean cloth, she draped it over the clay and stood. Perhaps a good ride would clear her head. But even as she made her way to the stable, she knew it was a futile endeavor.

Morgan pulled into his parking space at exactly 8:45 Monday morning and got out. He had only gone a few steps before he saw the black Dodge Ram parked several spaces over. A broad grin split his face. His strides lengthened. In a matter of seconds he was opening the door to his brother's private inner office.

"Didn't you two get enough of that on your honeymoon?" he asked when he caught Luke and Catherine kissing.

Luke Grayson slowly lifted his dark head. His arms remained around his wife's slim waist. "Nope."

"Hi, Morgan," Catherine said, standing easily in her husband's arms, her head on his broad chest.

Shoving the door shut behind him, Morgan crossed the room and hugged them both. "Welcome back."

"Thanks," Luke said with a wry twist of his mouth. "Bart faxed me every day for the past five asking when I was coming back. I almost said never."

"I reminded him that I begin a lecture series at St. John's next week, so we decided to start weaning ourselves, so to speak," Catherine said with an impish smile.

Morgan chuckled at the two still in each other's arms. "Doesn't look like it's working."

"We've only been at this thirty minutes. Give us time," his sister-in-law said, then glanced adoringly up at her husband. "It would help if your brother wasn't such a hunk and all mine."

Luke's face creased into a grin. "Why don't we call it a day and go back to the cabin?"

Catherine considered. "How about twelve?"

"Ten sounds better." Luke countered with a kiss on her forehead and one on each cheek.

"Ten it is. Then we can swing by your mother's on the way home."

"You can't do that," Morgan told them, a stricken look on his face.

"Why?" they both asked almost in unison.

Morgan shoved his hand over his head. "Just look at you two. You can't keep your hands or your eyes off each other. Once she sees you, she'll be more determined than ever to marry me off."

"Since I've stood in your shoes, I know how you feel." Luke placed his hand on his brother's shoulder. "But when it's all said and done, if you find a woman half as good as Cath you'll die a happy man."

"I want to live a *single* happy man." He glanced at Catherine. "No offense. I just don't want to be married and neither do the rest."

Catherine snuggled closer to her husband. "Neither did we until we found each other. I can't imagine living one day without Luke."

"I feel the same way."

Morgan didn't want to recall Daniel saying the same thing. "Just because you two fit doesn't mean it will be right for the rest of us."

"Morgan, let's look at this from a logical point of view, shall we?" Catherine said, taking his arm and leading him to a chair in front of Luke's desk. "Please sit down."

He sat out of respect, but whatever she had to say wouldn't change his mind.

"As I see it, you have no control over what your mother does, just as Luke didn't."

"Here's a seat, Cath." Luke placed the other leather armchair beside her. "This might take a long time."

"Ha. Ha." Morgan folded his arms across his chest.

Catherine took the seat and crossed her long legs in navy pants over the other. "Don't mind Luke."

"He should be happy you're getting free advice that would cost one-fifty an hour to anyone else."

"She's a child psychologist," Morgan pointed out.

"Men sometimes act like children, but that's beside the point." Catherine ignored the raised brows of her husband and those of her brother-in-law. "As I was saying, Ruth believes in what she's doing and thus won't be swayed by anything you say or do. She wasn't by Luke even when he threatened to move to Albuquerque to escape the parade of women. I was the twenty-eighth."

Groaning, Morgan slid deeper into the chair. "I'll commit hara-kiri."

"There is a simple solution to this that you, Brandon, Pierce, and Sierra have failed to see and that even your mother can't control."

He straightened and leaned forward in his chair. "What's that?"

"Don't fall in love," she said simply.

"What?"

She sighed, then sighed again as Luke grazed his knuckles against her cheek.

"Luke, stop that!" Morgan told his brother. "Of course I'm not falling in love, so what's your point?"

Catherine's hand lifted to join her husband's. "As much of an irritant as it may be to be the subject of women hoping to be 'the one,' none of them matter if you don't love one of them. Ruth wants all of you to be happy, and that means with a mate who makes your heart beat faster, one whom you can't get out of your mind. It's more than sex; it's a need to comfort, to see them smile 'just because.'"

She glanced at Luke before continuing, "Love is a combination of the simple things. You Graysons won't settle for anything less. So no matter how many women Ruth throws in your path, unless one clicks on all cylinders you have nothing to worry about."

Morgan's jaw became unhinged. She had just described how he felt about Phoenix.

"From the look on your face, Mama may be two for two," Luke said.

"You should be a stand-up comedian instead of a private investigator." Morgan came to his feet. "I'd better get to work."

"Who is she and when can we meet her?" Luke asked.

In certain situations lying was permissible, but never with his family. Morgan rubbed the back of his neck. "I'm not in love. I want to make that clear."

Catherine and Luke merely stared at him.

"She's just someone I met," Morgan felt compelled to say. "I don't think she's had an easy life and her employer is on a maniacal ego trip."

"A vulnerable woman has a certain appeal to men." Catherine rested her cheek against her and Luke's joined hands. "I thank God every day that Luke was there for me when I thought my world was coming apart."

"I'll always be there for you." Luke kissed her hand.

Morgan shoved his hand over his head. "Stay with me, you two. Just because I care what happens to her doesn't mean anything."

"You're right. But if you find yourself more concerned with her happiness than your own, you may want to examine more closely what your true feelings are for this woman." She gazed up at Luke, her love clearly shining in her eyes. "That's when I knew Luke was the only man for me."

"I would have done anything to keep Cath safe and happy. It never entered my mind to do anything else." Luke pulled her to her feet and into his arms.

"You were my salvation then. You still are." She met him halfway. Their lips touched as their bodies molded to each other in a familiar way.

Knowing they'd already forgotten about him, Morgan left quietly and went to his own office down the hallway. His and Luke's offices took up the entire fourth floor of the building.

Florine was sitting at her desk and looked up when he entered. "Good morning, Morgan. How was the weekend?"

She'd asked him that same question every Monday morning that she'd worked for him. For the first time he didn't know how to answer. "I'm beginning to think it was worse than I thought."

Concern flitted across her face. "Anything I can do to help?"

"I wish there was."

Inside his office, Morgan took a seat, propped his elbows on his desk, and placed his chin on top of his steepled fingers. He wasn't a novice where women were concerned. Deep in thought, he tried to remember if he'd felt any differently toward any of them. He was shocked to find their faces kept slipping away and all that remained was Phoenix.

He started to panic; then he recalled something about himself and relaxed in his chair. He had been the one to sever most of the relationships. When it was over, it was over. He had moved on with no regrets and no looking back. No walking down memory lane or thinking of what might have been.

Phoenix slipped so easily into his consciousness for the simple reason that she was the one he was interested in at the moment. It was healthy sexual attraction, pure and simple.

They'd enjoy each other's company for as long as it pleased them both; then they would go their separate ways, just as he had always done with the women before her. Dragging his attaché case closer, he pulled out the contracts for a merger and settled down to study them.

He shouldn't have been so worried. Catherine was right. Love was the only thing that would trip him up, and just like he kept telling everyone, he had no intention of falling in love.

8

Morgan stared at the phone in his home office for a long time before he picked it up that evening. He had purposely put off calling Phoenix just to prove that he could. He'd almost given in a couple of times to find out how she was feeling, but had resisted. Now, as the phone rang for a fifth, then a sixth time, he began to question his actions. The fact that he was didn't go down easy with him.

Nothing with Phoenix followed a predictable pattern. After the tenth ring, he hung up, then redialed. Maybe he had dialed the wrong number. It was past seven. Where could she be?

The absurdity of the question had him standing and pacing. She was a beautiful woman. She could be any number of places. Santa Fe might not offer the nightlife of Boston or New York, but there were clubs, and barhopping was an old and honored tradition. The city had over two hundred art galleries and several world-class museums, but they were closed at this time of night. Santa Feans tended to want to be home when night fell.

He hung up the phone on the twelfth ring. She could be at a restaurant, the movies. Or she could have fallen from Crimson. He had his car keys and was out the door in five seconds.

He prayed to the Master of Breath and God all the way to her house. He threaded the roadster through the traffic with skill and precision. He didn't breathe easier until he saw light shining through several windows in the house. Coming to a screeching halt, he hopped out of the car without benefit of opening the door and rushed up the walkway.

He jabbed the doorbell, listened to the chimes, then jabbed again. "Come on, Phoenix."

He was about to head to the stable to make sure Crimson was in his stall when he recalled her comment that she worked in back. Becoming increasingly concerned, he pounded his fist on the door. "Phoenix! It's Morgan!"

Just when he thought his hand would go numb, he heard the lock disengage. The door opened. Phoenix stood in the doorway in a long robe. Once again her feet were bare. Her hair was tousled as if her hand had run through it a thousand times. His relief was short-lived.

"I was about to lie down. Was there something you wanted?"

The coolness in her voice had him narrowing his eyes. "I was worried about you."

"As you can see, I'm fine." The silk robe slid off her

bare shoulder. She pulled it back in place. "Thank you for coming, but I've had a tiring day. Good night."

His hand kept the door from closing. "What is it? Why are you acting as if nothing happened between us? Is it Duval?"

"Nothing happened between us except a few kisses."

"Phoenix, I know what we both felt."

Her hand swept through her hair again. "That was then. This is now. I'm going out with someone else, if you must know. He should be here any minute. Now, if you don't mind. . ."

Morgan stared at her a long time. "My mistake."

Turning away, he went to the car and drove away. He didn't look back.

Phoenix closed the door, then leaned her back against it and slid down to the floor. Drawing up her knees, she crossed her arms, braced them on top, and lowered her head. She'd heard the doorbell and known it was Morgan. Cicely wouldn't come out this late to visit and no one else had visited since Andre had left except Raymond. From the persistent knocking, it hadn't sounded as if Morgan would leave without talking to her.

She'd thought it would be difficult but hadn't imagined how badly the hurt look on Morgan's face would wound her. Her stomach was still in knots. Her throat ached. This time she refused to let the tears fall. She'd cried too many useless tears in her life. No more.

Morgan would go on with his life and forget her. The ache deepened because she'd never forget him.

Swallowing the lump in her throat, she pushed herself up. All she had to depend on was herself. Every time she reached out to someone, she ended up being hurt. But this loneliness she lived with daily was slowly draining her. She wasn't sure how much longer she could continue in her solitary world.

Morgan shaved the drive time to his place by five minutes. Always careful of his possessions, he didn't slam the door to the roadster, but he wanted to. Activating the garage door, he went inside and straight to his study, determined to put Phoenix behind him.

So he'd misjudged her. He'd get over it.

He was behind his desk when the phone rang. He glanced in its direction and saw his sister's name and cell number. He debated a few seconds before picking up the receiver. "Hello, Sierra."

"Hi, yourself," came her bubbling reply. "I'll be there in ten minutes to pick you up. We're all going to Mama's."

He swiped a hand across his face. His intuitive family would know in seconds something was wrong. He wasn't up to twenty questions. Even if they were well-meaning. "I've got a lot of paperwork." Which was the truth, but nothing that couldn't wait.

"Tell me about it. But Mama isn't accepting any excuses. She's ecstatic because Luke and Catherine are coming over. It will be the first family get-together since he got married. She's cooking her famous lasagna."

The food would stick in his throat. "You go on. I'll come by later if I can."

There was a slight pause. "What's the matter?"

He'd flubbed it. Family was important. His not wanting to be there made her suspicious. "I'm just tired."

"I'll be there in five. We'll talk."

Morgan hung up the phone. He wasn't looking forward to the conversation. Going to his room, he changed into a pair of jeans, hand-tooled boots, and a starched white shirt. He grabbed a lightweight jacket out of the closet, then headed back out the door.

He had just emerged from his room when he heard the doorbell. Grimacing, he went to answer it.

Sierra took one look at his face and hers clouded. "What did she do to you?"

A dark eyebrow arched. "Who said it had anything to do with Phoenix?"

"Who said anything about Phoenix?" she asked, stepping inside the wide foyer and closing the door.

Morgan could have gladly kicked himself. He knew better than to offer information and he could dodge questions with the best of them. "That's the 'her' you've been so concerned about lately. Let's go."

"All right. Have it your way, but you know I'll find out."

"There's nothing to find out." He concentrated on setting the alarm and not on his sister's prediction. Luke often said if Sierra hadn't found her niche in real estate, she could have followed him into the FBI, where he had been a top agent before he opened his own private investigation firm. She had an uncanny knack for ferreting out information people wanted to hide. For a second Morgan thought of asking Luke to find out about Phoenix; then he dismissed the idea. Phoenix was out of his life.

As he closed the door, Sierra touched his arm and stared up at him. The porch light illuminated her concerned face. "Would it help if I took her on a camping trip into the mountains and left her stranded for a couple of hours?" Sierra was fiercely loyal. You didn't mess with her brothers.

"There is no 'her' to strand."

"Have it your way." She went to the driver's side of her vehicle and got in. "But if you change your mind, just let me know."

"What's the matter?"

If Morgan heard it one time, he heard it a dozen. He didn't mind their asking as much as he minded his inability to forget a woman who had forgotten him. "The only thing wrong with me is that all of you seem to think there's a problem."

"If you can't share with your family in time of need, who can you share with?" his mother said from the head of the table that sat eight.

Morgan looked across the table at Luke, saw his furrowed brow. They often had an uncanny ability to share thoughts. Morgan hoped this wasn't one of those times.

"Morgan, what's this I hear about you wanting to test the political waters?" Catherine asked. "If you're serious, my mother would be a great asset."

Unexpectedly, Catherine, not Luke, had come to his rescue. "A city councilman is hardly in the same league with a senator," Morgan said.

"Politics is politics." Luke cut into his lasagna. "We're with you."

"I meet some pretty wealthy and influential people," Sierra said. "I could test the waters for donations."

"With me in charge of your campaign funds, every penny would be accounted for, and, like Sierra, I can help solicit funds," Pierce added.

Brandon offered his support. "We could have the launch and victory party at my restaurant. Of course, I'd want to have the name prominently displayed, but you'll get everything below cost. We'll have to talk about the liquor. Some political hanger-on-ers drink like fish."

Laughter rang out around the table. They were all trying to help. But what made Morgan's laugh uneasy was that his mother had not joined in.

Ruth Grayson knew her children well. Morgan might try to hide a problem, but she knew better.

She bided her time and waited until she could get him alone. Her chance came when he went into the kitchen with his plate. When Pierce started to get up she shook her head. Picking up her plate and flatware, she followed Morgan, closing the French doors separating the dining room from the kitchen.

"It's nice having all of you together again. I can't

imagine a better daughter-in-law than Catherine," his mother said.

Morgan looked at her, then at the closed doors.

Ruth scraped the bits of food on her plate into the garbage disposal. "No matter how old your children are, you still feel at times as if they're little and you can take away all their hurts."

The only sound was Morgan scraping his plate.

"I heard today that you had taken Phoenix Bannister, Andre's assistant, to the opera. I wouldn't have thought you'd be interested in her."

His head came up. His eyes narrowed.

"Is she as beautiful as they say?"

"Yes."

"Ah," his mother said.

"What does that mean?" Morgan asked.

"Nothing. Will you be seeing her again?"

"No." Turning to the sink, he flipped the switch on the disposal.

As soon as Ruth headed into the kitchen after Morgan, Pierce said what was probably on everyone's mind: "Must be trouble between him and Phoenix."

"Looks that way." Brandon leaned back in his chair and cast a knowing glance in the direction of the closed door. "Mama is probably trying to get it out of him."

"She won't get any more out of him than we did." Concern knit Sierra's brow. "He's hanging tough."

"Doesn't mean he's not hurting inside." Luke's

arm circled Catherine's shoulder. "What's your take on it, Cath?"

As Luke's siblings turned toward her, Catherine once again felt the strong bond among Luke's family, which was now hers. "Since we don't know all the facts, the best thing we can do is give him the space and support to work through this by himself."

Sierra sighed. "I'm certainly not going to jump to conclusions like I did with you and Luke." She'd been ready to throw Catherine down a deserted mine shaft for hurting her brother.

Catherine smiled across the table at her fiercely loyal sister-in-law. "For all we know, Phoenix is just as miserable."

"Whoa," Brandon said, bringing everyone's attention back to him. "If Morgan has feelings for Phoenix, and it certainly is pointing in that direction, wouldn't it be to our advantage to leave things alone?"

"Would you trade Morgan's happiness for your own?" Catherine asked softly, although she already knew the answer.

"No." Brandon braced his arms on the table. "Besides, I'm made of sterner stuff than Luke or Morgan."

"You'd better be." Pierce frowned and finished off his iced tea.

"Excuse me, but how did we get from Morgan having feelings to him standing in front of the altar?" Sierra inquired. "Morgan isn't the type to date a woman just for sex, but that doesn't mean he's ready to propose."

All three men frowned at her as if she wasn't supposed to know about sex, let alone say the word. She ignored them and said to Catherine, "I plan to do some fact-finding. I'd ask you to come with me to see Phoenix, but I doubt if Luke will let you leave the house before nine."

Pierce stroked his chin. "Perhaps I should go with you. Look at it from a man's perspective."

"You just want to ogle her again," Sierra told him.

Pierce's dark eyebrows lifted. "I don't ogle. I'm too much of a gentleman for anything so crass. I observe and appreciate."

"Yeah, right," his sister said. "But I'm going alone and I'll let you know what I find out."

"Sierra," Luke cautioned, "I'm not sure we should meddle. You could do more harm than good. What if we're all reading this wrong? What if Morgan called it off and just regrets ever getting involved?"

"What do you think, Catherine?" Brandon asked. "Don't worry about speaking freely. Luke's not the kind of man who can't take his wife disagreeing with him."

"I wouldn't have married him if he was," Catherine pointed out.

Luke kissed her on the cheek. "Guess she told you."

"In my opinion, his actions indicate that whatever happened in the relationship was not his idea. Before you began questioning him, I couldn't tell anything was wrong. He's very self-contained. Therefore, it must have come out of left field and he hasn't had time to deal with it."

"Catherine, please do me a favor," Brandon said, his face deadly serious.

"Name it."

"Don't ever try to analyze me."

"With your brain, I don't think you have anything to worry about," Sierra said with a laugh, just as the door opened and her mother entered. The conversation quickly turned to the upcoming Indian Market.

Sierra liked to sleep late in her huge four-poster draped with voile netting. Tuesday morning when the alarm went off at eight, she cocked one eye open and stared at the Italian clock on the nightstand, then tossed back the covers and headed for the shower. She'd learned that if she lay there too long she'd go back to sleep and sleep through the second alarm.

Fifteen minutes later she pulled on a pair of designer jeans that cost almost as much as her handmade black boots. She stuffed a cream-colored silk blouse into the narrow waistband, treaded a turquoise belt through the loops, grabbed her satchel bag, and was out the door.

Her first appointment wasn't until ten, so she had plenty of time to ferret out information. Walking though the lush wooded area of her exclusive gated condo community, she hadn't a doubt that she'd be able to find out something. She had a natural talent to put people at ease. . . . She also had a hell of a temper.

Wrinkling her mouth, she climbed into the BMW, backed up, and drove off. This morning she'd be her sweetest. She didn't like seeing Morgan unhappy. She'd just have to take him at his word that he wasn't planning anything long-term.

Fifteen minutes later Sierra rang the doorbell at Andre Duval's house for the third time. She'd already tried to peep through the curtains, but they were tightly drawn. Hands on her slim hips, she was trying to decide what to do when she heard the nicker of a horse.

She started for the stable. Couldn't hurt.

At the entrance to the barn, she didn't see anyone. She stepped into the interior and saw a beautiful roan stallion. A lover of horses, she started toward him. She was less than fifteen feet away when she heard the faint voice.

It took her a moment or two to realize it was Phoenix. Ten feet away the words became clearer, plaintive and wistful.

"I wish I had a friend. Someone I could talk to, but that's impossible. I try to remember, but I can't help wanting to have someone in my life who just likes me for me. Andre says I must accept it, give myself to my art, but I don't think I can be happy without people in my life who care if I live or die."

The horse neighed again.

"You understand, don't you, Crimson? Morgan probably would have, too, but he's gone. I sent him away. I have only myself to blame. He'll never forgive me, because he thinks I'm seeing another man. Wouldn't he be surprised to know I haven't dated anyone in over a year.

"I'm almost finished with drawing your picture to remember you, not that I need it any more than I needed Morgan's. I have to stop thinking about him. I can't see him again. Ever."

The conversation was obviously private. Sierra knew she shouldn't have listened and that her sin would be compounded if Phoenix realized she was there. Quietly she retraced her steps until she was at her vehicle.

Morgan had been right. Phoenix hadn't had an easy time of it. Sierra could well understand what she was going through. It hadn't been easy at times being a child of mixed heritage. But Sierra had always had the assurance of the love and backing of her family. What must it be like to have no one?

She glanced at the barn and recalled Phoenix's comment the other night at The Red Cactus. Sierra hadn't spoken to Duval, but it was easy to tell from his demeanor that he wasn't a warm man. She hadn't thought much of Phoenix's life before. If she had, she supposed she must have thought it was a jet-setter's life and, as she was Andre's assistant, some of the limelight that shone on him touched her as well.

That wasn't the case.

Sierra looked back at the stable. She had the information she'd come for, but telling Morgan what she'd learned didn't seem right. But dare she follow through on what she was thinking? Whatever the reason Phoenix had taken the drastic steps to turn Morgan away from her, would the reason in the long run hurt him more?

Morgan had always defended the underdog. If he ever heard the longing in Phoenix's voice, saw it in her face, he'd do whatever it took to help her. There was no way of predicting what might happen if they spent time together. He cared about her and wanted to be with her.

Just because their mother was trying to marry him off didn't mean Phoenix was the woman he was meant to spend a lifetime with. They were just two adults enjoying each other's company.

Did she try to rectify the situation or leave it alone? Was Morgan better off never seeing Phoenix again?

Leaning inside the SAV, Sierra hit the horn for two quick blasts. If there was anything that could be done to take the unhappiness from Morgan, she was going to do it.

She'd count the cost later.

9

Phoenix's head snapped up along with Crimson's at the sound of the car horn. *Morgan*. The thought and the pleasure went through her before she took another breath. She was up and out of the stall before the improbability of her thought hit her as she recalled too well the coldness in his voice last night.

The smile on her face dimmed, her steps slowed.

She recognized the slim, beautiful woman standing by the luxury vehicle immediately. Wind-tossed strands of Sierra's wavy black hair swirled around her shoulder. A moment of unease hit Phoenix. What if Sierra came to ask her to leave? Andre would be livid. He lived off the goodness of others, seldom incurring any expenses. He had perfected the art of ingratiating himself to others so much that they acted as if they thought he was doing them a favor by living with them or on one of their properties.

It was only as Phoenix got closer that she saw

Sierra's mouth was curved into a warm smile. Which somehow made less sense.

"Good morning, Phoenix," Sierra greeted her, stepping away from the SAV to meet her. "I rang the doorbell and when there was no answer, I thought I'd try the horn in case you were riding nearby."

"Good morning, Sierra. Sorry. I wasn't expecting anyone." Phoenix clutched the sketch pad to her chest, still unsure why Sierra was there.

Sierra waved her words aside. "My fault entirely. I should have called. I had some time on my hands before my first appointment, and I thought I'd take you up on your offer to stop by and see Crimson."

She was offering friendship, but Phoenix wasn't sure the other woman would feel that way once she spoke to Morgan. It had been easy to see what a close-knit, loving family they were. "Have you spoken to Morgan lately?"

"We had dinner at Mama's house last night," Sierra answered easily. "Luke, my oldest brother, and his new wife, Catherine, were there. Why?"

Her grip on the tablet tightened. "We're not seeing each other anymore."

Whatever she was expecting, it wasn't the elegant shrug of Sierra's shoulder. "If I had to stop being friends with the women my brothers stopped dating, I'd be very lonely."

While her words were comforting on one hand, on the other they weren't. "Morgan dates a lot, I guess."

"Not as much as Brandon or Pierce, but more than Luke before he married. He's very selective and picky."

Sierra wrinkled her nose. "Our Morgan is a perfection-
ist. You should see his house. Not even a magazine out
of place."

"I'm not very neat," Phoenix murmured.

Sierra smile broadened. "Neither am I."

They grinned at each other.

Suddenly Sierra put her hand on her flat stomach.
"Sorry. My stomach is telling me to feed it." She
looked forlorn. "Brandon's not open for breakfast. I'd
go by his place and wake him up, but he's a grouch
before nine."

"I can cook." The words just slipped out of
Phoenix's mouth.

"Great!" Taking Phoenix's arm, Sierra steered her
toward the house.

Phoenix wasn't sure how it happened, but she found
herself in the kitchen taking instructions from Sierra
on how to cook an authentic northern New Mexico
breakfast burrito . . . eggs, bacon, and potatoes rolled
up in a tortilla. Although Sierra generously ladled red
sauce over hers, Phoenix stuck to mild picante sauce
they'd discovered in the cabinet.

"Good thing the kitchen and freezer were well
stocked," Phoenix commented, savoring her burrito.

"I made sure of that." Sierra sipped her coffee.
"Nothing worse than being hungry at night and the
fridge and cupboard are bare. I check before each
renter moves in to ensure that at least they have the
staples."

"My stomach appreciates your foresight." Finished, Phoenix picked up her juice. "That was good."

"Must have been. You ate three."

Phoenix flushed.

"I was joking." Sierra placed her mug on the table. "I put away two myself."

"Sorry." Playfulness was not a part of Phoenix's relationship with Andre. Nor could she imagine Ben or Cleo bantering with her.

"Forget it. I'll help you clean up the kitchen and then we can go see Crimson." Standing, Sierra reached for her flatware.

Phoenix reached it first. "You'll do no such thing. I'll get it later." Stacking the plate on top of hers, she placed them in the sink. "Come on; I'll show you Crimson."

"I probably should argue, but I detest washing dishes," Sierra admitted. "Growing up, I got out of it every chance I got. I could usually get Luke or Morgan to do them for me. How about you? Any brothers or sisters?"

The smile on Phoenix's face froze. Picking up the jars of hot sauce and salsa, she returned them to the refrigerator. "No. Just me."

Sierra waited until she came back for the flatware. "Where did you grow up?"

A fork and knife clanked on the stone floor. Phoenix stooped to pick them up. "Indiana."

Sierra didn't push it, although she'd bet her new Ralph Lauren hot pink alligator bag she'd had to wait six months to get that Phoenix was lying. Not very well, either, which was in her favor. The deceit wasn't ingrained. "We've lived in Santa Fe since I was a little girl. Mama took a teaching position at St. John's after our father died."

"I'm sorry," Phoenix said, longing and sadness in her voice. "Morgan told me. That must have been difficult for all of you."

Sierra watched her closely. "It was, but we had each other and that helped."

Phoenix's hands clenched on the place mats she'd just picked up. "Yes. Having someone to love you would have helped."

Sierra didn't comment on the odd phrasing; she just stored it away for future thought. "After we look at Crimson, I'd like to ask you a favor."

Weariness entered Phoenix's face. "What?"

"Help me close a deal?"

Phoenix blinked. "Me?"

Easily removing the place mats from Phoenix's hand, Sierra looped her arm through the other woman's and started out of the kitchen. "My new client is a noted art collector. Knowing how satisfied Mr. Duval is with the leased property would go a long way toward helping me close the deal."

Phoenix walked through the front door Sierra opened. "I don't know."

"It wouldn't take long and you'd be doing me a huge favor." They started down the path to the barn. "I know it's asking a lot."

"No, it's not."

"Great; then you'll do it. I'll pick you up at eleven and afterward we can lunch at Brandon's place."

"All right."

Sierra didn't let her triumphant smile show. One down and her stubborn brother to go.

Morgan's mood was only slightly improved from last night as he worked his way though the standing-room-only crowd in the foyer of The Red Cactus. He nodded greetings to the hostess and kept going. He just hoped he didn't have to go through another well-meaning third degree.

He didn't need or want another analysis of his feelings. He would have turned down Luke's request to meet him for lunch if he hadn't said it was important.

No matter how Morgan had tried to play it off, they'd known better. He wasn't up to a replay of last night. He had beaten himself over the head enough without his family ever learning the entire extent of what a gullible fool he'd been.

He thought he was too smart to be conned. He'd been proven wrong.

He'd swallowed Phoenix's innocent act, hook, line, and sinker. Every time he thought of her standing there in the doorway wearing silk and moonlight waiting for another man he wanted to smash something.

Controlling the impulse wasn't easy. He wasn't used to being on guard around his family. That added one more reason never to want to set eyes on Phoenix Bannister again.

He stepped around a departing group of diners and came to an abrupt halt. Phoenix was sitting at their family table. He couldn't get there fast enough.

"What are you doing here?"

Phoenix's head came sharply around at the whiplash in Morgan's voice. "I-I . . ."

"I invited her," Sierra said from beside her. "She helped me sell a house and the commission is going into my business fund."

Morgan kept his hard gaze fixed on Phoenix. He refused to be swayed by the undisguised delight he'd initially glimpsed in her face. He much preferred the wariness he now saw. "I don't want her here. She doesn't belong."

Phoenix lowered her head. "Let me out, please."

"Morgan, sit down and then apologize," Luke ordered.

He chose to stand. "You don't know how deceitful she can be."

Phoenix flinched. Morgan's fists clenched. He wouldn't feel bad that he'd hurt her.

"Morgan, sit down."

Morgan had heard that tone in Luke's voice more than a few times. Luke had been the undisputed leader of the family since the death of their father. Not so much because of his age, but because he led by example and, like their mother, could make you feel two inches tall.

Morgan sat. His gaze locked on Phoenix's downcast head for a long moment; then he turned to Luke. "Make it fast."

Luke looked at him, then nodded toward Phoenix.

Morgan didn't see it at first and when he did his stomach clenched: the steady drip of moisture on the paper napkin in front of her. He wanted to believe it was all acting. He had to believe it.

"Here's the food." Brandon set a large platter in front of them. He cut a disapproving look at Morgan. "Why did you have to show up? I was hoping the next time I asked Phoenix out, she'd accept."

"I don't care what she does."

Brandon was taken aback. "For that, you don't get any."

"I'll survive," Morgan said.

"Not if you don't have teeth to eat," was Brandon's rejoinder.

Phoenix looked alarmed. "Please. I don't want this. I'll leave."

"Please let her out, Sierra," Catherine spoke from beside Luke for the first time.

"Morgan," was all Sierra said before she stood.

Head down, Phoenix quickly scooted out. She looked anywhere but at Morgan. "Thank you. I'll get a cab back. Good-bye." She took a couple of steps, then turned to Morgan. "I wish things could have been different. I guess I forgot for a moment." Battling tears, she walked away.

"You made her cry," Brandon accused. Next to food, Brandon loved women most.

"You don't know her the way I do," Morgan defended himself.

"You don't know her at all."

His gaze cut to Sierra. "Don't be fooled by that sweet innocent act."

"Morgan, it's not an act. If you don't go after her, you'll be sorry," Sierra told him. "Is whatever she did really that bad?"

He opened his mouth to say yes, then snapped it shut. Phoenix had a right to date whomever she wanted. Her careless dismissal of him had bothered him more than he cared to admit, but it didn't give him the right to crucify her. With any other woman he would have wished her well and forgotten her by the time he reached his car. With Phoenix he couldn't.

His inability to control his feelings toward her annoyed him, but not as much as his harsh treatment of her. To her a couple of dates didn't signify a commitment to see each other exclusively. How was she to know he didn't date casually or share? She would, though. No man was taking her away from him.

Phoenix was going to be his.

Morgan's mind made up, he was strangely at peace. He glanced around the table at the accusing faces. "I owe her and you an apology."

Brandon moved the platter of food back in front of him. He was forgiven.

Phoenix easily found a cab in the Plaza to take her home. Paying the man and adding a generous tip, she let herself into the house. The sensation in her chest hadn't lessened. Morgan detested her so much that he didn't want her around his family. Until then she hadn't admitted to herself how much she had hoped they could still be friends.

Her hand was on the button of her blouse when the doorbell rang. Her heart rate quickened when she saw Morgan's car through the window. Her first impulse was to not answer.

Apparently Morgan thought as much. He banged on the door as he had last night. "Stop hiding, Phoenix! I know you're in there."

The more he banged, the angrier she became. He'd treated her abominably and she'd taken it. Just like she always had. She was a spineless wimp. She stalked across the room and opened the door.

"I don't want you here."

His black eyes narrowed as she tossed the same words back at him he'd said earlier to her. "Did you really have a date last night?"

She almost faltered, then stiffened her spine. "That's none of your business."

"I say differently." He stepped over the threshold, causing her to back up. He shut the door behind him. "I don't know how they do it wherever you've been living, but here, after a man and woman get to the kissing stage, it pretty much says they're seeing each other exclusively."

Her gaze flickered to his sensual mouth. She wasn't sure what to say.

His hands settled possessively on her waist. "Your mouth was made to be kissed. By me. By only me."

Her entire body sighed; then she snapped straight and stepped back. The reason for her sending him away last night was still there. "I don't want that."

His eyebrow lifted at the obvious lie.

"I mean it," she said, hearing the trembling in her own voice.

"All right, have it your way. For now." He extended his hand. "Let's go see if they left us any food."

She wanted to take it so badly. "I can't."

His hand didn't waver. "I shouldn't have said the cruel things I did. It seems I'm rather possessive. From now on I'll be on my best behavior. Besides, my family will probably disown me if I don't bring you back."

"I like your family."

"They like you, too." He closed the distance between them and took her hand in his. "My ears will probably be ringing until next week."

"Family is too important to be at odds."

"Families argue. Didn't yours?"

There it was again, a question about her family, and they wouldn't stop. At least in this she could be totally honest. "Yes."

"It will be all right. Trust me."

"I want to, but it's hard," she told him with aching sincerity. "It hurts too bad when people let you down."

"Like I did earlier."

She shook her head. "It wasn't your fault."

"Thank you for excusing my bad manners. If any

man had treated Sierra that way he'd have me to answer to."

She didn't doubt him, but there was another truth
she'd learned. "Sierra can take care of herself. You
don't have to worry about her. She also has a way of
talking people into things before they know what hit
them."

He laughed. "She was born to sell."

Phoenix was fascinated by the way the light
played on his face. She wondered if any artist could
do it justice.

"Did I grow another head?"

She flushed. "No. I was thinking how challenging
it would be to sculpt you."

"You want to try?"

She was already shaking her head. "I'm not ready."

Morgan absorbed the new information. "Who says?"

"Andre," she admitted slowly. "But after the show
in Seattle he promised to talk about letting me show a
few pieces with his."

"What have you done? Can I see?"

Unhappiness clouded her features. "Andre says
I'm not ready."

Morgan's mouth tightened. "He could be wrong."

"He's the best there is. His opinion is highly respected internationally."

"Since I don't want to have another argument, let's
agree to disagree about Duval and go eat lunch." His
hand in the small of her back, he urged her out of the
house.

Aware she still hadn't said yes, she got inside the car. "Why don't you like Andre?"

Morgan paused in closing the door. "Why do you like him?"

"He saved my life."

He saved my life.

Morgan replayed Phoenix's words over and over in his head as he sat with her and his family at The Red Cactus. They were still plowing their way through the enormous platters of food Brandon had served them.

From across the table, Luke gave him a nod of approval. Catherine did the same.

They were obviously delighted to see Phoenix. A person might dupe one or even two of them, but not his entire family. So that left the conclusion he'd already come up with: Phoenix was exactly the sweetly shy woman he'd thought her to be when they first met.

Which brought him back to what she had meant. Duval might have fooled some people in the art world, but not Morgan. Duval was selfish, vain, and egotistical . . . just the type of man to want the world to think he could have a beautiful young woman at his beck and call. Phoenix might not like the way Duval ordered her around, but she took it.

Dangling the bait of letting her show her work kept her in line. Morgan's hands fisted beneath the table. Duval was the worst kind of user. He thought of himself first, last, and always. He wouldn't cross the street to help anyone if it didn't benefit him in some way. So why had he helped Phoenix?

Morgan couldn't figure out the answer to that question any more than the reason Phoenix hadn't wanted to see him again. It didn't take long to recall she was fine until Cramer and Rodgers had spoken to him about running for office. Had that been a coincidence or had she begun to have second thoughts about becoming involved? Duval certainly wouldn't approve if he knew.

Morgan was no closer to an answer when he took Phoenix home and walked her to the door. Taking the key from her hand, he unlocked the door and handed it back to her.

She made no move to go inside. "You were quiet during lunch."

He brushed a strand of hair behind her ear. "Just thinking."

She stuck out her hand. "Thank you."

He'd let her call the shots, but he'd also wanted her to know he'd only pull back so far. He took her hand, raised it to his lips and kissed the inside of her wrist, felt her pulse leap. "I thought we had settled that we established that we had moved to the kissing stage?"

She flushed. "Morgan, please try to understand. It can't be the way you want."

"Why?"

She hadn't expected it to be easy. "It just can't be."

"It was going great until Snake, and then the night of the opera. You have something against policemen and politicians?" He had meant it half-teasingly, but her expression instantly became wary.

"The incidents reminded me that our lives are going in different directions. I'm leaving here soon," she told him. "There is no sense in becoming involved with someone I'll miss."

His dark eyes narrowed. "So you'd rather live your life alone?"

"If it means not getting my heart trampled on, then the answer is yes." She started inside then she heard Crimson neigh. She stopped. The sound was weak, as if he was in pain. "Crimson!"

She took off running. She had only gone a couple of steps before Morgan caught up with her and took her arm.

"It could be nothing," he said.

Phoenix didn't say anything, because if he really thought that, he wouldn't be running, too.

Her anxiety grew when she didn't see Crimson's head over the stall door. She ran faster.

Morgan opened the stall and Phoenix rushed inside. She dropped to her knees beside the horse on his side. The horse's pitiful neighs tore at her heart. She stroked his neck, said nonsensical words to soothe him.

Morgan came down beside them. "Has he ever been sick before?"

"No." She continued stroking the animal's long neck. "The owner supplied me with Crimson's health record."

"Let me take a look." Morgan moved in front of the horse, murmuring softly, then moved to the side and ran his hand along the horse's belly, down his legs, then lifted it to look at the bottom of his hoof. "The pads are inflamed and swollen. He's foundered because it's too painful to stand."

Phoenix glanced from Morgan to the horse. "Are you sure? Couldn't it be something else? It will take over an hour for someone from the stables to reach here. I don't want him in pain all that time."

"He won't be." Morgan pulled his cell phone from the inside of his jacket pocket. "I know someone closer."

Richard Youngblood was one of the best veterinarians in the area, and that was saying a lot considering Santa Fe was world-renowned for its veterinarians. Today he was taking off early. He smiled as he bid his receptionist Becky good-bye and headed for his truck. He had it all planned. He'd pick up Naomi from her apartment and go then they'd go to an early movie and swing by the day care center to pick up Kayla, and go eat.

It had been a humongous hurdle for Naomi to let Kayla get used to being away from her mother before she started kindergarten in the fall. It had been a tough few weeks for both of them, but they had adjusted well.

Smiling to himself, Richard parked in front of Naomi's apartment building and bounded up the stairs to the second floor. If anyone had told him he'd be so happy to have a date at three in the afternoon to go see a movie, he would have fallen over laughing.

A lot of things had changed since Luke and Catherine had come to his clinic to check on Hero and suggested he give a woman who was down on her luck a job as his receptionist. Since his receptionist had run off and he was desperate, he'd agreed. The next morning he'd knocked on the door of the hotel room Luke had gotten for the woman and her little girl, and Naomi had answered.

Then Richard hadn't known that she was running from her abusive ex-husband. He had just accepted that there was something about her that made him want to see her smile, help ease the fear for herself and her daughter.

He rapped softly on the door and thought of the day he'd come to pick her up for work as usual and her ex had been carrying a screaming Kayla to his car. Naomi had been hysterical and helplessly running after them. Richard had called the police and they'd stopped her ex with Naomi and Kayla in his car on their way back to Texas.

Now she was free and able to live her life without looking over her shoulder. That part of her life was over. Richard intended to make sure of that.

The door opened, and Naomi stood there, a shy smile on her pretty face. "Hello, Richard. You're sure you can take off?"

"Positive." He came inside the neat apartment and shut the door. One day he and Catherine would get Naomi to the point that she believed she and Kayla were important to them. "Ready?"

Nodding, Naomi picked her purse up from the

pretty sky blue sofa she'd wanted but hadn't been
able to afford. After he and Catherine had a talk with
the store's owner, the good-hearted man had let her
have it and the rest of the furniture for the room and
Kayla's bedroom at cost.

Naomi had cried all the way home from the furniture store. She told him she'd gotten up that night just
to make sure she hadn't dreamed it. In another month
or so, he planned to see that she had a new bedroom
set. He didn't like it that Naomi did without.

She went still. "Something's wrong."

Richard could have kicked his backside. He'd forgotten how closely she watched people. Naomi trusted
him, but it was as if she thought any minute someone
would take everything away from her.

"Nope. Just wondering if the popcorn will be any
good." Smiling to put her at ease, he held out his hand.

Visibly relaxing, she slipped her hand in his without a moment's hesitation. He'd waited four long
months for her to trust him that much. "I haven't been
to an adult movie in years."

"Then let's get going." He led her out of the apartment and to his truck. Her ex had a lot to answer for.
If he ever brought his sorry behind back to Santa Fe,
Richard planned to have a close and personal talk
with him, then call the police and report him for vio-
lating his restraining order.

Richard backed out of the parking space just as his
cell phone rang. Becky had strict orders not to call
unless it was an emergency.

He felt Naomi's worried gaze on him.

She'd been one of the best receptionists he'd ever had. "You'd better answer it."

Stopping at a signal light, he jerked the cell phone from his belt loop and looked at the display screen. "It's Morgan." He put on his headset. "We're still on for that movie," he told Naomi, then into the receiver said, "Hi, Morgan. Make it fast—"

Then, "I'll be there in ten minutes." The light changed and he made a U-turn, talking quickly so Naomi wouldn't worry. "A friend of Morgan's has a horse down. I need to get out there right away."

"Then we'll go."

He threw her a grateful smile. He'd quickly discovered her empathy for animals as well as people when she worked for him. He just wished she'd be a little bit selfish and think of herself.

10

Morgan was surprised to see Naomi behind Richard as he rushed into the barn nine minutes after he hung up. Opening the stall door, Richard came inside. Naomi stayed by the door. "Phoenix Bannister, Richard Youngblood and Naomi Reese."

"Thank you for coming," Phoenix said, remaining on her knees by the animal's head.

"I think he's foundered." Morgan moved to the other side of Phoenix.

"You've been around enough horses to know." Richard knelt by the horse and ran an experienced hand over the animal's quivering stomach and down his legs until he'd examined all four hooves. "You're right." He opened his bag, took out a nail pick, and stared at Morgan. "I need to clean around his shoes before I can apply the antibiotic ointment and bandage him up. He's not going to like it."

Morgan nodded his understanding. "Phoenix, move out of the way."

"But he needs me," she protested, refusing to budge.

"Miss Bannister," Richard said softly. "A thousand-pound horse has a lot of power behind a kick. I'd feel better if you'd move aside and let Morgan take your place."

"Morgan can't hold him, either," she told Richard.

"I won't need to," Morgan said. "Just trust me, Phoenix."

After a moment's hesitation, she stood and moved back a few feet. "Just be careful. Both of you."

"Richard." Naomi's hands curled over the top of the stall door. "Why don't you sedate him?"

He gave her a reassuring smile. "I don't have a large enough dose in my bag. Besides, I have Morgan."

Morgan moved in front of Crimson and sent a river of words flowing to the animal for what seemed like an eternity before nodding to Richard. Phoenix was just as amazed as she had been the first time and almost missed seeing Richard quickly pick up Crimson's hoof, clean it, then move to another.

Finished, he reached for his bag. A frown puckered his brow. Naomi was kneeling beside him, surgical gloves in one small hand and an open jar of ointment in the other.

Richard's eyes narrowed; then he snapped on the gloves. As soon as he spread the ointment, he reached behind him, his palm up, and she placed a thick roll of gauze in it. In a matter of minutes both of the animal's back hooves were wrapped. Naomi quietly left the stall. Richard stared after her until he felt Morgan's gaze on his. He pulled off his gloves and put them in a disposable plastic bag.

"Crimson will be fine. The main thing is to keep him off his feet for the next twelve to fourteen hours and let the medicine work." Richard snapped his bag shut and came to his feet. "He'll probably stay down by himself for that time, but watch him just to make sure."

"I will." Phoenix looked at Richard with grateful eyes.

"I imagine you will," he said. "His bandage won't need to be changed until the morning with a special ointment I use. There's not enough of it left. I'll have it and some pain pills delivered."

"Thank you." Once again, she knelt by the animal's head. "I don't know what I would have done without you and Morgan."

Richard smiled. "What did Morgan do? I did all the work."

She brushed her hand gently on the animal's neck. "He found you even after I questioned him, and he kept me from falling apart." Her gaze went to Morgan. "I'm sorry I didn't trust you."

"The main thing is that Crimson is going to be all right," he answered easily.

"Because you were here. I panicked," she admitted.

"That's natural when someone you love is sick," Naomi said quietly from the open stall door.

Morgan was as astonished as Richard appeared to be. Naomi didn't enter into conversations without being prompted, and now she had done so twice. She had certainly changed from the frightened, jumpy woman he'd met some months ago. Morgan had an idea it was because of Richard's influence.

Richard came out of the stall. "Now, if you'll please show me where I can wash up, I think we may be able to catch another movie before we have to pick up Kayla from day care."

Remorseful, Phoenix came to her feet. "I'm sorry. I didn't mean to spoil your afternoon."

"You didn't," Naomi reassured her. "Richard is too good of a man and a veterinarian to let an animal suffer. Your horse was more important."

Morgan lifted a brow. He'd been right. *So that was the way the wind blew.* He wondered if Catherine suspected anything. His mother had brought Luke and Catherine together, and in turn they had brought Richard and Naomi together.

"I can certainly tell," Phoenix said. "Dr. Youngblood, if you'll send the bill with the medicine, I'll send a check back with the delivery person."

"Please call me Richard, and there's no hurry." Richard took Naomi's arm.

Phoenix's attention switched back to the animal. She knelt in the hay. "Morgan, I don't want to leave Crimson. Would you please show Richard into the house? The guest bath is the first door down the hall."

Morgan didn't like being dismissed. He liked it even less that she thought she could get rid of him. "I'll be back."

Her hand paused; then its gentle stroking of the horse's neck continued. "That isn't necessary."

He didn't bother answering. Richard's mouth was twitching enough. He'd probably tease Morgan when he saw him again. Women usually did their best to gain his attention, not ignore it. That would be all right if he did. Morgan planned to do some teasing of his own about Naomi.

When seconds turned into minutes and Morgan didn't return, Phoenix tried to convince herself that she really had wanted him to leave. It was for the best, she kept telling herself, but that was difficult to believe when she so desperately wished he was there.

"We both will be fine without him." Saying the words aloud didn't reassure her any better than it had the other times. She was alone just as she had been since her mother's death. There should be at least one person whom she could talk to, tell her fears and hope to, someone who would stay in spite of her past.

But there was no one. The few men in her life before Morgan had all had ulterior motives for dating her. Even Andre had his own reasons for helping her. The closest she had come to inspiring loyalty was with Ben and Cleo, yet they'd never jeopardize their jobs for her.

Why couldn't she inspire loyalty? Why couldn't just one person care about her? Just her?

"I'm back with his medicine."

Her startled gaze lanced upward to see Morgan opening the stall door. Emotions swirled through her. Denial was impossible. No matter what her earlier thoughts, she was ridiculously glad to see him. She'd lied to herself because she sensed Morgan could hurt her more deeply than anyone before. Letting herself care for him when she knew what might happen was a risk she couldn't afford to take.

"I thought you had left," she said, unaware of the longing mixed with deep misery in her voice.

"I did. To get this." He held up the squat brown jar and a bottle of pills. "Richard's regular delivery person was out on another call." Squatting beside her, he moved in front of the animal.

Once more Phoenix was aware of the strange connection he had with Crimson as he uttered a seamless current of words that settled the animal. He held out his large hand. "Pour the pills in my hand. They're to ease the pain."

She complied without question. Crimson took the pills from Morgan's large hand as readily as if they were the sugar cubes he loved. "Thank you," she said when Morgan finished.

"Anytime." Instead of moving away, he crossed his long legs and sat beside her. His muscular thigh brushed against hers, sending shivers over her body.

"Shouldn't you get back to your office?" Her voice sounded husky to her own ears.

"Already called and told my secretary I wouldn't be back until tomorrow."

She tried again. He disturbed her in too many ways,

made her want things she couldn't have. "You're too busy to spend the time with me. I have to call Mr. Jones at the stables again anyway and let him know how Crimson is doing. Maybe he can send someone."

"You can call the owner, he can send someone if he wants, but I'm still staying," Morgan told her flatly. "You might want to go and change into more comfortable clothes."

"I'm not leaving."

"Suit yourself."

What would suit her was if he would move. It was too tempting to lean into him, draw on his strength, his tenderness. Pretending to get more comfortable, she shifted until their bodies no longer touched. Head down, she resumed stroking Crimson's neck.

"Never thought I'd be jealous of a horse."

The words shook her, but they also made her wonder how it would feel to have the freedom to stroke Morgan's body, feel the resiliency and warmth of his naked flesh. Her gaze lifted and saw the passion in his dark eyes that he made no attempt to hide. Her body heated, yearned. "I think I'll go change after all." She sprang to her feet and away from temptation. "I'll be back shortly."

"Take your time." He shifted to where he could look directly into the animal's eyes.

A frown worked its way across Phoenix's forehead. "How do you do that?"

Slowly Morgan's gaze lifted. "Do what?"

"Get him to accept you," she told him. "His trainer at the stables is a woman. She was off the day I picked him up. The man in her place could hardly do anything with him."

"Nothing special," Morgan said in a nonchalant way. "It's not so difficult when he understands he can trust me. It's difficult for some animals, just like people."

He was too close to the truth. "You want anything?"

The corners of his sensual mouth lifted. "Yes, but it can wait."

Her body, which had begun to cool, was suddenly infused with a burning need to give in to the pleasures his voice and eyes promised. Then what? Loving Morgan and then losing him would be worse than any pain she had ever endured. Opening the stall door, she left without another word.

Morgan watched Phoenix leave. She wanted him but for some reason was fighting it. He had decided it wouldn't do her any good. On some level, he'd known from the first moment he'd seen her that they would become lovers. His mouth wrinkled. He just hadn't known it would take this long or be fraught with so many problems.

But he was a patient man. Good things came to those who waited. And Phoenix was well worth the wait.

Phoenix chose a lightweight sweatshirt and jeans, then picked up a jacket. Although the temperature during the day ranged in the eighties, it could drop thirty degrees at night. She was headed out the door when she remembered Andre's nightly calls. Changing

directions, she went to the end table in the great
room, picked up the phone, and dialed.

"Hello, Mr. Duval's suite."

"Hello, Ben," she greeted him. "Is Andre there?"

"No, Miss Phoenix. He's visiting with the Baron
and Baroness of Hampshire."

Phoenix recalled the elderly couple as patrons of
the arts. Andre had met them at the clinic two years
ago. Since it was a very private facility and offered an
array of treatments from weight control to detoxifica-
tion, it was difficult to determine the reason for clients
being there. She quickly explained the animal's illness
and ended by saying, "I'll be in the stable all night."

"He'll be all right, won't he?" Ben asked with gen-
uine concern.

"Yes, thanks for asking. I'd just feel better if I was
with him."

"Certainly. I'll inform Mr. Duval as soon as he
comes in." There was a slight pause. "You should
probably expect a phone call at the stable."

Andre didn't trust her. But since the person he'd
warned her against was with her, she couldn't fault
him too much. "I understand. Good night."

"Good night, Miss Phoenix. Sleep well."

Hanging up the phone, Phoenix left the house.
Sleep would be impossible with Morgan there with
her.

Morgan glanced up when she entered. His lazy gaze
swept over the baggy gray sweatshirt and slim-fitting

jeans. Draping the fleece-lined jacket she'd carried under her arm over the stall door, she moved past him. If she had put on the sweatshirt to disguise her figure or to make him want her less, she had wasted her time.

"Did he do all right?" She sat down a couple of feet away from him.

"Fine. Richard is the best."

"I don't know how I'll ever be able to thank you," she said, pulling long legs that he could easily imagine wrapped around his waist under her. "I'm going to hate to leave Crimson when I go."

He didn't want to think of her leaving. "How long have you been riding?"

"Five years," she answered, her attention on Crimson.

"So you learned in Europe?"

She threw a quick look over her shoulder. "Yes."

So she didn't like talking about her past. "Your instructor must have been pretty good."

"He was." Her hand paused; then she continued stroking the animal's long neck.

"How long have you been with Andre?" Morgan asked, watching her closely.

Her hand paused, then slowly resumed. "Since I was nineteen."

"I take it your father didn't object."

"He was glad to get rid of me," she admitted, unable to keep the bitterness from her voice.

Morgan didn't say anything, just moved beside her. "Don't push other people out of your life because of what he did."

Amazement on her face, she jerked toward him, then quickly glanced away. "I don't know what you're talking about."

"So many of the kids at Second Chance want to be loved, but because they've been rejected or mistreated so many times in the past, they're afraid to try," he said softly from beside her.

Feeling exposed and vulnerable, Phoenix scooted over until his thigh no longer brushed against hers. "I'm not a child."

"No, but you were apparently hurt as one. Often those wounds are the deepest and hardest to heal." He moved closer and drew his legs under him. "You going to let me take a peek at your work?"

Her startled gaze flew up to him. "Why do you care?"

"The question is, why shouldn't I?"

She moistened her lips. "I'm just some woman you met."

"Are you?"

His voice stroked her; his question confused her. She turned back to Crimson. "I can certainly believe you're a lawyer. You keep asking questions instead of answering them."

"Irritating, isn't it?"

She opened her mouth to say yes, then remembered she was guilty of the same thing.

"Nothing to say?"

She didn't know what to say anymore. She just knew she was tired of being on guard. "My mother made beautiful pottery. I used to love watching her create things out of nothing but her imagination and clay. She did it for the enjoyment it gave her, not the money."

"Sounds like she was a wonderful woman."

"She was," Phoenix said softly, aware she hadn't talked about her mother to anyone since her death. "After she died in an automobile accident my father destroyed every piece of pottery in the house. I begged and pleaded, but he wouldn't listen."

"Perhaps it was the only way for him to cope with losing her," Morgan suggested gently.

Phoenix turned on him, unaware of the moisture in her eyes. "What about me? He left me with nothing of hers. He stripped the house and my soul bare. He wouldn't even talk about her."

She blinked away tears and found Morgan kneeling beside her. "No one can ever take her from your heart, Phoenix. That's the thing about love: it lives on long after the person is gone."

She knew he wasn't just mouthing words but speaking from experience. "But you weren't alone."

"No, and now neither are you." His arms closed around her. "Tell me about your mother. What was your first memory? What was your favorite food she used to prepare just for you?"

The knot in her throat threatened to choke her. "She loved me."

He kissed her cheek, then sat and pulled her into his lap. "Tell me."

Her hand clutched his shirt. "She was coming to school to pick me up because it was raining. She . . .

she never made it." Tears ran in rivulets down her cheeks. "I used to think Daddy blamed me because she came for me instead of letting me ride the bus that day."

Morgan's arms tightened. "It wasn't your fault."

"There was a pileup on the freeway." She sniffed. "I know it in my head, but . . . but . . ."

"But what?" he asked gently.

"It's hard when your own father won't look at you," she admitted, her eyes closed in shame.

Warm lips pressed against her closed eyelids. "Then think of how much your mother loved you and the happiness she wanted for you. Think of her and mourn the loss of your father and move on."

He'd said the words she'd never said aloud. It was like losing both parents. "How can I?"

"By living and finding the joys in life your mother would have wanted for you."

"To be a sculptress," she said quietly. "While she worked at the pottery wheel I used to work in the clay by hand, trying to make people and animals."

"Then do it and don't let anyone stop you," he told her.

She raised up and looked into his fierce eyes. "Wanting something doesn't mean I have the talent."

"Do you believe?"

"Andre—"

"No. Not what he thinks. Do you believe in there?" He pointed to her heart.

She had to be honest. "I don't know."

"Then work your tail off until you can stand up to

anyone and tell him he's a liar if he says you aren't the best," he returned.

"It's probably easy for you—"

"Why do you think it was easy getting where I am?" he interrupted. "I'm part Muscogee, part African-American. Some people count me out just because of the color of my skin and my heritage. Their ignorance is no excuse for me giving up. It makes me work harder. If you want something, then fight and keep fighting until you have it."

"I don—" His hard glare made her clamp her mouth shut. "I'll try."

His gaze saddened. "Then you might as well give up. Trying isn't good enough."

She was the one glaring this time. "You're so . . . so . . ."

"Right," he supplied.

She sighed. He was. It was time she stopped feeling sorry for herself. "All right. I'm going after what I want."

"Good." He pulled her back into his arms. "Hopefully starting with me." His head lowered, his warm mouth found hers.

"Dinner is served," Sierra said, grinning at them over the stall's door.

Phoenix scrambled to her feet, embarrassed to have been caught kissing Morgan. "Sierra, I—I didn't expect you."

Sierra cocked a brow. "Obviously." She lifted the picnic hamper so it could be seen. "Brandon sent everything you ordered, Morgan. You two go eat and I'll babysit."

"Thanks." Morgan glanced at his watch, then reached for the medicine bottle and gave the horse his 7:30 dose for pain. Finished, Morgan easily came to his feet and took Phoenix's arm.

She balked. "You go on."

"We're both eating," he told her. "Sitting here staring at him is not going to help him get better any faster."

"I know; I just don't want him to feel I've abandoned him."

"We'll be back before he misses you." Ushering her firmly out the stall's door, Morgan took the basket from Sierra's hand and started toward the house.

Phoenix glanced over her shoulder, then at Morgan. "We could have eaten in there."

Morgan shook his head. "I'm as partial to horses as anyone, but I draw the line at eating with one."

She sighed and continued to the house. In the kitchen he set the hamper of food on the island and went to the sink to wash his hands. "I'll get things ready if you'll get the plates and flatware."

"You do this often?" she asked as she took her turn at the sink.

"Order takeout, yes. Have Sierra deliver food, no." He began pulling food out of the hamper. "Brandon loves to cook and I like to keep him happy."

The aromas were wonderful. "This is very nice of all of you."

Morgan pulled out a chair. "Then thank us by sitting down and eating. You can tell me about the places you lived in Europe."

Phoenix sat, her stomach settling. Morgan had given her notice they were going to keep the conversation light. She bowed her head as he said grace. Even with Crimson sick, she felt better than she had in a long time. She wasn't alone.

They had finished eating and had cleaned up the kitchen when Morgan dropped a bomb. "Where do you keep the extra pillows and blankets?"

"I beg your pardon?"

"It's going to get cold tonight in the stable unless you're going to be sensible and sleep in the house and set your alarm to check on him."

She went to the linen closet and came back with a pillow and a blanket. "I had a jacket, but this will be better."

"We're sharing?"

Her mouth gaped like a fish. With a smile of pure devilment, he lifted her chin, then took the things out of her arms. "I guess that means no. I'll take these."

"You don't have to stay," she told him.

He started for the door. "Go get yourself a pillow and a couple of blankets."

Instead of trying to talk him out of staying, she did as he requested. When she returned, he opened the door and they went to the stable.

Sierra rose nimbly to her feet when Morgan opened the stall door. "The patient is doing fine."

Seeing Crimson sitting up, Phoenix quickly went to the animal and hugged his neck. "You scared me." She looked up at Sierra. "Thank you for sitting with him and bringing out the food."

"No problem." Sierra eyed the bed linen Morgan placed in a corner of the stall. "You plan to stay here all night?"

Phoenix felt heat climb up her neck and flush her face. "I've tried to get him to leave."

"You're stuck with me."

Sierra looked between the two. "I'd better be going. Call if you need anything."

"Thank you again," Phoenix said.

"Don't be surprised if the others show up," Sierra told them as she left the stall.

Phoenix's eyes widened. "You mean your brothers?"

"The same." Sierra stared at Morgan. "You think she'll find out?"

Settling on the blanket, he propped his back against the wall and laced his fingers behind his head. "There's not a shred of doubt in my mind."

"You think she'll show up?"

"I wouldn't put it past her."

"Oh, well." Sierra looked from the animal to Phoenix. "Couldn't be helped, but remember what I said. Night."

Phoenix's hand clutched her stomach in rising misery. She wanted to shout at him for making her trust him, then disappointing her like everyone else. But he had helped her. "If you need to go before she gets here, I understand."

"Wouldn't make any difference," he said lightly. "She'd find me."

Another thought struck Phoenix. "You have a stalker?"

"A mother." At the puzzled frown on her face he continued. "One who loves her five children and is determined that she marry us off one by one, from the eldest on down." He made a face. "She successfully picked out a bride for Luke and now it's my turn."

Her eyes widened as pain splinted through her. "You're engaged."

The expression that crossed Morgan's face was a comical mix of disgust and horror. "No, and I plan to keep it that way. But that hasn't stopped my mother from throwing women in my path in hopes I'll be the next Grayson to walk down the aisle. She's wasting her time. I am not getting married."

Phoenix should have felt relieved that he wasn't engaged, but she didn't. One day he would be, and the woman wouldn't be her. Despair clutched at her heart. Instead of giving in to it she busied herself arranging her blanket over the straw. "There must be a lot of women who want to marry you."

His answer was a grunt.

She glanced over her shoulder at him and once again thought how magnificent he was and how utterly unobtainable. "Most people want to get married."

He crossed his long legs, his gaze holding hers. "I'm not most people."

She'd known that from the first. Morgan was one of a kind. He would bow before no man. Unlike Andre or many of the other people she'd met, he'd give without expecting anything in return. Perhaps if she'd met someone like him in the beginning her life wouldn't be shrouded in lies and lived in fear.

His eyes narrowed as he leaned away from the wall. "You all right?"

"Of course," she quickly said, straightening the already smooth blanket. He read her too easily. "Just thinking how lucky the kids at Second Chance are to have you in their corner."

"I lost my best friend our senior year in high school to drugs," he said, his voice tight with anger. "It was a senseless waste. Gene had so much going for him."

Sitting on the blanket, she drew her legs under her and pulled the pillow tightly against her chest, hoping to still the tremors that suddenly rippled through her body. "I'm sorry."

"Gene and I had planned to go to Harvard Law School together." He looked away. "I couldn't save him."

The anguish and regret in his voice moved her. Morgan was a strong man, yet he wasn't afraid to show the pain he felt. If only her father had been as courageous. She didn't count the cost; she just went to Morgan and placed her hand on his tense shoulder. "But you saved others, and you'll save more."

As he turned his head, his gaze locked with hers. "Sometimes the ones you want to save won't let you. Those are the ones that haunt you."

Phoenix swallowed. He was talking about her. "Maybe they can't be saved."

He shook his head, his hand sliding up her arm and stopping at the back of her neck. "I don't believe that. I won't believe that."

His warm breath fanned her mouth and beckoned her to close the short distance between them and forgot about the consequences. If she just had herself to consider she might have risked one last maddening taste of his mouth. She went back to her side of the stall. "If you change your mind about leaving, I'll understand."

"Get some rest, Phoenix," he said, his voice weary. "I won't need it, but I've set the alarm on my watch for eleven-thirty to see if he needs any pain medication and check his bandage."

She wasn't sleepy, but she pulled the blanket over her and closed her eyes anyway. It was safer to ignore Morgan than to admit she cared about him. Being a coward had always been easier. Angry at herself and the situation, she tossed off her blanket and sat up.

"Can't sleep?"

"No." She glanced at Crimson, then back at Morgan, arms folded, looking perfectly at ease in a cotton shirt and dress pants to a tailored suit. There had to be a dozen things he could be doing and probably as many women he could be doing them with, yet here he was staying with her to watch a sick horse. "Why is your mother trying to marry you all off?"

"Because she's under the misguided impression that we'd be happier."

"In my case she was right."

Morgan angled his head around, knowing he'd see Luke standing beside Catherine. He came to his feet. "Hi. Sort of expected you."

"Hello, Phoenix," Catherine greeted her, a warm smile on her face. "I hope you don't mind us dropping by."

"Oh, no," Phoenix quickly assured her, and stood. She was somewhat at a loss as to what to say. The only reason people paid her any attention was her connection to Andre; otherwise she was ignored. "It was nice of you to come."

"Pierce has a business meeting he couldn't get out of and Brandon's tied up at the restaurant." Luke propped one arm over the stall door, the other around Catherine's shoulders. "I see you plan to spend the night."

Phoenix moistened her lips. "I don't want to leave Crimson."

Luke affectionately glanced down at Catherine. "Where have I heard that before?"

Catherine laughed, then explained, "When Hero, a wolf hybrid I befriended, was injured, it was difficult to leave him at Richard's clinic."

"I can't thank him or Morgan enough, and you for coming," Phoenix said. "Sierra came by earlier."

"That's what friends are for," Catherine said. "If you need anything, call. Our cabin is about ten minutes from here."

"Thank you." Phoenix had never met anyone quite like Morgan and his close-knit family.

"We'll be going then." Luke glanced at his brother. "Like Cath said, call if you need us."

"Everything's fine. Go home." Morgan smiled. "The honeymoon will be over next week."

Catherine smiled and gazed up into her husband's face. "Not for us it won't."

Luke briefly kissed her lips, then lifted his head. "Good night."

"Good night." Phoenix watched them leave, their arms around each other. "I'd dreamed, but I wasn't sure that kind of love existed."

"Then you'll have to meet the others."

"Others?" she questioned, turning to him.

A half smile on his lips, he walked over to her. "The other happily married cousins and in-laws. They can't keep their hands off each other." His own hands settled on her waist. "Although I can't blame them. Some women were meant to be held, kissed, loved."

Each word seemed to sink deeper into her heart and fill the void that had been there so very long. She knew she should stop him but somehow found herself on her tiptoes meeting his lips.

Maybe just this once she could have what she wanted without counting the cost later.

His warm lips settled against hers. Phoenix quivered, then melted into him. The kiss was long and languid, a relearning and welcoming. Her hands speared through the thick hair at the nape of his neck. She pressed closer, then closer still.

From a distance she heard a ringing noise. It took a few moments to realize it was the phone and another to realize who the caller was. Her eyes flew wide. Her hand pushed against the wide chest she had moments ago pressed her body enticingly against. "I have to get that."

Morgan's lips nibbled on the curve of her neck, her cheek. "They'll call back."

"I-I . . . It's Andre."

His body stiffened immediately. Lifting his head, he released her and stepped back.

Phoenix would have given anything to see the return of the teasing smile on his face instead of the mask of disapproval. "Please try to understand. He's my employer and I owe him more than I can ever repay."

His face didn't soften. "So you say."

Threading her fingers through her hair, she went to the phone near the tack room at the end of the barn. "Hello."

"Where have you been? What took you so long?" Andre fired the questions at her.

"I was taking care of Crimson," she replied, feeling bone weary.

"The horse looked healthy to me," he told her.

The implication on top of everything else was too much. "Looks can be deceiving, as we both know, Andre."

His sharp intake of air hissed through the phone. "You forget yourself."

She rubbed her temple, which had begun to pound. "If only I could."

"What is happening to you? I should have brought you with me."

Her arm wrapped around her waist, she leaned against the wall. "I've just had a lot of time to think, Andre, and I want to show my work now. If not with you, perhaps another artist or patron would be willing to sponsor me."

There was a long tension-filled silence before Andre spoke. "You'd turn your back on me when so much is at stake? No other artist can do for you what I can," he reminded her. "Think where you would be if not for me. I'm the only one you can count on; remember that."

Her head came up and she saw Morgan, arms braced on top of the stall door, watching her. She knew exactly where she'd be, and Morgan and his entire family would despise her.

"Phoenix, are you listening to me?"

"Yes. I have to go. Good night." Hanging up the phone on him, something she wouldn't have thought of doing in the past, she retraced her steps.

"You all right?"

Nodding, she started past him but found herself caught instead. Slowly her gaze moved up his wide chest to his face. "I'm just tired."

"Phoenix, don't let Duval or anyone dictate how you live your life. Fight for what you want and don't let anyone stand in your way or tell you you aren't talented enough."

Tears stung her eyes. "Some of us aren't as brave as others."

Gently he pulled her into his arms, his hands sweeping up and down the curve of her back. "Then lean on me until you can stand alone."

What would it be like to know that someone as strong as Morgan would always be there for you no matter what? She hadn't experienced that feeling since her mother's death. "It's better if I don't. You won't always be around," she said, already dreading that day. She'd tried not to care for Morgan but found it was impossible when he was all the dreams she'd ever dreamed but dared not let herself believe.

"I'm here now and I'm not going anywhere." He shifted.

Her eyes flew wide when she found herself lifted in his arms. "W-what are you doing?" she spluttered.

"Putting you to bed, such as it is." He placed her on her blanket, then pulled the second one up to her chin. "Go to sleep. I'll be here when you wake up."

She thought of resisting, then gave in. "Not many people win an argument with you, do they?"

He smiled. "I'd be a poor lawyer if they did."

No one except her mother had ever treated her as gently as Morgan. Was he asking too much of her or was she asking too little of herself? She glanced at Crimson nearby, then back at Morgan. "You'll wake me if he's not doing well or you need help with his medicine, won't you?"

"You have my word."

She closed her eyes. Morgan's word was as inflexible as the mountains surrounding them. She'd trust him with her life. She just couldn't trust him with the truth.

11

Phoenix woke wrapped in a cocoon of warmth. Smiling, she snuggled closer, her chin rubbing against something smooth and soft. Slowly her eyes opened and she saw . . . Morgan, his handsome face inches from her, smiling lazily up at her.

A wild shriek tore from her lips as she attempted to scramble up, which took time, considering she had been sprawled on top of Morgan, her legs inserted between his, her arms wrapped around his neck. "W-what are you doing over here?"

"Trying to sleep until you decided you wanted to use me as a mattress."

Heat climbed from her neck upward. She gestured wildly where his blanket had been when she'd dozed off. "You were on the other side of the stall when I went to sleep."

"The temperature dropped in the night, and after I gave Crimson his medicine and rebandaged his hoof this morning you were huddled up in a ball. I spread my blanket over both of us and you just gravitated to the heat. Every time I'd move, you'd move." He grinned. "Since I enjoy holding you, I decided not to look a gift horse in the mouth, so to speak."

It made perfect sense. She was cold natured. Besides, they both still had their clothes on and Morgan wasn't that hard up for a woman. "I-I'm sorry."

He grinned roguishly. "I'm not."

Her heart thumped. She wasn't, either. She quickly busied herself folding up her blanket, then saw Crimson standing. Laughing, she wrapped her arms around the horse's neck. "You had me so worried."

The horse neighed and she laughed again.

"I like that sound."

Still smiling, she turned toward Morgan. "You didn't wake me up to help you last night or this morning."

"Crimson and I did all right." He finished folding up his blanket. "Why don't you show me where you keep his feed?"

"You've already done enough," she said, absently rubbing Crimson behind the ear. "You should go home."

"I will." Opening the stall's door, he held out his hand. "Come on. Let's get him taken care of, then go get our own food. I'm starving."

She opened her mouth, then closed it and placed her hand in Morgan's. "What would you like?"

His eyes narrowed on her lips. His head dipped, his lips finding hers. Her eyes had barely drifted closed before his mouth was gone.

"That's for starters. I can wait for the rest." Having

thoroughly confused and aroused her, he pulled her out of the stall.

She'd say one thing: he sure knew how to start the day.

They cooked breakfast together. Morgan's contribution was to mix the eggs for the omelets and set the table.

"Breakfast was great," he said, sipping his second cup of coffee.

Phoenix smiled across the table at him. "You weren't kidding about leaving all the cooking to Brandon."

"Nope." He placed his cup in the saucer. "When there are five children and a working mother, you quickly learn to trade off."

"So what did you trade off?" she asked, shoving her plate aside and placing both arms on the table.

He paused for a moment. "Babysitting Sierra."

A frown worked its way across her smooth brow. "That doesn't seem like it would have been that big of a deal."

He laughed. "You don't know Sierra. Being inquisitive and headstrong is a bad combination in a child who likes having her way."

"How did you keep her in line?" she asked.

Morgan picked up his plate and started to the sink. "Who said I did?"

Phoenix followed and stared up at him. "You have a strong sense of responsibility and what's right.

I can't imagine you not taking the best possible care of your sister."

Her words pleased him. Perhaps he was getting closer to her trusting him. He took her dinnerware out of her hands. "Thanks."

Folding her arms across her chest, she watched as he rinsed the dishes and loaded them in the dishwasher. "So give."

"Family secret." One he hoped would never be revealed.

Phoenix added dishwashing detergent and a rinse agent and turned on the machine. "Although my curiosity is running wild, I won't push. I'm too grateful for all your help with Crimson."

He pulled her into his arms and tried to keep the smile on his face when she stiffened. "Then you'll be my date for this weekend at the Indian Market."

"The weekend?"

"The event kicks off Friday night with a reception and ends Sunday at six," he told her. "Over twelve hundred artists from one hundred tribes will be there selling authentic handmade items. It's an experience of a lifetime."

She pushed out of his arms. "I have a lot to do."

Morgan wasn't sure if she did or was simply avoiding him again. In either case, he wasn't having it. "We're expecting over a hundred thousand people from all over the world. There's Native American food from chile stew to fry bread." He played his trump card. "There's also sculptures made from an array of materials."

Interest flickered in her beautiful eyes. "What kind?"

"No bronze, of course, but there's wood, clay, sandstone. I know several of the artists personally. I'll be happy to introduce you to them," he told her. "Maybe you can get some ideas."

"Maybe," she said slowly.

He'd never had to work so hard for a date. "If you really want to thank me you'll come."

Puzzlement knitted her brow. "How?"

"I told you I'm on the board of the SWAIA. If I'm by myself, I'll be inundated with problems like I was last year. I didn't even get to eat the first day and barely snagged food the next. If I have a date, I can enjoy myself for once," he explained.

"How many years have you been on the board?" she asked.

"Three," he answered promptly. "And before that I volunteered since I was in high school."

"And you've never had a date the entire time?" she asked suspiciously.

"Not once," he said, not adding that by the end of the first day he'd always had a date for the weekend event. "I'd really like to enjoy the market and just have fun. Please say yes."

Her hands slipped into the pockets of her pants. "I'm afraid I have to say no."

He resisted the urge to pull her into his arms. "I don't suppose there's anything I can say that will make you change your mind."

"No, but thank you anyway."

"I'd better go so you can get some rest." Going to the front door, he opened it. "Call if you change your mind."

Her answer was a heartbreaking smile. Brushing his fingertips along her cheek, he walked out the door, closing it after him.

Phoenix stared at the snowcapped mountains in the distance, the piece on her worktable forgotten. She'd tried to work after Morgan left but had given up after an hour or so when she realized she was simply shifting clay and not creating. For the rest of the day she'd done nothing but mope.

Andre had been right about one thing: to create required passion and vision. She had neither. How could she when the reason she couldn't be with Morgan filled her thoughts? It didn't take much reasoning on her part to know that he didn't have to search or plead for a date.

It was both exhilarating and frightening to realize a man like Morgan was interested in her. Just her. Unlike the other men in her life who had tried to use her in one way or another, Morgan had nothing to gain—in fact, he'd lost money, because of his association with her.

So what was she going to do about him? Her hand massaged her temple. She could waste time worrying about the implication of her past on his political career . . . if it was discovered . . . or take what she wanted . . . a chance with Morgan.

Her head lifted. Why couldn't she? Morgan wasn't

looking for anything permanent. She certainly couldn't afford to think beyond the time they'd spend together in Santa Fe.

It wasn't likely anyone would try to investigate every woman he'd dated if he decided to run for office. Her past couldn't hurt him. She'd just enjoy the time they had together and not think about tomorrow. The more she thought about it, the more the idea appealed to her.

She slid off the stool to call Morgan just as another thought struck: what if he'd changed his mind about waiting and asked another woman? Or worse, maybe one of those women he said his mother kept throwing at him had asked him out and he'd accepted.

Phoenix couldn't get to Andre's Rolodex in his office fast enough. Finding the number to Morgan's office, she quickly dialed.

"Grayson Law Firm. How may I help you?" asked an efficient-sounding voice.

"Morgan Grayson, please," Phoenix requested, her palm damp with perspiration.

"I'm sorry. Mr. Grayson is out of the office. Would you like to leave a message?"

Disappointment slumped her shoulders. "Please ask him to call Phoenix Bannister. He has the number," she said, then quickly added, "It's about the Indian Market."

"Ms. Bannister, he's in court and I don't expect him until very late," the woman explained. "However, I'll make certain he gets the message when he returns."

"Thank you." Phoenix hung up the phone and slumped back into the chair, her fingers dangling over the armrest. By the time he got her message he could have a date . . . if she waited.

She was standing on her feet the next instant. Perhaps she could reach him on his cell phone. The woman who answered the phone might not give it to her, but Phoenix knew where to find one person who would.

Morgan sat alone in the family booth at The Red Cactus, shoving his food from one side of his plate to the other. He had struck out before, but he didn't recall a time when it had bothered him more.

Usually he'd move on, but somehow he couldn't this time. Perhaps it was the aching loneliness he'd glimpsed in Phoenix's face and her voice that made him keep trying. The sadness that surrounded her drew him as much as her beauty and sensuality.

"Something wrong with the fish?" Brandon asked.

Morgan's gaze flicked up to his brother, then back to the barely touched seared tuna. "It's fine."

"Then why aren't you eating it?" Brandon slid into the booth across from Morgan. "When you came in you said you only had thirty minutes for lunch because you had to get back to court. You've wasted most of it playing with your food."

"Just thinking." Morgan lifted a small bite of the tuna because Brandon was watching him.

"You'd better be glad Sierra isn't here or she'd

grill you." Brandon leaned farther over the table. "I don't suppose this has to do with Phoenix again?"

Morgan considered evading. "She turned me down for a date. Again."

"What did you do or say to her?" Brandon asked, his eyes narrowing.

"Nothing." Brandon had always championed women.

"Then why did she turn you down?" Brandon asked. "Anyone with eyes could tell she's attracted to you."

Tired of pretending to eat, Morgan shoved the plate aside. "I don't know, but I plan to drive out there after court today and find out." Placing a generous tip on the table, he came to his feet. "See you later, and thanks for the meal."

"Next time, eat it," Brandon said, standing as well.

Morgan nodded and grabbed his attaché case. He turned to leave and came to an abrupt halt.

Brandon's gaze followed the direction of Morgan's. "Looks like you won't have to wait to find out your answer." He stacked Morgan's dishes expertly. "Hi, Phoenix, have a seat."

Phoenix was grateful for Brandon's intervention. She made her feet move closer. Facing Morgan was more difficult than she had imagined, especially since he wasn't smiling. "Hi, Morgan. Brandon."

"What will you have? I hope your appetite is better than Morgan's." Brandon gave the dishes to a passing busboy.

"Nothing, thank you," she said, her gaze on Morgan.

"Wrong answer," Brandon said. "Try again, or shall I order for you?"

"Please bring her salsa, chips, and iced tea for starters," Morgan told him.

"I'll get that right out," Brandon said. "I don't want to make you late for court."

Phoenix's hand clamped on the strap of the handbag slung over her shoulder. "I don't want to make you late, either."

"I have a few minutes." Morgan took her arms and seated her in the booth, then slid in beside her. "Everything all right with Crimson?"

"Yes," she said, clutching the handbag in her lap, then glanced up at him. "This was a lot easier when I was imagining it."

His hands closed over hers. "Just say it."

She moistened her lips. "If . . . if the invitation is still open for this weekend, I'd like to accept. I mean, if you don't already have a date."

"Going with someone else never entered my mind," he said. The restlessness that had plagued him since he last saw her disappeared. "It's you or no one."

She could have walked on air. She couldn't keep the pleased smile from her face, nor did she try. "I want to go."

"Then we'll go."

"Morgan, you'd better scoot." Brandon placed the food on the table in front of Phoenix. "Or you'll be in jail on a contempt of court charge and I'll have to take Phoenix to the Indian Market."

Morgan grunted, then stood. "I'll drive out this evening. It will probably be close to six."

"I'll be waiting. I'll cook."

"See you then."

Phoenix's head snapped up at the sound of the doorbell. Her frantic gaze saw that the sun that had shone so brightly when she had begun work in the studio was gone. The doorbell sounded again.

"Oh, no!" she cried, coming off the stool. Her unused muscles protested. "Ouch." Bending, she quickly massaged the calves of her legs, then hurried out of the room. The doorbell sounded again just as she opened the door and saw Morgan, an indulgent smile curving the sensual line of his mouth.

"I was working in the studio and lost track of time. Dinner will be ready in—"

Warm, persuasive lips cut off her flow of words. Her arms curled around his neck as she let her body sink into his.

After a long moment, he lifted his head. "Hello."

She sighed and smiled up at him. Morgan could scatter her brain faster than anything or anyone. For the time being she wasn't going to worry about it, just count her blessings that he could. "Hello," she said, then remembered and straightened. "Dinner will be a little late. I'm really sorry, especially after seeing how little you ate earlier."

"I'll survive." He kissed her again, this time a teasing

brush of his lips across hers. "Can I see what you're working on?"

She didn't hesitate. "Yes, but not until it's finished."

"Then I'll try to be patient. How is it going?"

"Fantastic," she admitted, her smile growing. "The inspiration hit while I was driving home. I went to the studio as soon as I got back and have been there ever since," she said, then glanced down at the faded sweatpants and -shirt. Flushing in embarrassment, she pushed out of his arms.

"Please excuse the way I'm dressed. I'll go change."

Chuckling, Morgan grabbed the hem of her sweat-shirt as she turned to run. "You look beautiful."

She glanced over her shoulder and her heart did a little dance. He was magnificent. He had to be the most gorgeous man she'd ever seen. That he thought she was beautiful made her want to purr and curl up in his lap. She'd never met a man like him. He was without equal.

"I grow another head again?"

Without thinking, she came back to him and ran one finger from his high cheekbone to his chin. "I wish I had the talent to sculpt you."

"Anytime you want to try, I'm available," he said easily.

"One day." Taking his arm, she headed for the kitchen. "Since we already know this is not your terri-tory, I'll get the food ready and you can set the table if you don't mind. Brandon got things ready."

"He let you near his precious kitchen?" Morgan asked, following her.

"Not exactly." She flipped on the overhead light on the way to the sink to wash her hands. "I asked him what you liked and he made suggestions. After we came up with a menu he brought everything out in to-go bags."

"That's Brandon." Morgan took his turn at the sink. "He's very possessive about his kitchen. All his chefs have to pass a demonstration and an oral test."

Phoenix opened the door to the built-in refrigerator and took out two large marinated T-bones and placed them on the counter near the grill on top of the stove. "With his reputation for excellence, I don't blame him." Her hands clamped on the long-handled fork in her hand. Her mouth firmed. "Once you lose your reputation, it's difficult to get it back."

Seeing Morgan staring at her strangely, she rushed to divert him. "When the table is set, would you mind pouring me a glass of tea? It's in the refrigerator."

"Tea coming up."

"On the way back I went by Richard's clinic to pay him." She placed the steaks on top of the heated grill, then accepted the glass of tea. "He said you're going to pay the bill in October. What did he mean?"

Morgan wrinkled his nose. "Bachelor auction I let him talk me into. If it wasn't for a good cause, I'd balk."

Her fingers tightened around the glass. "I'll be gone by then."

Placing his glass on the counter, he pulled her to him. "Then we'll just have to make sure the time we spend together is memorable."

"I'd say we're off to a good start. Now stop

distracting me and tell me about your case today," she said, and went back to tending the steaks.

"I like distracting you," Morgan said, but he told her about the litigation case for a large development company.

Thanks to Brandon's help, they were sitting at the table in less than thirty minutes. "I'm looking forward to the Indian Market."

"It's great. I'll pick you up around seven Saturday morning before the traffic gets so bad. We'll take Crimson to be boarded." Morgan sliced into his beef. "Once he's settled at Richard's place, I'll show you your hotel room and we can have a leisurely breakfast on the terrace before starting out."

"Hotel room," she repeated dully, her food forgotten.

"The city's population almost quadruples during market, and with the closing of streets for the vendors it's next to impossible to get around," he explained. "Even people who live there generally check into a hotel. It isn't over until Sunday."

She swallowed. "I see."

He put his fork down and stared across the table at her. "You can trust me, Phoenix, but if it makes you uncomfortable I'll bring you back home."

Less than twenty-four hours ago she'd slept safe and secure in his arms. He didn't have to resort to seduction or tricks to get a woman. "I trust you, Morgan. It just took me by surprise." She cut into her own steak. She was grabbing every moment. "Will your family be staying there?"

Relieved, Morgan returned to his food as well. "I made reservations for all of us at the same hotel."

Her eyes went wide again. "Your mother will be there?"

Morgan couldn't keep the look of horror off his face. "No way. For all of our sakes, I made her reservation at a different hotel."

Phoenix had to smile. "She can't be that bad. You and your brothers and sister couldn't be so close if you didn't have a wonderful mother."

"She's the greatest woman in the world," Morgan admitted. "Until she starts meddling in our lives."

Phoenix relaxed in her chair and sipped her tea. "She sounds like an unusual woman. Maybe we'll meet."

A look of dread crossed his face. Morgan's fork paused midway to his mouth.

Phoenix's smile wobbled. So he didn't want her to meet his mother. She shouldn't care, they were just getting to know each other, but her stomach felt as if the food she'd just eaten had turned to lead. "Tell me more about the market."

Instead of doing as she asked, Morgan placed his fork on his plate and rounded the table. As he took her hands in his, his thumb skimmed across the top of her hand. "Every woman my mother sees me with since Luke married has become a potential bride. Some of the women I dated saw themselves the same way. I'd just about stopped dating until I saw you."

"You're going out with me because your mother

doesn't know me?" The hurt was unmistakable in her trembling voice.

One hand lifted to tenderly cup her face. "From the first moment I saw you riding Crimson, elegant and beautiful, I was attracted to you. Hearing your laughter clinched it for me. You were a woman I simply had to know better. Any other questions?"

Her hand briefly covered his. "Not at the moment."

"Good." Coming to his feet, he went to sit down. "When we finish I'll help with the dishes and then we can go check on Crimson. Afterward we'll come back here and indulge in my new favorite thing to do."

"What?"

"Long, hot kisses."

Her grin was slow and wicked. "Let's hurry."

12

Saturday morning Morgan picked Phoenix up promptly at seven. After getting Crimson settled at Richard's place, they went to the hotel. Phoenix had promised herself she'd be mature about staying there but found she couldn't quite manage.

"It will be all right," Morgan said, then reached out to take her hand.

She looked into his face and the fears receded. She wanted to be with him. A smile took the worry from her face. "I know."

"It's about time you made it," Sierra said, walking up to them. "Morning."

"Good morning," Phoenix greeted her. She had barely gotten the words out before they were joined by Pierce, Brandon, Luke, and Catherine. Their appearance at the same time couldn't have been coincidental.

Her gaze went from them to Morgan, who had her luggage and his own in his hands. "Thank you."

"I've already checked all of us in," Luke said. "Our

rooms are on the same floor, so we can all go up together, then come back down for breakfast."

"Pour some coffee down Brandon and wake him up," Sierra said.

Brandon yawned. "Excuse me. Late night at the restaurant."

Pierce slapped his sleepy brother on the back. "I know a quicker method to wake him up." He leaned over and whispered, "I saw the Kent sisters check in earlier."

Brandon's eyes widened. "Really?"

"Men." Sierra turned to Phoenix. "Come on and let's put our luggage up before they get started and embarrass us."

Phoenix followed Sierra into the beautiful hotel nestled within walking distance of the Plaza. The adobe-looking building was surrounded by century-old trees and beautiful gardens. The rest of the family joined them on the elevator. If anyone saw them together they'd assume she was with Sierra. Morgan had gone to a great deal of trouble to put her at ease, and his loving family had helped.

"Thank you," she told them.

Morgan smiled knowingly down at her as they stepped off the elevator. "They do have their moments."

Luke stopped in front of the third room, opened the door, then handed Phoenix the key with the overnight case and garment bag that Morgan had passed to him on the elevator. "We'll see you in the lobby in five minutes. That's probably as long as Sierra and Pierce can wait to eat."

Phoenix noted Morgan stopping in front of the door next to hers. Despite her nervousness, a small thrill raced through her. "I'll hurry."

Her room was lovely, with a fireplace and beamed ceiling. She couldn't help but notice there was a connecting door and wondered if it would be used. She hoped so. Morgan's kisses were addictive.

Coming out of her musing, she went to put up her things. If he didn't use the door, she just might.

Breakfast was fun and filled with laughter and bantering. Morgan was pleased to see Phoenix relaxing. His family obviously liked her. It was easy to see why. Beneath the shyness was a warm, caring woman with a sharp wit and keen intelligence.

"Well, it's nice to see my family so happy."

Every person at the table froze. They all were like a deer in headlights.

Ruth Grayson chuckled. "Someone say something."

They all spoke at the same time. But Ruth's attention had already moved to Phoenix sitting next to Morgan. "I don't think we've met. I'm Ruth Grayson."

Phoenix stood and accepted the hand extended to her. "Phoenix Bannister, Mrs. Grayson. It's nice to meet you."

Frowning, Morgan came to his feet as well. His mother knew where they were staying of course, but since they usually straggled in at different times she'd never joined them for breakfast. So how had she known? It certainly wasn't a coincidence. "Would you like to join us, Mama?"

"Thank you."

Luke had stood as well and was reaching for a nearby chair, but his mother claimed Morgan's. Morgan had no choice but to pick up his plate and take the seat on the other side of the round table. "What would you like, Mama?"

"Anything." She smiled at Phoenix. "Morgan said you were beautiful."

Phoenix threw a quick look at Morgan. "Thank you."

"I'm glad we're finally meeting."

Phoenix's eyes widened. "You are?"

"Of course," Ruth said, accepting the coffee the waitress put in front of her. "I'm with the arts council. We're very proud to have Mr. Duval here."

"Of all the cities we've visited, and I know Andre would agree, this one has been the best," Phoenix told her. "Your hospitality and graciousness are unmatched."

Ruth nodded as if she expected no less. "It's easy being hospitable to those who deserve it. I trust you're seeing some of our beautiful city and not working too hard while Mr. Duval is gone."

Once again Phoenix's gaze went to Morgan. Ruth's followed.

"I'm showing her around," Morgan admitted.

"I see." Ruth looked at the plate-size blue corn–piñon pancakes the waitress placed in front of her. "This looks wonderful. Thank you, Morgan. You're such a good son and always make me so proud."

Her children traded looks. They didn't know if she was speaking generally or specifically. One thing for certain: they knew their mother was up to something. They just wished they knew what.

"Your mother is very nice," Phoenix commented later that evening as she and Morgan wandered through the maze of vendors at the Indian Market. An array of crafts from jewelry, to sand painting, to sculptures surrounded them.

"That's why you can't stay upset with her." Morgan pulled Phoenix closer as a group of young children ran past them.

"I kind of noticed that." Phoenix laughed. "I think all of you have a healthy fear of her. Brandon and Pierce left as soon as they finished their breakfasts."

"Darn right. Mama is a tactician. She'll lull you into a false sense of security, then *wham*." Morgan shook his head. "She can be lethal."

The smile left Phoenix's face as she thought of his mother's desire for him to get married. Ruth Grayson wouldn't fail, and Phoenix would lose Morgan. Her eyes closed against the emptiness she already felt.

"What's the matter?" he asked.

Opening her eyes, Phoenix stared up at the man she was becoming increasingly fond of. She couldn't possibly tell him how she felt. He was a man too easy to care about. Then she heard an evocative sound coming from the next booth. "What's that music?"

"A flute," he answered.

"It's haunting and so sad." And so reminiscent of her own life.

"Come on. I'll introduce you to the artist." Morgan maneuvered them through the milling crowd to behind the long table loaded with CDs and flutes for sale.

"Glad to see you back, Ellis." Morgan shook hands with the trim elderly man. Snow-white twin braids hung from beneath his black Stetson. He wore a leather vest, blue shirt, and starched jeans.

"Morgan," Ellis greeted him. "You always manage to find the prettiest flower in the garden."

Morgan shook his head. "Stop it. I had to work too hard to get this date for you to try to steal her from under my nose. Phoenix Bannister, this is Ellis Free of the Cherokee Nation of Oklahoma, an old friend of the family."

Phoenix shook the older man's hand. "Your music is beautiful."

"If it touches your heart, then it must be," he said.

Phoenix smiled up at him, then picked up a CD and opened her purse. "I have to purchase this. I've never heard anything like it."

Ellis looked at Morgan. "You haven't played for her?"

Morgan shifted uncomfortably. "It hasn't come up."

Ellis reached over, picked up a flute, and handed it to Morgan. "What did I teach you all those summers you came to visit your grandparents for? Play."

"Ellis—"

"Play."

Lifting his other arm from around Phoenix, Morgan put the flute to his mouth. You didn't argue with your elder and a man you respected.

Morgan's eyes closed as the melody flowed out of the instrument. It told of a proud young warrior who lost his love to another and was destined to roam the earth in search of her.

At the end of the last lingering note, applause erupted. Morgan opened his eyes to see Phoenix. Tears rolled down her cheeks. His heart turned over at the sight. If he wasn't careful, Phoenix would prove to be a difficult woman to walk away from.

It was past seven when they arrived back at the hotel. Phoenix had been tempted to buy so many things . . . vases, jewelry, sculptures . . . and had purchased nothing.

"You're the strongest woman I know," Morgan said as they walked down the hall to their rooms. "You didn't buy one thing."

She shrugged. "We travel too much to have a lot of possessions. Besides, I enjoyed just looking at everything."

He didn't look as if he believed her. "If there was something you wanted, you'd tell me, wouldn't you?"

She didn't want him feeling sorry for her. "I'm fine. I think I'll go in and take a long hot bath. I can't remember when I've walked so much."

"Knock on the connecting door when you finish. I'll order dinner and we can eat on the patio."

Her pulse accelerated. "All right."

Phoenix tried to relax in the tub but couldn't. Giving up, she quickly dressed in a teal-colored sweater and pants to match. Her knock on the connecting door was answered almost immediately.

Morgan had changed as well, into a black sweater and pants. He looked handsome and dangerous. "You look beautiful."

"So do you," she said, then blushed.

Chuckling, he pulled her into the room. His head lowered, his mouth finding hers. The intoxicating kiss made her feel warm and mellow. "Dinner is waiting on the terrace and afterward we can go dancing."

"We're going out?"

"No," he answered as they stepped onto the terrace, where a small table draped in blue linen with two flickering candles on top waited. "If you don't mind, we'll stay in. I don't want to share you with another person."

"I'd like that."

"Good." He kissed the nape of her neck. She shivered and wondered what else the night would bring.

Wrapped in each other's arms, their bodies aligned with each other, Morgan and Phoenix danced to another

Vanessa Williams song. "Did you give Cicely a hint of the music to play at the dance?"

"I might have," he admitted, rubbing his cheek against hers.

Phoenix sighed. "Your selections were excellent, but I'm enjoying this more."

"So am I. I'm glad you decided to come."

She lifted her head. "Because you finally got to enjoy the market without people demanding your attention?"

He stopped and gazed down at her. "Because of this." His mouth found hers. Desire struck him hard and fast. He pulled her roughly to him. "I'm not sure this is a good idea any longer."

"I trust you."

His laugh was ragged. "I know, and that's the only thing that's helping me keep it together."

"I've never known a man like you. You make me . . ." Her voice trailed off.

Strong fingers lifted her face. "What?"

Her eyes closed, then opened. "Nothing. Nothing at all."

His hands cupped her face. "If you trust me, then trust me all the way. Let me help you."

Her smile was unbearably sad as her hands cupped his. "You already have. You make me believe for the first time in what seems like forever."

"You're going to blow the socks off the art world."

She'd been referring to him, not her work. "You haven't seen anything I've done."

His eyes were intense. "I don't have to. I just know."

"How?"

He smiled into her troubled face. "Just as I knew that one day I'd hold you like this, kiss you like this." His tongue traced the seam of her mouth. On a trembling sigh she opened for him, forgetting fears, forgetting everything except the man and the slow, burning kiss.

Reluctantly Morgan lifted his head. "I think you'd better go to bed while I can let you go."

She wasn't sure if she wanted to leave.

"My mother might show up in the morning."

Phoenix jerked upright. Her eyes widened.

"Yeah," Morgan said.

Despite her initial embarrassment, Phoenix smiled. "Good night, Morgan. I had a wonderful day."

He walked her to the connecting door. "Sleep late if you want. The market doesn't open until twelve."

She shook her head. "I usually get up early because I work better in the mornings."

"In that case, knock on the door and we'll drive out and check on Crimson."

She kissed him on the cheek. He always thought of what made her happy. "Thank you. Good night." Opening the door, she went into her room.

Sunday was just as much fun as Saturday. After checking on Crimson, they returned and met the rest of the Graysons for breakfast. His mother hadn't shown. Finished, they all went to the market together.

Phoenix quickly learned that she was not the only one who thought the Grayson men together were magnificent. Women actually stopped and stared. The men didn't seem to notice.

Phoenix was pleasantly tired when she arrived home. After putting Crimson in his stall, they went back to the house. "You think you'll be rested enough to see a movie tomorrow night?" Morgan asked.

She didn't hesitate. "What time?"

His hands settled on her slim waist. "Six. You'll probably forget to eat."

"Probably. I'll be ready. Good night."

"Night." He kissed her; then he went to his truck. With a wave he got in and drove off.

Closing the door, Phoenix went to her room, a small smile on her face. Maybe, just maybe, this time wouldn't end in misery and heartache.

13

Friday night Phoenix had just finished putting on her makeup for her dinner date with Morgan when she thought she heard a sound from the front of the house. Her hand clenched over the tube of lipstick in her hand. She strained her ears to listen.

Voices floated to her. Her heart thumped in her chest until she recognized one of them.

Andre.

Anguish swept through her. Her idyllic time with Morgan was over . . . if she let it be. They'd been together every night since the Indian Market. It didn't matter what they did as long as they were together. The tube of lipstick still in her hand, she stared at herself in the mirror, looking for a hint of the strong person Morgan thought she could be.

"Phoenix, we're home," Andre cried. "Phoenix, where are you?"

Placing the lipstick on the dresser, she went to the great room. She was just in time to see the backs of Ben and Cleo as they carried Andre's luggage to his room. "Hello, Andre. Why didn't you call to let me know you were coming?"

"I wanted to surprise you." His gaze ran over the knee-length black dress she wore, the high heels, the pearl earrings. "It appears I achieved my purpose."

She chose to ignore his baiting words. "Everything is on schedule. The pieces arrived back from the foundry yesterday. I spoke with Mr. Simmons and production is on schedule for *Courage* to be unveiled at a private reception the first week in December."

Instead of looking pleased, Andre's mouth firmed. "You've been busy."

"I followed all of your instructions," she told him.

He went to the bar and expertly poured a splash of water and whiskey in a glass. He drank before he faced her. "All except one, it seems."

"Hello, Miss Phoenix."

"Hello, Cleo." Phoenix's attention went to the housekeeper/cook, a slender woman with dark chocolate skin and kind eyes.

"Mr. Duval, would you like Ben to finish unpacking or would you rather retire for the night?" Cleo asked, standing just at the beginning of the hallway leading to the master suite.

"Leave us," he snapped, his hard gaze on Phoenix.

Phoenix flinched at the venom in his voice. Andre left the bar and came to stand within inches of her. "Who is he? What man are you seeing behind my back?"

"How do you know I'm seeing anyone?" she asked,

aware that she wasn't going to be able to put off the inevitable for long, wondering why she even tried.

The squat glass banged against the top of the coffee table. "Do you think I'm a fool!" he demanded. "Your pitiful excuses that you put on the answering machine at night because you were working didn't fool me. You've always worked best during the day. Despite my warning, you've been seeing *him* behind my back."

"Andre, my personal life is my own."

He sneered. "We're both aware that it isn't. You stand there because of my generosity. Grayson wouldn't look at you twice if he knew our little secret."

She flinched inside, but she refused to knuckle under to him again. She'd done too much of that already. "We both know I'm not the only one with a secret."

He paled and took a step back. "You dare threaten me after all I've done for you?"

"It's not a threat, Andre, simply a statement of fact. We're essential to each other's well-being, but I plan to live my life from now on as I see fit." She took a deep breath. "If that angers you, I'm sorry."

His hard stare drilled into her. "You'll regret this."

Phoenix's knees shook, but she wouldn't let herself cower. "I don't think so."

The sound of the doorbell cut into the tense silence. "If you answer that door, you're throwing away everything you've worked for. You're so close. What if he found out? Do you think he'd still want to be seen with you?"

She hesitated. How many times had she asked herself the same question?

Andre smiled. "I'll get rid of him."

"No," she said, stopping Andre in his tracks. "I want this time with Morgan and I'm taking it."

"You'll be sorry."

Refusing to listen to any more dire predictions, she went to open the door. "Hello, Morgan."

He frowned at the stiffness in her voice. "Honey, what's the mat—" Seeing Duval, Morgan had the answer to his question. He nodded. "Duval."

The other man glared.

"Come on; let's get out of here." Morgan took her by the arm. Her resistance sent a shaft of dread and anger through him.

"Wait; I need to get my bag."

Relieved, he loosened his hold, but he didn't breathe easier until he saw her rushing back with the large handbag over her shoulder. His arm curved around her slim waist and he felt her shiver.

"Good night, Andre," she said.

Dead silence.

Morgan closed the door and took her into his arms. "That wasn't easy."

"No. No, it wasn't."

He palmed her face. "Forget about him and concentrate on being with me and enjoying each other."

"I want to, but . . ."

"Perhaps this will help." His mouth found hers, shaping the sweet lushness of her mouth to his. She melted against him, her body molding effortlessly to his as she met and matched his passion, so easily ignited in her. "Let's get out of here."

His arm around her waist, he led her to the car and closed the door. When he started around the car to the driver's side he saw Duval standing in the window. Open hatred stared back at Morgan.

Dismissing the man, Morgan got inside the car and drove off. "Why don't we see what we can scrounge up to eat at my house instead of going out?" he asked as he pulled onto the highway heading back to town.

"I'd like that."

His hand squeezed hers reassuringly for a few seconds before he picked up his cell and canceled their dinner reservations. In less than ten minutes he was in his kitchen pulling out the ingredients for a chicken Caesar salad. Hating the lost look on Phoenix's face, he wished he had Duval in front of him.

"I've seen Brandon do this enough times so it should be good." He handed her the leaf lettuce. "Wash this off, please, and I'll get the rest of what we need. There's a bowl under the counter."

Opening the cabinet, she obtained the bowl and went to the sink. "Thanks for being civil even though he wasn't."

Morgan stopped dicing grilled chicken and kissed her on the cheek. "My mother's training and respect for you."

Her hands were wet, so she rubbed her cheek against his. "Whatever happens, I'll always be thankful that we met."

His eyes went cold. "Are you afraid of Duval?"

She quickly tucked her head and continued washing the lettuce. "Not in the way you think."

"What—"

"Please, can we just forget it for now?"

If her voice hadn't trembled, he might have pushed it. "Hurry up with that lettuce. I'm almost ready. We can light a fire and eat in front of the fireplace."

"That sounds wonderful." Grabbing a handful of paper towels, she dried the lettuce, then tore the leaves into chunks. "Then I can give you your surprise."

Morgan thought of the surprise he'd like, the glow of fire on Phoenix's beautiful naked skin. "What?"

"You'll see." She dumped the lettuce in Morgan's bowl, then took the forks from him and mixed everything herself. "I'll finish this while you get the plates."

Morgan did as directed. He was sure his surprise wasn't going to be the one he'd just fantasized about, but he was curious just the same.

He didn't know what to say. Morgan stared from the twelve-inch bronze rearing stallion to Phoenix's anxious face as she sat beside him on a rug in front of the burning fireplace in the great room. The detailing was perfect.

"Don't you like it?"

Morgan thought it was magnificent. The artist had captured exactly the fierce proudness of the animal, his yearning to be free. Morgan wondered how he could refuse it without hurting her feelings. He didn't want anything of Duval's. He'd never acquired any of the other man's pieces for his collection because they simply had not moved him. Morgan didn't buy for investment purposes. He wanted to enjoy whatever he spent his money on.

"Phoenix, I don't know how to say this."

Her face clouded, then cleared. "You think it's Andre's work, don't you?"

"Isn't it?"

"No!" she cried happily. "It's mine. I made it."

"You?" Morgan's gaze went from the statue in his hand to her proud, glowing face.

"Me." Her fingers gently swept the horse's mane. "I never thought I'd get this right."

Morgan was still confused. "This is superb. Why haven't you been in Duval's openings or had your own show?"

The happiness slid from her face. She drew her hand into her lap. "Andre says I'm not ready, but he told me we'll talk about it after the Seattle opening."

"Bull." Morgan's heated word caused her eyes to widen. "He shows Raymond Scott's work and he hasn't a thousandth of your talent."

"Raymond is in a different medium," she said, then continued, "Although the critics have been rather cruel, Andre says it makes for a better showing to mix different types of art."

"And you believe him?"

"He's world-renowned. He's the best." She hated to admit that she had so little self-confidence.

Morgan snorted. "You're as good as he is."

A mixture of emotions he didn't understand clouded her eyes. "You've never liked him."

"True, but I'm also a good art critic." He looked at

the statue in his hand again, then stood and held out his hand to her. "Come on. If you don't believe me, I'll take you to someone you can believe."

Their first stop was at Persians, the gallery that had had the opening for Andre. The owner wasn't in, but the general manager, Howard Canton, was. Explaining that he wanted a moment of Mr. Canton's time to look at the work of a new artist, Morgan pulled the manager aside and unwrapped the statue.

The man's eyes immediately widened with excitement. "May I?"

"Of course," Morgan said, glancing back at Phoenix, but her attention was fixed on the manager's reaction.

Mr. Canton turned the statue this way and that, letting his hand follow the smooth line and ripples of muscles, over the nostrils, the forelegs lifted in supremacy. "Magnificent! I want to meet the artist. If he has at least six pieces, I'd be willing to have an opening for him."

"He's not ready to go public just yet." Morgan held his hand out for the bronze.

Reluctantly the gallery manager relinquished it. "I hope you'll consider us when he is."

Carefully rewrapping the statue in a soft towel, Morgan stuck out his hand. "I'll let the artist know. Thank you for your time."

Leading Phoenix from the gallery, Morgan pulled her aside on the crowded street. "Told you."

"I still can't believe it."

"You will. There are a couple of other galleries I want to show this piece to. Luckily, it's Friday night and they're open late."

"But they'd be too busy to look." She sounded disappointed.

"Don't worry." Morgan curved his arm around her shoulder and set off down the well-lit, busy street. "I'm on the arts council. None of them would dare refuse me."

Phoenix soon learned Morgan was right. But she also discovered it wasn't just being on the board that gave him weight; it was who he was. As with the first man, the other two managers genuinely liked and respected Morgan. The contrast between him and the other men in her life was never more evident. One manager, a woman, appeared to like Morgan a little too much.

"I got the impression she wanted you as much as the statue," Phoenix grumbled, then clamped her hand over her mouth. "I didn't—"

"Yes, you did. Now move your hand so I can kiss you."

She moved her hand. "Sorry."

He gave her a quick kiss. "I'm not." They started back to his car. "After watching you fend off men, including my brothers, it's nice to see you're a little possessive."

"I've never been that way before," she said almost to herself. For so long there had been little she could call her own.

"I'm glad to be the first." Arriving back at his car, he helped her inside and then closed the door and got in. "I'm also proud to be the owner of the first of many pieces by Phoenix Bannister." He started the motor. "I think you should go only by your first name. When do you want to have a show?"

"Wait. This is happening too fast." She covered her face, took a deep breath, and was surprised when she giggled. "Let me think."

"All right. Let's go back to my place and celebrate."

Morgan would have chosen a vintage wine he kept for guests and clients, but Phoenix wanted what he was drinking: sparkling cider. "I don't want anything to cloud my senses tonight. I'm too happy."

He'd filled the Baccarat flutes and handed her one. "To tonight being the first of many successful showings."

Their glasses touched. They drank. Sitting in front of the fireplace, they stared into the low-burning fire. "You can't possibly know what you've given me."

His arm around her shoulders, he kissed her. "Yes, I do. The beginning of a new life that you're in control of."

She stared at him in surprise, then leaned her head against his shoulder. He understood her better than anyone. "Thank you."

His arm tightened. "Your gift to the world is enough."

"Really, this is for you." For the first time, she was

the aggressor, her mouth finding his, her body align-
ing with his naturally as they lay on the rug. In the
searing kiss, she tried to show him the immeasurable
gift he had given her.

"You're so happy, you're glowing," he said, threading his fingers through her hair.

"It's because I'm in your arms." Firelight danced
on his strong features. "I've never felt this way about
anyone. You make me believe anything is possible."

Passion darkened his eyes. He rolled, and she was
beneath him, his tongue mating with hers. Her hands
tugged his shirt from his pants. She wanted to feel
his skin. She wanted it all.

His breathing ragged, he clamped his hand over
hers. "No."

"You don't want me?"

His laugh was tortured. "I can't stop wanting you,
but I don't want you to think you have to pay me with
your body."

Her fingernails closed into a fist. "You think I'd
give myself to you out of gratitude?"

Morgan knew he was in trouble. Either way he answered, he had a feeling he'd end up taking another
long shower and, worse, hurting Phoenix. "You're a
beautiful, special woman. I don't want me or anyone
else taking advantage of you."

Her hands uncurled as her body softened beneath
his. Her lips brushed across his once, twice. "You'd
never do that. I want to belong to you. But you'll have
to help since this is my first time."

Morgan's entire body went still. Gently he pulled

her to him. No words had ever scared him so much or taken him to such heights. "If you change your mind anytime, tell me."

"I'm not going to change my mind," she said, looking into his deep black eyes. "To tell you the truth, I've wondered."

Morgan came off the floor with her in his arms in one fluid motion. "So have I." He quickly strode to the bedroom and set her on her feet. A flip of his wrist tossed the duvet aside. "We'd better start in here or else we won't make it."

Phoenix shivered.

"Cold or change your mind?" he asked, picking her up again, his gaze intense.

Her arms went around his broad shoulders. "Anxious."

Air hissed over his teeth. He wanted everything all at once. Most of all he wanted her to experience the ultimate satisfaction. He started a slow assault on her senses, taking his time, building the passion and the need. With each layer of clothes that came off, he stopped to savor that which he had uncovered. By the time he dragged the silken stockings from her long legs and trailed a path of kisses to her insteps, she was whimpering with need.

"Morgan."

Quickly sheathing himself, he moved over her and then stared into her passion-glazed eyes. "Now it begins," he breathed, as he brought them together. The fit was exquisite.

His body worshiped hers as he took her to the

height of pleasure, again and again, wringing cries of ecstasy from her lips. Completion came, leaving them both shaken and too weak to speak. Morgan had just enough strength to roll to one side and gather Phoenix in his arms.

Phoenix had never felt so content and mellow in her life. Stretched out on top of Morgan, she felt like a contented cat sunning itself after a bowl of cream. "Now I understand why you were so taken with *Everlasting.*"

His large hand swept up and down her bare back. "More than the statue, it was seeing you shortly before that did it."

She lifted her head, and her hands stroked his face, trailed through his unbound hair. "I'd like to sculpt you. You're magnificent. Sleek, powerful, sensual. You remind me of a beautiful panther, all grace and power." She glanced at the clock on the bedside table and sighed with regret. "It's after midnight. I have to leave."

His indulgent smile disappeared. His arms around her waist tightened. "You don't have to go back. I've shown you that you don't need Duval."

"I won't desert him now. The two shows coming up are important."

"How can you willingly go back to being abused? You can't enjoy it."

She rolled from him, pulling the sheet up to cover her naked breasts. "No, but I gave my word. Please try to understand. I have my code of honor, no matter what Duval says or does."

He came out of bed heedless of his nakedness and stared down at her. "If he yells at you again, I won't be responsible for my actions."

"Then perhaps you shouldn't come inside tonight."

His eyes narrowed. She dropped the sheet and curved her arms around his neck. "This has been the most beautiful night of my life. Please don't spoil it for me."

"You don't fight fair."

"Do you mind?" she asked, rubbing sensuously against his hard length.

"Yes, but I'll get over it." His mouth took hers and they tumbled back into bed.

Duval was waiting for Phoenix when she let herself into the house that night. "Good night, Morgan."

Morgan looked past her to Duval, disapproval in every line of his thin body. "Call me on my cell in ten minutes. If you don't, I'm coming back and taking you with me."

It was the best she was going to get. Stalking panthers weren't known for their niceness. "I'll call."

Morgan shot Duval a hard glare, then turned to Phoenix. "Make that five minutes."

She watched Morgan walk to his car, then steeled herself for the inevitable confrontation. "You didn't have to wait up for me."

"You slept with him!" Andre accused. "I can see it in your eyes."

"Good night, Andre." She started for her room.

He crossed to stand in front of her. "You're throwing everything away for a man who only wants your body. He won't want that when he learns you have a police record."

Phoenix flinched. This time she couldn't deny Andre's prediction.

"Just stop and think about what you're throwing away," he cajoled. "You're almost ready."

"I *am* ready. Morgan showed *Freedom* to three gallery managers and they all like the bronze and want to give the artist a show," she told him proudly.

Andre waved her words aside. "One piece does not make an artist."

"I can make more."

"And how will you survive if I decide to let you go? You live this life by my good grace alone. Without me, you have nothing and no one." He slipped his hands into his pockets. "Forgetting that because of lust would be foolish and costly. Grayson may want you in his bed for now, but he hasn't asked you to be a permanent part of his life, has he?"

"I won't discuss my personal life with you. Good night," she said, and stepped around him.

"He's just like the rest of the men who wanted to use you," Duval yelled after her. "With me you can have everything. Don't throw your life away."

Phoenix kept walking, unwilling to give Andre the

satisfaction of knowing he'd succeeded in ruining the
night for her. Entering her room, she sat on the bed,
her fingers linked tightly together.

She trusted Morgan. He wouldn't use her, but neither was he looking for anything permanent in their
relationship. Continuing to see him would only make
it more difficult to leave when the time came. Her
heart ached just at the thought of never seeing him
again. If only she could tell him the truth.

Morgan drove half a mile down the road, then
stopped the car and got out to watch the house. If he
got any indication that things were going badly, he
was going back there and, whether Phoenix wanted to
or not, she was coming with him.

He glanced at his watch again. Two minutes more.
He wasn't known for his patience. This time he had no
choice. As difficult as it was for him, he had to give
Phoenix the opportunity to make the break herself.

His concern didn't lessen when the lights in the
front room went out. His cell phone rang exactly two
minutes later. "Are you all right?" he asked as soon as
he answered.

"Yes."

She didn't sound like it. "I'm still on the estate
down the road a bit. I'm on my way back to pick you
up." He reached for the door handle.

"No. Please."

"Dammit, Phoenix. I don't want you living under
the same roof with that sadistic bastard," Morgan riled.

"There are some things you don't understand."

"Then tell me so that I will," he snapped, his concern for her straining his patience.

"It's not that simple."

He intensely disliked hearing the weariness in her voice when she had been so happy in his arms. "I'll pick you up for breakfast and we can spend the day together."

"I can't. I'm not sure what he has planned for me to do tomorrow."

"Let him get someone else. You don't need him." He rubbed the back of his neck in frustration.

"You don't know how I wish that were true. I'll call you tomorrow. Good night."

"Phoenix. Phoenix!" He listened to the dial tone. The bastard had something on her and Morgan was going to find out what.

14

Morgan had a bad night and his morning wasn't better. He'd called Duval's house twice. Both times the butler had said Phoenix was at the stable with Crimson. Morgan's temper was on a short leash when Luke finally arrived at his office.

His brother took one look at Morgan and said, "Come into my office." Unlocking the door, Luke led the way into his inner office, and closed the door behind them. "What is it?"

"Phoenix."

Luke pointed Morgan to a chair in front of his desk. "Sit down. You don't look like you've slept."

Morgan slumped into the seat. "I had this all worked out in my head, but now I'm not so sure."

"Start from the beginning."

Morgan came out of the chair. "That's just it. There is no beginning." He rubbed the back of his neck, then went to stand and look out the window at the early-morning traffic. "I think Duval has something on Phoenix."

"You want me to find out what it is?"

Morgan turned. Luke was the best at this type of work. "I did last night."

"And now?"

Morgan shoved his hands into the pockets of his pants. "What if it's something that could mean serious repercussions for her?"

"You think there's a crime involved?"

"I don't know what to think. Duval has some kind of hold on her that is stronger than anything I say to her."

Luke folded his arms across his chest. "Are you sure it isn't that she simply places Duval's wishes above what you want?"

Morgan's mouth tightened. "He treats her like she's his property."

"Morgan," Luke said patiently. "We've both been around long enough to know that people seldom thank us for interfering in their lives when it's not asked for. If Phoenix is keeping a secret, she's not going to thank you for bringing it out in the open."

Morgan nodded. "That and the possibility that it might hurt her kept me up last night."

"Looks like you've made your decision."

Luke knew him so well. "I'll wait and see, and pray whatever it is, she'll tell me on her own."

Phoenix was in the studio when the sun came up the next morning, her hands shaping a new project, a stalking panther. As she worked, she realized what she had refused to admit until now. She couldn't bear to see the hatred in Morgan's eyes if she told him the truth, and she couldn't continue to see him and keep that truth from him.

She loved him too much.

Her eyes shut. She loved him. It was impossible not to. He called to everything within her. He was everything she wasn't: brave, honest, self-assured.

She'd started this knowing it wouldn't last, but she hadn't counted on how much heartache it would bring. Her eyes opened, and she continued to work. If pain was required to shape an artist, she was destined to be the best.

Glancing at the angle of the sun, she came off the stool and went to the living room. She couldn't put off the call to Morgan any longer. He answered his cell phone on the second ring.

"I've been trying to reach you," he said. "Are you all right?"

Phoenix was momentarily puzzled about how he knew it was her before she recalled that almost everyone had caller ID. "I'm fine, Morgan. Don't worry."

"I'm just finishing up some paperwork in the office. I'll be through within the hour and I can pick you up and we can spend the day doing nothing," he suggested.

She'd never wanted anything more. "I'm sorry, Morgan. Andre has me swamped. I might not be able to get away for a while."

There was a long silence. "Define *a while*."

Her hand shoved through her hair. "I don't know. Perhaps four or five days."

His breath hissed. "If not for me, do it for yourself. Leave Duval. Take your life back. Fight. Lean on me."

"I have to do this myself," she told him, unable to keep her voice from trembling.

"Three days, and that's pushing it. That's all I'm giving you, and then I'm coming for you."

She shivered from the promise in his voice. "Three days. Good-bye, Morgan." Slowly she hung up the phone. In three days she'd be gone.

Morgan couldn't stop thinking or worrying about Phoenix. If he hadn't learned early to compartmentalize his thoughts, he would have been completely useless in the litigation case he was the lead defense lawyer for . . . but it was a near thing. In the past he'd always prided himself on his ability to give his clients his undivided attention. Now that was impossible.

No matter what Phoenix said, he was sure she was in trouble. He couldn't help her unless she trusted him more than she feared Duval. So far, Morgan kept coming up the loser.

Two nights after they'd made love, Morgan sat in his great room staring at the fire. His chest felt tight. He recalled Phoenix there with him, laughing, loving. He'd never felt that way about a woman or missed one more. He couldn't wait another day. He was going to see her tomorrow. Just the thought put a crazy grin on his face.

When you aren't with the woman you love, you're thinking about her.

He jerked upright as Daniel's words played in his mind. "It can't be!" he said, trying in his mind to out-run what his heart already knew.

Seconds later laughter echoed off the walls. "Brandon, Pierce, and Sierra are going to kill me." Grabbing his car keys, he raced to the car.

In record time Morgan rushed up the walk to Duval's house and rang the doorbell. The one person he most wanted to see opened the door.

"Morgan. I—I thought you weren't coming until the day after tomorrow."

"This couldn't wait." A wild exhilaration shot through him. He felt as if he were invincible. "Believe me, it came as a surprise to me as well."

Phoenix's brows bunched as she closed the door behind him. "I don't understand."

Laughing, he curved his arms around her waist. "I'm sorry if I'm not making very good sense, but you'll have to forgive me. I've never done this before, so I'm not sure how it goes."

"Morgan, what is it?"

"I love you. Will you marry me?"

She stared at him, her mouth gaping; then her head fell forward against his chest.

"That's not the response I was hoping for," he said, trying for levity when his palms were sweaty with fear.

Her head lifted. Misery stared back at him. "Before

I answer, there's something you need to know. I can do this better if you're not holding me."

His hands flexed. Suddenly he wasn't so sure he wanted to hear what she had to say.

"Please, Morgan. Help me be as strong as you."

His hands dropped to his sides. "All right."

She took a step back and clamped both hands together. "You already know that my mother died when I was nine and the difficulties I had with my father afterward. We were both relieved when I went away to college to major in art. I studied and worked hard because I didn't want to go back home and be miserable around my father.

"I found my passion in clay, a way of connecting with my mother and, as she did, creating something out of nothing. I was a sophomore when I met a man and found a different kind of passion."

The harshness that came over his face almost made her quit, but she had to go on. "Royce Cummings was a handsome man who said he loved me, and I foolishly believed that he did."

"I don't want to hear any more," Morgan told her. "That's all behind you now."

"I wish that were true. His uncle owned a flower shop and Royce worked for him. One afternoon when I was there a rush order came in for a box of long-stemmed roses. Since they were busy I offered to take them. I was so proud to be helping the man I loved, who appreciated me, always had time for me, unlike my father." She swallowed the knot in her throat.

"What I didn't know was that the flower shop was a front for a drug ring."

Morgan stiffened. "What?"

She wanted so badly to reach out to him but was afraid he'd reject her. "I might have remained ignorant if the police hadn't received an anonymous tip about a drug buy." Her voice wavered, then firmed. "The strange thing was, the apartment I was supposed to deliver the flowers to was vacant. The police arrived while I was ringing the doorbell. They found four small packages of cocaine beneath the tissue paper. I was arrested for possession of cocaine with intent to distribute."

An odd mixture of disbelief and fury stole over his face. "You're a convicted felon?"

Her heart cried out at the rage in his voice. "No. Andre hired a lawyer who was able to get the district attorney to grant me deferred prosecution. I'd never been in trouble before. If I complete my eight-year probation without any problems, no charges will ever be presented to the grand jury. My time is up in six months."

His face didn't soften. "Deferred prosecution is a way for rich kids to break the law and get a slap on the wrist. The felony arrest will remain on your record."

"Yes," she pushed the word out. How she had agonized over the decision to go along with Andre's lawyer to confess to a crime she didn't commit, but going to trial and trying to prove her innocence had been too risky, especially after learning Royce's uncle was a suspected drug dealer.

"Where was your father?" Morgan asked, his voice as cold and as cutting as shards of ice.

Her stomach knotted. After all these years her father's abandonment continued to hurt. "He didn't want anything to do with me when he found out. I wrote him while I was in Europe, but he never answered. About a year ago the last letter I sent came back marked 'addressee unknown.' I haven't talked to him since the night I was arrested."

Morgan stared at her. She looked beautiful, vulnerable. How many times had he heard the same story with different variations about the drugs being planted?

Tears of defeat crested in Phoenix's eyes. "You don't believe me, do you?" When he didn't answer she went to the front door on legs that refused to steady, and opened it. "I'll make this easy for you. Good-bye, Morgan."

As if in a trance Morgan walked through the door, feeling as if his entire world had crumbled.

Feeling a pain so deep she could hardly stand, Phoenix turned to go to the studio and saw Raymond and Andre in front of his study. Andre wore an I-told-you-so look on his thin face. Raymond had a smirk. Obviously they'd heard everything. Her secret wouldn't be one for long.

She refused to be ashamed. She'd done nothing wrong. Lifting her head, she continued to the studio. She was barely settled on the stool in front of the panther when she heard the door open and close. She didn't want to talk to or see anyone, but she couldn't get the words out.

"I tried to warn you," Andre said, a note of glee in his voice.

Hoping he'd leave, she simply shook her head.

He crossed to her and patted her awkwardly on the shoulder. "Don't worry about Scott. He wants my support too much to say anything. Your secret is safe. If it does get out, artists can be forgiven their shameful pasts."

The injustice of it all finally worked through her misery. Her eyes blazed as she rounded on him. "I did nothing to be forgiven for! I didn't do anything wrong and I'm tired of living as if I did!"

Startled by her outburst, Andre staggered back. "Calm yourself."

"Why?" She laughed raggedly. "My life is ruined. I lost Morgan. He couldn't even stand to look at me."

"Forget him!" Andre snapped impatiently, his hand closing over her upper forearm. "You don't need him."

"I love him!"

"You loved Royce, too, but you got over it," he said snidely.

How could she explain to a man who was devoid of love for anyone except himself the difference between infatuation and real love? Royce had been so attentive, so caring, and so vastly different from her distant father. She had confused gratitude with love.

The police had told her that she was one of many girls Royce had showered attention on before using them as runners. He hadn't cared about her.

"I think it's time we moved on, in any case. I've already contacted the Arts Foundation in Seattle. They'll be ecstatic to have us early. There's nothing to keep us here."

Only her life.

"I've decided to definitely let you show a couple of pieces at the New York show."

It was what she had hoped and prayed for. But it had come too late and at too high a price.

"That's less than two months away." He frowned at her when she remained silent. "You should be pleased."

How could she be when she felt like she was bleeding to death? "I can't think now. I'm going down to visit Crimson."

"Very well, but call the stables you rented him from when you get back and tell them to pick that horse up first thing in the morning," he ordered.

"No," she said, never pausing. "I don't want to lose anything else tonight. He can be picked up the day before we leave."

"All right," Andre said. "Now, go grieve if you have to, and then remember who you are. We'll leave within the week. Grief is an artist's best friend. Just look at Picasso and Renoir. As long as we have art, we don't need anyone else."

Opening the door, she glanced back at him. "You're wrong, Andre. One day you're going to find out just how wrong you are." Shutting the door, she closed her eyes. Unfortunately, she already knew.

Morgan was on automatic. He didn't know where he was heading until he pulled up in front of Luke's cabin in the mountains. For a long moment, he just sat there.

I was arrested for possession of cocaine with intent to distribute.

No wonder she had been scared about giving her statement. She had been afraid the police might do a background check. Of all the scenarios that had gone through his mind, he had never imagined that.

She was too shy and innocent. Drug dealers weren't shy or innocent. His hand swiped over his face. No matter how he tried to picture her dealing, he couldn't.

"You all right?"

Morgan glanced up to see Luke standing by the car. His chambray shirt was open. His unbound hair hung past his shoulders. It wasn't hard to imagine why. "Didn't mean to disturb you."

Luke opened the door. "Get out and let's talk."

Morgan leaned his head back. "I don't know where to begin."

"Then the quicker you start, the better."

As if every movement was an effort, Morgan climbed out of the car. He saw Hero on the porch. "Still protecting Catherine, I see."

Luke shut the car door. "You might say they're protecting each other. As long as he stays with us, he won't be captured and euthanized because he bit the bastard who tried to discredit her."

Morgan dropped wearily down on the porch, his feet on the middle step. Bright golden light from the wrought-iron porch lanterns on either side of the door spilled over him. "It wouldn't matter that the man was trespassing. Criminals love to cry foul."

Luke came down beside him. "Does this have anything to do with Phoenix?"

"Everything." Morgan told him about her arrest and finished by saying, "For once, I don't know what to do."

"What does your heart tell you?" Luke asked.

Morgan frowned at his brother. "I'd expect something like that from Catherine."

"Think, Morgan. It's what you're best at." Luke twisted toward him. "You've always been able to read people. What does your gut tell you about Phoenix?"

He lowered his head. "How the hell should I know? I love her."

"We'll worry about what Brandon, Pierce, and Sierra will probably do to you later when they hear. From me, congratulations."

"The woman I love has a felony hanging over her head."

Luke stared back at his brother. "In a room with five hundred people I saw a perverted picture of Cath with two men. She didn't have to say a word for me to know the picture had been altered. When it's right, you just know."

Morgan digested the words quietly. "I trust Phoenix." Just saying the words made the heaviness in his chest lighter. "She could never be willingly involved in anything illegal. I have to find out what happened and clear her name."

"Most crimes are committed for revenge, financial or personal gain, or pure meanness," Luke said.

Deep in thought, Morgan stared into the thick darkness surrounding the cabin. "It must have been a setup from the start. Whoever called to tip off the police meant for her or her boyfriend to be busted."

Luke nodded his agreement. "But which one? The DA probably figured the same thing or she would have been given serious time, Andre's influence and clean record or not."

Morgan felt chilled, imagining Phoenix behind bars with no one to help her or care about her. "Her father should have been there for her."

"She's got you now."

"Yes, she does." Morgan twisted to Luke. "Since it was an empty apartment, her boyfriend probably had never delivered to that address before. Like most dealers, until you're a regular, he'd send an underling to make the sale. They don't care if it's a sting and the underling gets arrested. If the caller was into the drug scene he or she would have known that." His face and voice harshened. "Whoever made the call was after Phoenix."

"She was set up," Luke confirmed that he was thinking the same thing. "The question is, who and why?"

Morgan came to his feet. "We won't find out sitting here."

Luke stood as well. "If you weren't my brother and I didn't like Phoenix, I'd send you off and go back to my wife."

Morgan smiled and slapped his brother on the back. "I know. Isn't love wonderful?"

Both men laughed.

Phoenix wouldn't let herself cry. After she'd checked on Crimson, she'd gone back to the studio, determined not to fail again. Work was the only thing she could control or put her faith in. She'd finally learned that painful lesson.

Just as her hands shaped and molded the clay, she'd mold her life the same way. Morgan had taught her a valuable lesson: that you had to fight for what you wanted. Andre had helped her, but she had also helped him. She'd repay her debt and then she would be free.

Morgan had a restless night and was up before dawn for the second day in a row. Every time he closed his eyes he'd see Phoenix's haunted face just before he had walked out. He wished a thousand times that he had handled things differently, but he'd make it up to her . . . by clearing her name. She wouldn't have to be afraid any longer.

He'd left several messages for her to call, sent flowers, and even driven out there, but the servant always said Phoenix didn't want to see him. Morgan couldn't blame her. He just hoped and prayed that after a few days she'd forgive him.

Just thinking about what she must have gone through, was still growing through, made him want to pound his fist into the person responsible. He'd have that pleasure. There wasn't a doubt in the world. Luke was on the case, and he was the best there was.

Catherine had found that out when she needed answers to who was trying to discredit her, and despite the odds, Luke had solved the case. To help Phoenix, Luke was using his contacts in the FBI and on the police force to find out all he could. But it would take time.

Sitting at the breakfast nook with a cup of untouched coffee, Morgan picked up the small bronze statue that Phoenix had given him. She was so gifted. And once her name was cleared she'd be able to leave Duval and show her own work, which, in Morgan's opinion, was every bit as moving as *Everlasting*.

Studying the bronze closer, he twisted it over in his hand and mentally compared the two pieces. In both, attention to detail was flawless. Both had the same fluid lines and grace. Both pulsed with life.

A frown worked its way across his brow as he continued to study the bronze in his mind. There were so many similarities between this piece and *Everlasting*. He had collected and seen enough art to know each artist had his or her own distinct style that was as traceable as fingerprints.

As he stared at the statue, his thumb grazed over the horse's mane that rippled in an unseen breeze, over the muscular legs that would carry the animal for miles, over the flaring nostrils drinking the wind. Each detail took time, talent, and a steady hand. Then Morgan recalled something else, the black gloves Duval always wore.

His hand tightened as suspicion swirled in his mind. If he was right . . . He *was* right. Getting up from the table, he quickly went to his study.

First he was going to make some phone calls; then he was going to see Phoenix.

Everything was ready. The handle of her suitcase clamped tightly in her hand, Phoenix took one last look around the bedroom to ensure she hadn't forgotten anything. Assured that she hadn't, she went to place her single suitcase by the front door, then started for Andre's study.

It had been two long days since Morgan had walked out of her life. She had grieved for the loss. She couldn't imagine going through a day, an hour, without regretting that he was no longer in her life, but she had to move on. Keeping busy kept her sane. If she stopped too long, misery would immobilize her.

Yesterday the foundry had picked up the new piece, *Unbowed,* a statue of a woman with tears on her cheeks but a radiant smile on her face. Phoenix had given them instructions to have *Innocence* and the unnamed stalking panther delivered to her new address. Morgan might not have wanted her, but he had helped her find the strength to do what she should have done long ago.

Stopping in front of the study, she knocked softly.

"Come in."

Entering, she stopped abruptly on seeing Raymond Scott in front of Andre's desk. Raymond's expression was one of annoyance, while Andre almost looked relieved. The old Phoenix would have quickly excused herself and left.

"I'm sorry to interrupt, but I need to talk to you, Andre."

"Scott was just leaving," Andre said in his usual dismissive manner.

Raymond clenched and unclenched his fists. "On the contrary, we still have a lot to talk about."

Andre cut him a look that would have sliced through stone, then waved his hand in a dismissive gesture. "Wait outside."

For a charged second, Phoenix was afraid that Raymond would balk or, worse, round the desk and beat Andre to a pulp. "We haven't finished." Spinning abruptly on his heels, he left, slamming the door shut behind him.

"Impertinent bastard," Andre mumbled under his breath. "What is it, Phoenix?"

"I'm leaving," she announced, finding it as easy as she had imagined.

Andre slipped his other hand on top of the desk. "You didn't have to interrupt to tell me that you were going riding," he told her impatiently.

"No, I'm leaving *you*. Permanently."

His eyes rounded. His mouth opened, then snapped shut. He quickly rounded the desk. "It's him! You're giving everything up for that sanctimonious lawyer."

Phoenix's chin lifted. "Morgan may not have loved me enough to forgive my past, but he helped me realize I have to step out on my own."

"Don't be foolish and throw away everything!" Andre said. "You're too close to everything you've worked so hard to achieve."

She shook her head. "I've made up my mind. I'm tired of deceiving people."

Andre's face mottled in anger. "You'd leave me and run to him after what I did for you? Even your father wouldn't stand by you."

The words no longer had the power to hurt. Long before then she had lost her father. "I can't change what my father did, but neither will I keep living in shadows and fear, or continue this charade. After the last two shows, and *Courage* being put into mass production, your financial worries will be over. You don't need me anymore and I want my life back."

"But what about the shows to come?"

"You're on your own."

He gasped as if struck. "You won't make it without me," Andre warned. "You need me."

Once those words might have frightened her. "No, I don't. I'll always be grateful for what you did, but I can't stay here trying to repay you. It's wrong, Andre." She went to the door. "They picked up Crimson an hour ago. I wish you well."

"You can't do this!" he yelled, grabbing her forearm.

"Good-bye, Andre." She pulled her arm away. Grasping the knob, she started to open the door.

"You'd be in jail if it wasn't for me!" Andre yelled, his eyes wide and desperate with anger.

Tired of the arguing and realizing nothing she said

would make him understand, she started out the door and saw Morgan a few feet behind Ben. A startled gasp slipped past her lips as she came to an abrupt stop.

The rage in Morgan's eyes, his combative stance, were undeniable. Something inside of her died at the sight. He would never forgive her. She wondered briefly why he was there, then decided it didn't matter.

With monumental strength, she broke eye contact with the man she would love forever. She heard a snicker and turned her head slightly to see Raymond sitting on the arm of the sofa a short distance away from Morgan.

Her shoulders straightened, her head lifted. She would never be ashamed or cower again. Praying the taxi she'd called earlier was waiting, she headed for the door.

15

Just as she passed Morgan, his hand reached out and circled her forearm. Her body shivered in awareness even as her throat clogged with tears. "Please, I just want to leave," she told him.

"I can't let you go," he said, his gentle voice at odds with the unyielding grip on her arm.

"Get out of my house!" Andre ordered, rushing over to them. "Ben, call the police."

"Fine by me. Maybe they'd like to hear what I have to say as well." Morgan stared hard at Duval. "I'm sure the arts council and the rest of the art world would be interested as well."

Duval's eyes widened. He backed up a step. "What are you talking about?"

Instead of answering, Morgan faced Phoenix. "How long have you been doing Duval's work for him?"

Andre gasped. "How dare you make such a preposterous accusation!" Spittle flew from his mouth. "I'll sue you for slander! Get out of my house!"

His attention on Phoenix, Morgan ignored the rage of the older man. "I believe you were framed, and I'm going to prove it. You don't have to be afraid anymore."

"He's trying to trick you, Phoenix," Andre told her, careful to keep a safe distance from Morgan.

"Honey, I know you're upset with me, but I wouldn't lie to you," Morgan said, one hand lifting to gently touch her cheek. She trembled beneath his touch but remained silent. "I've collected enough art to be able to tell an artist's distinct style. So can many other people in the art world. That's why Duval didn't want you to have your own show. His secret would have been discovered."

"Don't listen to him, Phoenix. You know I planned to let you have a show with me in New York. Your triumph will be in every major newspaper and art publication in the world. Send him on his way," Andre almost pleaded. "We don't need him!"

Morgan's hand fell as he stepped back. "Your decision. But I have enough faith in you to believe you're woman enough to put this farce to rest. Trust me. Trust your heart just like I trusted mine."

"Enough of this drivel!" Duval reached for Phoenix, but she moved out of reach, her uncertain gaze going back to Morgan before settling on Duval.

"Don't let your loyalty be misplaced," Morgan said. "It isn't hard to figure out why Duval's work became more passionate and why he wore the black gloves. You're weren't just his protégée; you were his hands."

"That's a lie!" Andre spit. "Don't listen to him,

Phoenix. He walked out on you. If he cared he would have tried to contact you before now."

"I did, numerous times." Morgan nodded toward a silent Ben. "Ask him about the phone calls and the flowers. I drove out here yesterday, but he told me you didn't want to see me."

The regret in Ben's face confirmed Morgan's words, but she hadn't needed to see it. Morgan was the one person who had never lied to her. "Andre, how could you when you knew how much he meant to me?"

"I did it to protect you," he quickly said.

Morgan sneered. "To protect yourself, you mean."

"You have to believe me," Andre wailed, his voice high-pitched and desperate.

Morgan remained silent. The tenderness and love in his eyes helped her reach a decision. He made her stronger, not weaker, as other men had tried to do. She looked at Andre. "It is time."

"No! Send him away," Andre begged.

Shaking her head, she faced Morgan, her hand camped on the wide strap of her handbag. "You deserve the truth and you deserve to hear it from me. It began gradually. I'd studied under him for over two years when he asked, as a test he said, for me to finish the fine detailing of a woman's face and outline of her body. By then I had seen how the arthritis at times caused him a great deal of pain, but I didn't suspect anything. Afterward he said I'd done a fair job, but that I needed more practice, so I began finishing more and more of his work." She paused and drew a breath.

"I was so grateful and wanted to learn so badly that

I gladly helped him. By the time he began the pieces a year ago for his openings, the arthritis in the joints in his hands made it impossible for him to complete the sculptures. He kept hoping his treatments at a private clinic in Switzerland would restore the full use of his hands, but they never did. I do all the finished details for his sculptures." She glanced at Andre.

"He promised me an opening at the most prestigious gallery in the country, and that he'd explain that the similarities of our work were due to me studying under him for so long. With his reputation he said no one would dare question him."

"Lies. All lies!" Andre shouted.

"Then remove your gloves and show me your hands," Morgan asked calmly.

Duval took a step back, ramming both hands into the pockets of his loosely constructed jacket. "I-I don't have to prove anything to you."

"Yes, you do. To me and the art community." Morgan's eyes narrowed dangerously. "Your day in the sun is over."

Phoenix wrapped her arms around her. "I was uneasy and questioned him about the amount of work I was doing on the pieces, but he assured me it wasn't out of line with what other apprentices had done; besides, he had to be successful. He kept saying he had heavy unexpected financial obligations. I always knew he meant me. My lawyer was very expensive, and afterward Andre took me in." She ran a shaky hand through her hair. "I wanted him to succeed. I wanted to give back to him because he had saved my life when I had no place to go and no one else to turn to."

Morgan's gaze hardened. "It's going to be a pleasure watching you go down."

"She's lying, I tell you," Andre screamed, raising his hand to strike her.

Morgan pushed Phoenix aside and caught the man's thin arm. "Don't give me any more reason to forget you're an old man and give you a taste of what you deserve for framing Phoenix."

Duval's eyes bugged in his head, he shrank back. Morgan flung his arm away and the older man stumbled back.

"What? What did you say?" Phoenix asked slowly, her arms unfolding.

"I'm sorry, honey." Morgan went to her, hating that she had to endure more pain. "It was just too pat. I made some phone calls before I came out and learned Duval's last two shows hadn't gone well before he left for Europe. His work was no longer in demand. He's the type of man who thrives on the accolades of others. He needs that as much as he needs air to breathe. Didn't he ask you to study with him?"

"Yes, but . . . but I turned him down." She didn't like to remember why.

"You'd just started dating Royce and didn't want to leave," Morgan supplied the answer for her.

"How did you know?" she asked in surprise.

"Luke located your art professor. He's still at your old university and remembers how upset Duval was that you refused to study under him. Duval tried to get rid of the reason, but you were caught instead," Morgan said. "He used a high-priced criminal lawyer and his clout to get you free and made you indebted to him. To his sick way of thinking, it probably worked out better because you had to remain with him."

Stunned, she faced Andre. "Tell him he's mistaken. Someone else must have been responsible, someone after Royce. You wouldn't have done that to me. Tell him."

"Of course not," Andre said, trying to smile. "The man would say anything to discredit me and make himself seem like the hero. He just wants you back in his bed."

Morgan's hands fisted. If Duval weren't sixty-five . . . "The apartment you went to was empty. Whoever tipped off the police wasn't street-smart enough to know that your boyfriend would have never gone himself to sell to a new client." Morgan watched Duval closely. "They're going through the nine-one-one police records now looking for the tape. When they find it, and they will, a voice analyst will confirm what I already know."

Phoenix stared at Andre. Perspiration dotted his forehead. Realization was settling like a lead weight in the pit of her stomach. "You did it. You ruined my life all because of your own selfishness," she said, her anguished voice barely audible.

"He'll pay," Morgan said, sliding his arm protectively around her trembling shoulders. "Hell is too good for you, Duval, but I'll settle for the satisfaction

of seeing you locked up, your career in ruins for a
false police report and an attempt to buy drugs."

"No, no, please. I'll do anything you ask," Andre
pleaded, pulling his silk handkerchief from the
pocket of his jacket to dab his forehead. "Art is my
life. I'll sponsor her. She can show with me in Seattle
and New York. She'll be a star."

"How can you think a show will make up for ruining my life?" Phoenix asked, her incredulous voice
filled with contempt.

Bitter laughter erupted from the other side of the
room. "That's rich. The great Andre Duval will become
a pariah," Raymond said with gleeful satisfaction.

Andre rounded on him. "What do you know of art?
You couldn't paint by numbers. Not one of your
paintings has sold."

"We all know your work did, Duval. Once word
gets out, there will be a lot of angry people who'll
want your hide nailed to the wall, their money back,
and to see you charged with fraud." Morgan's grin
was feral. "Your time in jail is adding up."

Andre's shaky hand went to his throat. "Y-you
wouldn't do that. It would implicate Phoenix as well."

"I'll take my punishment," Phoenix said quietly.
"No matter my reasons, it was wrong to help you."

"You aren't the one responsible for this, Phoenix;
it's Duval," Morgan quickly sought to reassure her.
He could have throttled Andre for putting the fear
back in Phoenix's eyes. His arm tightened.

"And when it becomes known the extent he went to

to ensure your cooperation, he won't have a friend or an ally anywhere. With your beauty and talent, you'll have people everywhere ready to help you and tear Duval to shreds. I'll see to it personally that you're on every major talk show and newspaper and in every art publication in the country."

Andre licked his lips. "You don't have that much money or pull."

"I don't, but my cousin does. And when he learns you duped his mother and his favorite aunt, my mother, and tried to destroy the woman I love, there won't be a hole deep enough for you to hide in to escape."

"No one has that much power," Andre sneered, regaining a bit of his confidence.

"You want to tell him or shall I?" Morgan asked Phoenix. She deserved to have the honor.

"Daniel Falcon is his cousin," she said with relish.

Andre gasped, then groped his way to a side chair and sat down heavily. Raymond started to sneak toward the door.

"Sit down, Scott," Morgan ordered.

He stopped abruptly, but his tone and face were belligerent. "This has nothing to do with me."

"I'm not so sure." Morgan released Phoenix and went to the other man. "Phoenix's professor also remembers you being a junior art major, and how Duval had ridiculed your work. He was surprised you had improved so much from the showing you had three years ago, which was a dismal failure."

Raymond swallowed and tugged the misshapen knot in his tie loose.

Phoenix frowned. "I don't remember him."

"He was there all right," Morgan said.

Duval suddenly came to his feet. "Yes, yes! He was jealous of Phoenix. He's the one you should want to see, for what's left of his pitiful career, ruined. He suggested the whole thing. It was wrong and I was desperate. Blame him!"

"What?" Raymond cried, taking a step toward Morgan and Phoenix. "That's a lie!"

Duval kept talking, his voice desperate. "He's been blackmailing me. He threatened to go to the news media about Phoenix's arrest. Why else would I let him show with me?"

"You can't pin this on me!" Raymond talked fast. "I had nothing to do with it. I heard Duval tip the police about a drug buy. He was browsing in the gallery where I worked. I wanted to see if he would take another look at my oils and I followed him into the back. My guess is he wanted an alibi if things went bad."

"He's lying!" Duval's fearful eyes darted from Phoenix to Morgan.

"Check the phone record of the Anderson Gallery in Austin." Raymond stared hard at Duval. "You did it. I just thought you had the hots for her and wanted to control her. I never suspected it was because you were washed up. I'm *glad* you're through."

"So are you," Morgan said coldly. He grabbed the younger man by the shirt collar and shoved him back into his seat. "For what you helped put Phoenix through, you both deserve to rot in jail."

"Please, I'll do anything," Duval whined in desperation.

"Can you give me back the seven years of my life?" Phoenix asked quietly.

"I didn't know you would deliver the flowers. You have to believe me," Andre pleaded. "I was trying to protect you. He would have ruined your life. I came as soon as you called. I hired you the best criminal defense lawyer in Austin."

"But you didn't confess you had set up the buy," Morgan pointed out, and crossed to Phoenix.

Andre stared down at his hands encased in the black leather gloves, then sank back into his chair. "Don't you understand? I had no choice. These were becoming useless to me."

"You let me take the blame." Chilled, Phoenix wrapped her arms around herself. "All these years, you knew I was innocent and said nothing."

Andre's head came up, panic in his quivering voice. "I-I didn't know what to say."

"The truth." Morgan's arm tightened around Phoenix's shoulders. "Now you will or else."

"There has to be a way for us to keep this quiet." Duval came unsteadily to his feet; he looked as if he had aged ten years. "I made you into a great artist. You were privileged to study under the best. That has to count for something. Don't let him do this to me."

"You're pathetic. Even now you refuse to take responsibility for what you did. But you will or else," Morgan said, his voice cold. "Both of you will give a deposition confessing everything. You won't leave out even the tiniest detail. In exchange I've been authorized to tell you the DA is willing to give you the same deal he gave Phoenix, deferred prosecution and probation."

"Why would you do that?" Raymond asked, a hint of suspicion in his eyes.

"Because as much as I'd enjoy seeing Duval in jail for his crimes and you in the next cell for blackmail, Phoenix has been through enough. This ends today, so she can get on with her life."

Raymond came out of his chair and started for the door. "This happened in Austin. Neither you nor the Santa Fe police can touch me."

"I'm sure you've heard of extradition. The Santa Fe police will be only too pleased to detain you until the Austin authorities arrive." Morgan pulled a cell phone from the breast pocket of his suit jacket. "Push it if you want. You can't afford a high-priced lawyer like Duval if this goes to trial."

Raymond sat and traded glares with Andre.

"Wise choice." Morgan put his cell phone away and faced the older man. "Now, Duval, as for you, you're going to call off the show in Seattle in three weeks, or make a public statement that Phoenix assisted you on the pieces and deserves credit and recognition for her contribution."

Duval's eyes grew wider with each of Morgan's words. His mouth opened, but no words came out.

"Try to have the show and not give her credit and you'll regret it," Morgan warned.

Duval's mouth worked for a few moments longer

before he managed to speak. "But . . . but they'll know she . . . she . . ."

"She helped with the other pieces as well," Morgan finished for him. "That's why you wouldn't let her show her work, because you would have been exposed. You played on her sympathy and used her being grateful to string her along. It's a safe assumption that the previous buyers may want a refund. It's also safe to say that the furor that's bound to erupt may cause Morrison House to decide not to put *Courage* into mass production, although it was one of your earlier works."

Duval slumped back against the armchair. "I'll be ruined."

Morgan looked at the older man with loathing. "You only have yourself to blame, but at least you won't be in jail."

Crossing to the front door, Morgan greeted a young woman in a trim-fitting black suit. She had a black case the size of a laptop in her hands. "Hello, Marie. These two men have something they'd like to tell you."

Seventeen minutes later, when the woman closed her case and left, Phoenix was still trying to assimilate what she'd learned. She walked over to Andre and Raymond. Both looked defeated. "Because of your own selfish greed, you almost destroyed my life, but I'll survive."

She bent to pick up her suitcase by the door, but Morgan reached it first. Ben opened the door. His wife, who had come into the room moments earlier, stood nearby. Suddenly Phoenix realized they were out of a job. Andre wasn't frugal enough to be able to keep them. "Will you be all right?"

Cleo smiled. "After you said good-bye to us this morning we'd already decided to leave."

Ben nodded his graying head. "This just makes it sooner." He spoke to Phoenix. "Please forgive me for not telling you that Mr. Grayson had tried to contact you."

"I do. You didn't have a choice," Phoenix said. "I know how difficult it is to go against Andre."

The older man turned and extended his hand to Morgan. "Not for Mr. Grayson. Please accept my apology."

Morgan nodded and shook the other man's hand. "I do."

Ben smiled at Phoenix. "We won't worry about you now."

"Good-bye." Morgan tipped his head to the couple.

Phoenix hugged them both. "Good-bye, and thank you for everything."

"You just take care of yourself and show the world what a great artist you are," Cleo told her.

"I'll do my best." Hugging the older woman again, Phoenix went outside into the bright noonday sun. "I was always so grateful to Andre."

"He used it to control you." Morgan put her in his car, fastened her seat belt, and put her luggage in the trunk.

Weary, she closed her eyes and leaned her head

back against the headrest. "After it happened, I used to wake up in the mornings and think it had all been a bad dream."

"I'm sorry. I can't change what happened, but I can see that your name is cleared."

Turning her head slightly, she stared at him through misty eyes. "I thought you hated me."

His hand took hers as remorse hit. "You'll never know how sorry I am for letting you think for a moment I didn't believe you. I'll make it up to you. I swear."

"You already have." She lifted their joined hands to her lips because she couldn't help herself, because she'd never thought she'd be able to touch him again.

Morgan reverently repeated the motion, then started the car. "Let's get out of here."

She glanced around as they pulled off. "I guess the cab got tired of waiting."

"You don't need it anymore."

She debated only a moment before she said, "I'm afraid I do. My plane leaves for New York this afternoon."

Morgan's head whipped around. Fear congealed in his stomach. He might have lost her. "Were you going to call and say good-bye?"

"No," she confessed, her eyes dark with pain. "I'd already made up my mind to leave the day after we made love. I didn't want you to learn about my past."

He pulled onto the highway. "I should have insisted that I speak to you just like I did today," he said, unable to keep the self-derision from his voice.

"You came; that's important. Even my father didn't believe me."

"Do you want Luke to find him for you?"

"Perhaps later." She leaned her head against the headrest. "I'd like to wait until things settle more in my own head."

"Good idea."

Without lifting her head she turned toward him. "Andre will never admit that I did the finishing work. I finally realize that now. His ego is too huge and he's too proud."

"And selfish." Morgan made a sound of disgust as he stopped at a traffic light. "He'll run back to Europe, but the truth will emerge once people see your work. That's why I had to get a confession from him. He won't be able to lie his way out of this."

"The sculptures were beautiful. Before meeting you I didn't have the assurance to believe I was an integral part in their creation. I let Andre erode the little self-confidence I had left until I believed every lie he told me," she said, misery creeping back into her voice.

"He made sure of his influence by taking you out of the country and making you dependent on him." Morgan pulled through the light when it changed. "For his plan to work he needed you dependent and insecure."

She tenderly touched Morgan's face. "I might have remained that way if you hadn't come into my life. I finally see Andre for the shallow, manipulative man he is. It's just too bad the bronzes can't be appreciated for what they are rather than who created them," she said sadly.

Morgan's hand covered hers. "They will be."

Her head lifted. "How?"

He shot her a quick grin before pulling up into his driveway and activating the garage door. "I'm working on a plan."

The frown on her face didn't clear. "Is your cousin involved?"

"No." Morgan pulled into his garage and parked next to his truck. "Don't worry about it. You have enough on your mind right now." Retrieving her luggage, he led her into his house. He didn't stop until they were in his bedroom with the door closed.

As if coming out of a daze, Phoenix glanced around the masculine bedroom, then at Morgan. "Why am I here?"

Placing the suitcase on a padded bench at the foot of the bed, he started toward her. "It's where you belong."

She trembled as his lips found hers, then blazed a trail of heat to the side of her neck. "We need to talk."

His hands went to the hem of her sweater and drew it over her head. "I'm listening." He nipped her on the shoulder.

"Morgan." She shuddered, her legs giving way as his teeth closed over her nipple.

"I'm here, honey." Lifting her, he laid her on the bed and stared into her dazed eyes. "I'm here. I'll always be here."

His mouth, warm and seductive, captured hers again. He undressed her slowly, worshiping every inch of her body with hot kisses and slow hands. He wanted her to think of nothing but the two of them.

Resistance was impossible. Phoenix eagerly returned each erotic kiss, each feverish touch. She couldn't seem to get enough of him or him of her.

He moved over her. She felt the delicious heat and arousing hardness of his muscular body and shivered at the sensations sweeping through her as he began to ease into her. She wanted to suspend the exquisite moment and tell him to hurry at the same time. She moaned his name instead. "Morgan."

"Open your eyes."

With an effort she did, and shivered anew at the fierce passion she saw. "I'll always love you. You and no other." He joined them completely.

She welcomed him. With him she didn't have to hold back. Her legs and arms wrapped around him, drawing him closer. She gave him everything his body demanded. Pleasure swamped her, thrilled her, and finally completed her.

Afterward they lay curled together. "That was indescribable," she said, snuggling closer. "And sneaky."

"I'm a lawyer," he said dryly, stroking her back.

Lifting her head, she stared down at him, loving him so much her heart ached with it. "I love you."

Emotions swirled in his dark eyes. "I wondered if you'd ever get around to saying it."

"From the first moment we met, I knew you would matter to me."

His hand paused on her slim back. "Then why does this sound like good-bye?"

"I have to go."

"No you don't. You're free of Andre," he said.

Her hand tenderly cupped his face. "Thanks to you, but there's one more thing I have to do. I have to know if I can make it as an artist. Once this gets out, people will be even more skeptical about my work."

"You can prove yourself in Santa Fe and be my wife."

How to make such a proud, strong man understand? "I'd be in your shadow just as I was in Andre's," she said, willing him to listen. "It's time for me to try my wings. After seven years I need to know if I have the talent to succeed."

"I don't want you to go."

"But you understand that I have to. Will you call me a cab?"

He stared at her for a long moment, then crushed her to him. "Do you have enough money, a place to stay?"

She nodded. "Cicely's father helped me get a sublease in Manhattan. The foundry will deliver two pieces in the morning. A third should be ready in two weeks. Once I get settled and order supplies, I'll be able to begin work. I want six bronzes for the show."

"If you run short of funds or just need to hear my voice, like I'll need to hear yours, don't think, just call," Morgan told her. She opened her mouth to protest, but he talked over her. "This isn't the time for pride or stubbornness. This is your chance, but it's also ours. The sooner the art world confirms what I already know, the quicker you'll come back to me and we can be married."

"Morgan, my record might be cleared, but it still could jeopardize your political career." She took a deep breath. "I can't do that to you."

He set her away from him until their eyes met; his blazed with fury and determination. "I told you before, no one runs my life. The question is, do you love me?"

She didn't hesitate. "With all my heart and everything I am or hope to be."

"Then that's all that matters." His mouth captured hers in a heated kiss that left them both yearning for more. "What time is your plane out of Albuquerque?"

Caught up in the rapture of the kiss, it took her a few moments to understand the question. She glanced at the clock on the night table. "Three-thirty."

"Two hours. That gives us more than enough time." Instead of pulling her into her arms, he pulled her out of the bed. "Let's get showered and dressed."

Trying not to feel disappointed, she followed without protest. She had to start getting used to the idea that he could never be a permanent part of her life. But why couldn't it have waited until after they'd made love again?

16

"Which one do you like?"

Phoenix knew her mouth was hanging open, had been hanging open since she had entered the posh jewelry store with Morgan and he'd asked the salesman to show him his selection of engagement rings of at least five carats with an eighteen-karat gold or platinum setting. Her heart was beating so loudly she was sure the two elderly ladies who had entered the store behind them could hear it.

"Phoenix?" Morgan prompted.

Sitting on the red velvet-covered stool in front of the case of glittering rings, she closed her mouth and swallowed. But that seemed to create another problem. Tears. How could he do this to her? Offer her what she wanted more than anything? "You know I can't."

"If you want to be on that plane you will."

The inflexible way he spoke had her lifting her head. There was no give in this man. He wouldn't back down or take no for an answer. She clasped her hands together. "Please."

He took her hand, ignoring the clerk, the shoppers. All his attention was centered on her. "Do you love me?"

It was an unfair question and lawyer-tricky. "You already know the answer."

"Then, if you love me, you want to do what's best for me, right?" he asked, his tone reasonable.

Phoenix could see it coming. "That's why I'm leaving."

His gaze never wavered. "So you'd abandon the man you love even though losing you would hurt him more than he could bear."

Tears slipped down her cheeks. "Please let me go."

"As soon as you pick out your engagement ring." He dabbed the moisture from her face with his handkerchief and glanced at his watch. "Ninety-two minutes. Depending on traffic to Albuquerque and how the lines are moving through Security, you might miss your plane."

"What difference does it make if I pick one or not?" she asked, frustrated and angry at the situation. "I'm leaving."

He went down on one knee, touched her cheek with one hand, and held her left hand with his other. "Because every time you look at the ring you'll remember me waiting, loving you."

His words lodged in her heart, making her yearn, but she loved him too much. She tried again. "I can't wear it when I work."

"You have a heavy gold chain, Kent?" he asked without looking away from her.

"Be right back, Morgan."

Out of the corner of her eye she saw the salesclerk jump up from his seat. She finally noticed that several more customers had joined the two elderly ladies. "People are watching."

"What people?" His hands palmed her face. "I see only you. I'll love only you. You and no other."

Her eyes closed. The words were even more beautiful than the first time he'd said them to her. She couldn't help but lean her face into his hand. "I don't want to ruin your life," she whispered.

"Then wear my ring." Lifting her hand, he slid a flawless five-carat emerald-cut diamond surrounded by emeralds onto the third finger of her left hand.

"Morgan," she whispered, looking at him instead of the ring. "Please."

"We'll look at it as a friendship ring if it will make you feel better, but you're not leaving here without it," he said. "If you don't like it, pick another one."

The words were already forming on her lips to tell him she didn't like it until she looked at the ring on her finger, saw her hand lying loosely in his palm, and couldn't. She wanted this too much. "It's beautiful."

"You're beautiful." Gently he kissed her lips, then stood, drawing her to her feet beside him. "I'll settle with you when I get back, Kent. I have to get my special friend to the airport."

"Here's the chain." The grinning clerk handed

Morgan an eighteen-inch gold chain in a long velvet box. "Congratulations on your . . . friendship."

Phoenix bit her lip as Morgan hurried her out of the jewelry store. What had she done?

She should have been stronger. He might think her arrest didn't matter, but it did. What he wanted to accomplish, had already accomplished, with his life and Second Chance was too important to jeopardize.

Once she left Santa Fe she wasn't coming back.

Morgan wasn't surprised to see his mother's 4x4 parked in front of his house when he returned from the airport. Amanda Poole and her mother had followed him into the jewelry store. He didn't care then or now. It had been more important to show Phoenix that he was not letting her walk out of his life.

During the hour drive to the Albuquerque airport she'd alternated between staring at the ring on her finger as if it were someone else's hand and twisting the ring round and round. Knowing she had been through a great deal in the past few hours, Morgan hadn't tried to talk to her. However, the good-bye kiss he'd given her just before she got in line at the security checkpoint definitely said he wasn't going to settle for anything less than total commitment.

The mouthwatering aroma of green-chile stew, one of his favorites, welcomed him home. He supposed the meal was his reward for falling in love as predicted. Only neither of them had foreseen the possibility of a reluctant fiancée.

He found his mother at the stove and kissed her on her unlined cheek. "Hello. Thought you might drop by."

"Hello, Morgan." Ruth slid shredded chicken into the simmering pot on the stove. "I heard you had an interesting afternoon."

Grabbing a glass, he opened the refrigerator. Amanda probably had his mother on speed dial before he and Phoenix were two steps out of the jewelry store. "You want a glass of raspberry tea?"

Ruth folded her arms. "No. I'd rather know why such a persuasive man couldn't talk Phoenix into accepting that diamond as an engagement ring."

Morgan took a sip before answering. "Mrs. Poole always did have good hearing even when I was in her freshman English class at St. John's."

"Now is not the time to be eva—" Ruth began, then frowned and went to him, studying his drawn and tired face. Gently she pried his fingers from the glass and set it on the counter. "Is there anything I can do to help?"

He glanced out the double windows by the kitchen table to the mountains in the distance. "All the way back from the airport I kept telling myself she'll come back, but I can't be sure."

"Let's sit down, and you can tell me how I can help."

Morgan smiled in spite of himself. His mother didn't mind taking her children to task when needed, but she'd fight anyone or anything to keep them happy. He pulled out a chair for her at the oak table, then took the one next to her. He told her everything. She was incensed and angry.

"That's horrible. Poor Phoenix. What she must

have gone through, knowing she was innocent and unable to prove it, then to learn the man she thought helped her was responsible." Ruth's eyes glittered. "The career he coveted is over."

Morgan leaned back in his chair. "Phoenix's has just begun and it's taking her away from me."

"You think she'll choose a career over you?" his mother asked gently.

A sigh drifted past his lips. "It's not her career; it's her past that's standing in the way. She thinks if she married me, someone associated with her case might remember her and jeopardize my political career."

"Reasonable." Ruth propped her arms on the table. "But unnecessary. If she knew you better, she'd know you're your own man."

"Time wasn't on our side." He leaned forward. "Putting a ring on her finger was the only way I could think of to show her how much I love her. Her past doesn't matter. Without her, there is no future for me."

Ruth rested her hand on his tense arm. "Then you'll just have to wear down her resistance. She belongs with you."

Morgan opened his mouth, then narrowed his gaze. "What did you say?"

Ruth stared unflinchingly back. "If you love each other, then she belongs with you."

His mind rushed back to his mother throwing twenty-seven women in Luke's path when it was Catherine, number twenty-eight, whom she had picked out for him. Could Ruth have chosen Phoenix

for him? She *had* been instrumental in bringing Andre to Santa Fe. "I was just thinking. . . ."

"Thinking what?"

Morgan stared into his mother's calm black eyes,
knowing he couldn't read any more than she allowed
him. "You didn't choose Phoenix for me, did you?"

"You chose Phoenix for yourself." Getting up, she
went to the stove and stirred the stew. "What are you
going to do about Duval?"

He could push it, but he wouldn't get anyplace. His
mother could be a sphinx when she wanted. "See that
he knows how it feels when your life is ruined," Morgan answered, his voice harsh. "I plan to be in Seattle
the night of his show. It's my guess he'll cancel at the
last minute. When he does the same thing at the next
show in New York three weeks later, speculations will
run wild with reasons. By then Phoenix should be
ready to have her showing. When people get a close
look at her work, they'll soon realize the similarities.
She's brilliant."

"Can I see the bronze she made for you?"

"I'll get it." Morgan went to his office and returned. "See what I mean?"

His mother didn't say anything, just held out her
hands. She turned the statue over in her hands, let her
fingers sweep from the horse's flaring nostrils to his
haunches. "She's gifted. Her legacy will be powerful."

He stared at the bronze. "But is there a place for
me in her life?"

"If not, you'll make one." She handed him the

statue. "Set the table. Do you plan to visit Phoenix when you go to Duval's show in New York?"

"If not sooner." Morgan placed the bronze on the granite counter, then obtained the black woven place mats and flatware. "Six weeks is a long time."

"You'll need that time to get everything in place to clear her name and for her to have a show."

"You're right." Morgan took a seat beside his mother.

Ruth blessed their food. "The perfect time for Phoenix to have her opening is the night of Duval's second scheduled show. Student and teacher competing against each other will create a buzz."

"He won't show and he won't admit she assisted him." Morgan's grip on his spoon tightened.

"Not willingly, but you won't give him a choice."

Morgan looked at his mother. She was behind him. He hadn't doubted she would be, as would the rest of his family. Duval was going down and Phoenix was going to be his wife. "I'm glad you're on my side."

"Always."

They were halfway through their meal when they were interrupted by someone beating on his door and ringing his doorbell. He and his mother looked at each other.

She smiled knowingly. "It took them longer than I anticipated."

"Is that why you cooked such a big pot of stew?" Morgan asked, getting up.

"I'll set three more places." Rising, she went to the drawer for the place mats.

Morgan ignored his irate siblings. "Three? Brandon will be at the restaurant."

"He will be with Pierce and Sierra." Her smile was pure delight. "I can't wait until they find their own true hearts." She glanced up when he continued to stare at her. "Go answer the door, so we can have a celebration."

Morgan went, but he didn't see what they were going to celebrate. His reluctant fiancée had left him, and his sister and brothers were ready to run him out of town. He opened the door.

Sierra was in front. Black eyes narrowed and snapping, she advanced on him. "I like Phoenix, but I warned you."

"Did you really give her a ring the size of a marble agate?" Pierce asked.

Brandon, hands in his pockets, came in behind them. "I wonder if Mama will take suggestions on the type of woman I'd like."

"Of course I would, but I already know."

Morgan whirled around to see their mother beaming. He'd seen that beam a couple of times before. When Luke returned with Catherine after she'd left. And at their wedding.

"I'm too young to get married." Brandon went to his mother. "Can't you skip me and go to Pierce or Sierra?"

She punched him on the arm. "Coward."

"Survivalist," he countered.

"So, the rumor is true. You're engaged," Pierce said, looking a bit dazed, as if just realizing what that meant. "I think I need to sit down."

"Come into the kitchen. Dinner is ready." Ruth took Sierra and Brandon by the arm. "Morgan, bring Pierce. He looks a lot like the time he did when that investment with Tipton Industries went sour."

Pierce's head came up. "Please, Mama, don't bring that up. I trusted that old geezer, and he conned me and several of my clients."

"But you made full restitution," Morgan reminded him as he steered him into the kitchen. "Everyone was happy."

"Except my bank account." Shaking his head, Pierce took his seat across from Brandon. "After writing each check, I had to down an antacid tablet and a couple of aspirins."

Ruth took the seat Brandon held for her. "You've more than doubled your money and theirs since then. You're brilliant and resourceful."

"Does that mean you'll let me pick my wife in my own time?" Pierce asked.

Everyone's attention in the room centered on Ruth. "Of course."

Pierce didn't relax. There was a catch there, and he was afraid he knew what it was. "It was Luke's and Morgan's time, wasn't it?"

"I just said you were brilliant." She picked up her napkin. "Before you start in on Morgan again, I think he should tell you something about Phoenix. She'd been through a lot."

Morgan did and when he finished, his family was just as angry as he and his mother had been.

Sierra came out of her seat. "Duval gets out of the house tonight."

Pierce and Brandon stood as well. Both had their car keys in their hands.

"I taught you to respect and revere your elders even if they don't deserve it. Now sit down and finish your meal," Ruth said. "But if he's not gone by to-morrow night, I'll drive."

Morgan's sister and brothers erupted into laughter. Everyone took their seat again.

Sierra sobered and asked the question they all wanted to know: "Did you pick Phoenix for Morgan or did it just happen?"

"The answer is so simple I can't believe you didn't think of it yourself." Ruth took a bite of stew.

Her children knew better than to rush her and were always respectful, but Brandon was next on the hit list. "Mother, please."

She laid her spoon aside and beamed at them again. "They picked each other, of course. Just like each of you will when it's your turn."

Sierra looked skyward, Brandon groaned, and Pierce dropped his head into his palm.

Morgan chuckled and dipped into his stew.

She was miserable, but she'd been that way since she'd glimpsed Morgan for the last time at the airport. Now, five hours later, staring out the wide expanse of glass at the sublease apartment on Park Avenue, the misery was like a heavy weight pressing down upon her. She'd never felt more alone.

Her head rested against the cool glass. Coming to New York had been a calculated move. She needed to distance herself from Morgan. She couldn't have stood seeing the disgust in his face again.

Initially she'd made the decision to come to New York because of its reputation in the art industry, although she knew full well the Canyon Road in Santa Fe was just as renowned for its high-powered gallery district. Artists would do anything to have their work shown there. After Morgan asked her to marry him, it had been even more imperative that she leave. The lure in his eyes, the gentleness of his touch, the passion of his kisses and body would have been impossible to resist for long.

"This is for you, my love." Tears pooled in her closed eyes. Her hand clenched and she felt the impression of the unfamiliar ring. Opening her eyes, she stared at the sparkling diamond and emerald ring on her finger.

Morgan had stuck the velvet box containing the chain in her large bag just before she'd gotten in the security checkpoint line. If she was sensible, she'd take the ring off, put it and the chain in an envelope, and mail both back to him.

Phoenix knew she wasn't sensible at all. She could tell herself that she was afraid it would get lost in the mail, tell herself that it would be cruel to return the ring that way, or admit the truth. Even the false sense of belonging to a man as wonderful and caring as Morgan was better than the emptiness she'd feel otherwise.

Straightening, she started toward the bedroom. She might have appreciated the luxury and spaciousness of the apartment done in creamy silks and with modern art at any other time. Now she just wondered if she could go an hour without crying, wondered when the ache would go away.

Flicking on the light of the eighteenth-century French chandelier in the vaulted ceiling, she went to the trunk she'd shipped ahead. The phone rang just as she opened the locks. Her head came up and around. She couldn't stop the leap of her heart that was quickly followed by disappointment. She hadn't given Morgan the phone number.

As the phone rang for what must have been the tenth time, she gave up unpacking. Placing her sweaters in the drawer, she picked up the phone. "Hello."

"Hi, honey. I see you made it safely."

"Morgan!" His voice sent warmth and longing through her. She plopped down on the damask duvet on the king-size cane bed. "How did you find me?"

"Cicely's father gave me the phone number. We both wanted to make sure you were all right. I'll call him as soon as I get off the phone."

She shoved a hand through her hair. She'd been so steeped in her own thoughts and worries that she hadn't thought to call. "No. I'll call. I should have done so already. He did so much for me. The apartment is beautiful and cost me a fraction of what it's worth."

"There's no comparison to what you did for Cicely. She's back in school, not cutting classes, and dating Travis," Morgan said.

"I know. I spoke with her before I left." Phoenix stared at the sparkling ring on her finger again.

"You have a friend for life there. One of many."

Her arm wrapped around her waist. She could have been happy living in Santa Fe, but that was no longer an option. "Yes."

"You got a pen and paper? I need to give you some phone numbers in case you can't reach me. Another litigation case is starting and it promises to be a lengthy one. If you need anything and can't reach me I want you to be able to contact my family."

Her hand paused in reaching for the knob to open the drawer. "Do they know?"

"Yes. I told them tonight. Sierra was ready to put Duval out. Pierce and Brandon were ready to back her up."

There was one other person he hadn't mentioned. "W-what did your mother say?"

"That she'd raised them to respect and revere their elders even if they didn't deserve it and if Duval wasn't gone by tomorrow night, she'd drive them all over there to put him out. Mama can be a tigress when it comes to those she loves. You're included in that number now."

"Because of you?" Phoenix asked.

"Because of you. I showed her *Freedom*. She admires you and your talent. The same goes for me, but I also admire your body and wish I had my hands and mouth on it now. Got that pen and paper handy?"

She had until he'd mentioned his hands on her body. Picking up the pen from the floor, she tried without success not to remember those hands on her body and how they made her come apart. "Ready," she said unsteadily.

Morgan gave her so many numbers she had to turn the pad over. Cell phone, work number, home number, beepers of his immediate family. By the time she had written the last number she realized what he was doing. He didn't want her to think she was alone ever again.

"I told them you like to work during the day so not to call until after six. Any idea what you're going to do next?"

She did have one, but she wasn't ready to tell him. "It's something I've wanted to do for a long time."

"Whatever it is, it will shimmer with life and grace."

"Thank you," she said quietly.

"Well, I'd better let you get unpacked and get some rest. But before I go, you're still wearing my ring?"

I'm sending it back. If she could bring herself to pull it off. "Yes."

"Wish I was wearing you," he said, his voice husky and deep.

She quivered in every cell. "Morgan."

"You'll be back in my arms soon. In the meantime, follow your dream. Believe in yourself and work your behind off. This is *your* chance. Take it."

"I forgot and was feeling sorry for myself," she confessed.

"Well, stop it and plan your other pieces, because when your show is over I'm coming after you."

"Mor—"

"Good night, honey, and dream of me."

The line went dead. Phoenix placed the receiver back in the cradle. Morgan had given her warning, but he had also shaken her out of her desolation. Coming to her feet, she went to the tall windows and drew the silk damask sheers. The brilliance of New York sparkled in front of her.

Dreams here were lost, stolen, destroyed, but they could also be achieved. Morgan was right. This was her chance and she was taking it. And if he came to New York, she was taking him as well.

The next morning Phoenix was at the first gallery on her list, LeNoir. Prestigious and connected to the upper echelon of the art world, the gallery held some of the finest art in the country. If she could get a showing here, it would immediately bring attention to her work.

Her hands flexed on the hobo bag; then she took a deep breath and left the tree-lined street to enter the spacious gallery. Stretched out before her was an array of art in different mediums . . . clay, bronze, wood, metal, paintings . . . all artfully arranged as if they were a part of the room's setting. Every so often, the sleek design of a chair would invite browsers to sit and enjoy and imagine the art in their home. Clever without being intrusive.

"May I help you?" asked an attractive dark-haired woman in a stylish suit the color of fresh lemons.

Phoenix made herself let go of the bag's strap. "Mrs. LeNoir, I'm Phoenix Bannister; we met at the Bonelli estate in Rome a couple of years ago."

"Oh, but of course." She laughed lightly and leaned forward. "I refuse to wear my eyeglasses, but don't tell anyone." She glanced behind Phoenix. "Is Andre in the city with you? I'd love to see him again."

"No, ma'am. I'm no longer with Andre." Before she lost her nerve, Phoenix reached into her purse and pulled out the bronze of the little girl that had been delivered that morning. "This is my piece and I wanted to talk to you about giving me a show."

Twin furrows worked their way across the woman's flawless skin. "Come; let's go into the back."

Phoenix followed Mrs. LeNoir into her large office and took the seat she indicated with a wave of her slim hand on the way to her antique desk. She barely had the eyeglasses on before they were back on her desk. She was no longer smiling. "Are you sure this is your work?"

"Yes." Phoenix swallowed. She'd been afraid of this. "I know it looks similar to Andre's, but it's mine."

Mrs. LeNoir set the piece on the desk. "Please leave."

How to explain the lies, the shame? Out of nowhere came Morgan's voice: *Fight for what you want and don't let anyone stand in your way or tell you you aren't talented enough.* "Mrs. LeNoir, if you'll let me, I can prove it's my work."

"How?" The tone clearly spoke of disinterest and disbelief.

"I'll create another piece. A bust of a man. Strong, intelligent, fierce." She rose, an idea forming as she spoke. "I'll come here to do the work. It will draw attention and buyers."

The woman's thin, aristocratic nose lifted. "LeNoir does not need to pander to anyone for business."

"That's the reason why I came here. If I'm a fraud, I'd be a fool to pick the one place where I would be exposed to the entire art community." Phoenix took a step closer. "It will take me eight hours to do the piece. I can come back in the morning and stay until I finish. One day is all I ask. Please?"

Mrs. LeNoir unfolded her arms. She glanced at the statue again. "If you're trying some scam, you'll regret it. Be here tomorrow at nine sharp."

Phoenix trampled down the wild shout bubbling in her throat. "Yes, ma'am. You won't be sorry." She reached for the statue.

"Leave it. If this is a scam, at least this piece will be out of circulation."

Phoenix stared into the woman's dark eyes. Her decision wasn't debatable. "I'll be back at nine. Please take care of *Innocence*. I only have one other piece."

"Bring it tomorrow."

An order. "Yes, ma'am."

"Please stop addressing me as *ma'am*. I may be a widow, but I'm not much older than you."

Phoenix might have thought Mrs. LeNoir was vain if not for the warmth and unpretentiousness she'd shown her when they'd first met and when she recognized her earlier. "Yes, Mrs. LeNoir."

Phoenix left, going outside and dancing on the sidewalk, causing a group of camera-laden tourists to take a wide berth around her. Then reality hit. She rushed back into the gallery. "Mrs. LeNoir, do you happen to know where I can purchase clay and tools?"

17

Her bottom was numb, her fingers stiff but, after eight long hours, taking only short breaks, the clay bust was finished. She'd begun work in the back under the watchful eye of a security guard she hadn't seen the day before. As the face took shape and the features became more defined, Mrs. LeNoir moved her in front of the window. It seemed she was not above luring customers into the shop after all.

As expected, people came in to watch or stood outside. They'd leave and others would take their place.

Although she was finished, Phoenix couldn't keep her hands off the high cheekbones, the arch of the brow, the supple mouth. Somehow she had managed to capture Morgan's nobility, his fierce pride, his keen intelligence.

"He gave you the ring you wore on your finger yesterday and wear around your neck today while you work?"

Phoenix briefly clutched the ring hanging from the

heavy gold chain before she answered Mrs. LeNoir's question. "Yes." The gallery was now closed and only the two of them remained.

"You love this man?" Mrs. LeNoir asked.

"With all my heart."

The gallery owner walked in front of the bust. "I don't suppose you care to tell me why your and Andre's work are so similar?"

"For now, all I can say is that, as you know, I studied with him for seven years," Phoenix told her. "Andre will explain at his show in Seattle or in New York. If he doesn't, then I'll tell you everything. That is, if you plan to let me show."

"Let you?" Mrs. LeNoir laughed. "Two of my best customers have already made inquiries about your other two pieces and this one."

Phoenix's hand went back to the figure. "I'm sorry, Mrs. LeNoir. I didn't make it clear. *Defender* is not for sale."

Mrs. LeNoir opened her mouth, then closed it. "Call me Alix, and you had better create another piece just as intense."

Phoenix's trembling fingers touched the mouth. "That's impossible. Nothing could compare to him."

The woman threw up her hands and muttered in French about the man's probable sexual prowess.

Phoenix understood and blushed, but she lifted her gaze and said, "All that and so much more."

Alix chuckled. "From the longing in your voice, I suppose he's not in the city. You'll certainly have a reunion when he shows up."

"We certainly will," Phoenix murmured. "We certainly will."

Between the litigation trial and working on clearing Phoenix's name, Morgan kept busy for the next few weeks. He didn't call Phoenix, but his family did. Hearing she was doing well and had a show coming up with one of the most prestigious galleries in New York made him happy on one hand and scared on the other.

If he lost her . . .

Morgan shook his head. He wouldn't allow that to happen. Focusing his attention back on the milling crowd at the Hamilton gallery in Seattle, he looked for Duval. He didn't expect to see him but wasn't taking any chances. Raymond Scott's work was notably absent and unmissed. Morgan had learned he'd gone back to Detroit and was now working in a hardware store, selling paint.

"You were right," Luke said from beside Morgan. "All of Duval's work has a *Not for Sale* sign in front of it, and the gallery manager looks real nervous."

They'd been at the Hamilton gallery for the past hour. "I can't blame him with the press and over a hundred people here already." Morgan glanced at his watch and waved away a waiter with champagne. "Duval likes to make an entrance. We'll give it another thirty to forty minutes; then we'll have a discreet talk with the manager."

"Are you going to call Phoenix?"

Morgan glanced at his sister-in-law, wearing a long black gown and diamonds. Flawless and beautiful, she leaned easily against Luke, who had his arm around her slim waist.

Morgan had gotten used to her being with them as they'd worked on clearing Phoenix's name. In the three weeks since she'd left Santa Fe, they had flown to Austin twice and stayed overnight both times. Catherine had gone with them.

Like their cousins the Falcons and their friends the Taggarts, once married, Catherine and Luke preferred going to sleep in the same bed. Morgan just hoped and prayed he'd have the same opportunity with Phoenix. "As soon as we know."

"She scheduled her show the same night as Duval, as your mother suggested," Catherine continued. "Mrs. LeNoir has held back promoting the event because enough word of mouth was generated from the creation of *Defender*."

Morgan's chest felt tight. Phoenix understood him so well in some ways and in others not at all. "I plan to be there."

"We all do," Luke told him.

Morgan hadn't expected anything less. Family meant love and being there for one another. Soon he hoped Phoenix would be included in that number.

"Could I have your attention, please?" asked a tired-looking middle-aged man in a black tuxedo. "Due to illness, Mr. Duval will not be here tonight and has asked that we not allow any of his work to be sold."

Murmurs of protest came from around the room.

"So it begins," Morgan said. "But not soon enough."

"Phoenix will be all right," Luke told his brother.

"Will she?" Morgan said, his mouth tight. "Let's go talk to the manager."

Tonight was the beginning or the end. Her opening night had finally arrived. Phoenix was so nervous she hadn't been able to eat all day. Neither had she slept the night before. "What if they don't come?"

"They'll come," Alix assured her. "It's another hour before the opening. If you don't calm down, you'll be a nervous wreck by then."

Her arms wrapped around herself, Phoenix paced Alix's plush office. The long black gown she wore graced the sinuous curves of her body. "Believe me, I'm trying."

After a brief knock sounded on the door, it opened. The security guard stuck his head inside. "There's a group of people who say they're friends of Ms. Bannister. The Graysons of New Mexico."

Phoenix's eyes widened. Picking up her skirt, she ran to the front door. He'd come! Turning the lock, she opened the door and was in his arms, his mouth on hers seconds later.

"I guess she missed him," Brandon said with dry amusement.

Phoenix heard Brandon but couldn't seem to let go of Morgan to greet his family properly. She needed to feel his strong arms around her, have his hot mouth devouring hers.

"Welcome to LeNoir. Please come inside," Alix said warmly. "I think it might be a while before they join us."

"Thank you," Ruth said. "I'm Ruth Grayson and these are my children Pierce, Brandon, and Sierra. Morgan will introduce himself later."

After another long moment Morgan was finally able to release Phoenix's mouth, but he continued to hold her. "You didn't think I'd miss your opening, did you?"

She couldn't stop touching him. "Andre's opening is an hour before mine. I thought you'd be *there*."

His kissed her lips. "Luke, Daniel, and their wives are there. It was more important that I be here with you."

"I'm glad you came." She bit her lip. "What if no-body—"

He laid his finger on her lips. "They'll come, and they'll be as stirred by your talent as everyone else who has seen your work." His arms curved around her waist. "It's cold out here. Let's get you inside."

She hadn't noticed. "I want you to see what I've done."

Morgan reached for the door just as a limousine pulled up. The driver hopped out and quickly opened the back door. A middle-aged couple emerged. "Oh, good!" the woman in a ranch mink exclaimed. "They're opening early."

Phoenix glanced at Morgan, unsure of what to do.

"Hello, I'm Morgan Grayson, and this is Phoenix, the artist," Morgan said, introducing them and taking control of the situation as he extended his hand to the elderly gentleman.

"Eustace Powell. This is my wife, Corine," he returned.

Corine's gaze whipped from Phoenix to Morgan. "The bust is of you."

"I haven't seen it yet," Morgan said easily. "We were just about to go in. Would you care to join us?"

"We'd be delighted," she answered. "I can't wait to see the other pieces."

"I'm rather anxious myself." Morgan opened the door. When he spotted the owner coming toward them he said, "Mrs. LeNoir, I think the opening might start a little early."

Morgan soon discovered how right he was. The Powells weren't the only ones who had decided to get a jump on the crowd. In all fairness, Mrs. LeNoir wouldn't accept any bids until the time of the official opening. She'd been crafty enough not to set a price on the six pieces. By eight there was standing room only, and prices for each bronze steadily rose.

Standing in front of his bust with the *Not for Sale* sign, Morgan was as moved as he had been the first time he'd seen it that night. Out of the corner of his eye, he saw Sierra walk over to him.

"After seeing *Defender* and feeling its intensity I know that if you didn't love her, you would after you saw it." She looped her arm through his. "It would have been a shame for the world not to have seen this and her other work. Duval has a lot to answer for."

Morgan's gaze moved to Phoenix, who was surrounded by several admiring people. She was smiling now. The confident woman was never more evident. "Luke and Daniel are on their way over here. Duval was another no-show. He's gone underground."

"Do you plan to let him stay there?"

It was a question Morgan had asked himself when Luke had given him the information a week ago. "Yes. He can't hurt her anymore. She can gradually let it be known that she assisted Duval but then decided to go out on her own. Afterward, all the people who purchased the collaborative pieces will be discreetly contacted to see if they want to sell their work."

"If you need—"

"No." Morgan leaned down and kissed Sierra's cheek. "I have it covered. Thanks, anyway."

"Why aren't you over there with her?"

"Because this is her night," he answered, watching the ebb and flow of people around her.

"Is she going back with us tomorrow?"

"I wish I knew."

"You're a hit, Phoenix!" Alix exclaimed, excitement shimmering in her voice. "Every piece sold for more than expected. The media is clamoring for interviews. You're on your way."

"Yes," Phoenix said, grabbing her small beaded

clutch. The gallery had finally pushed the last person out ten minutes ago. "We'll talk tomorrow."

"Make it late," Alix almost purred. "Pierce is seeing me home."

It hadn't been difficult to miss the sparks flying between the two. "Late it is. Good night." Phoenix had plans of her own. She passed Pierce on the way to the front of the gallery. "Thanks for coming."

"My pleasure, and congratulations again." He hooked his thumb over his shoulder. "Morgan is waiting."

She hurried, then stopped on seeing Morgan by the door, his hands shoved deep into his pockets, his face unsmiling. "What's the matter?"

"We have to talk." Taking her arm, he led her out to one of two black limousines double-parked in front of the gallery and gave the driver her address. He didn't speak again until the driver pulled off. "Your dream has come true. With your talent and Alix behind you, your success is assured."

"Why don't you sound happy about it? If it's because of Andre, don't worry," she said, trying to understand the strange mood Morgan was in. "I'm not worried about him or the coming interviews. I can handle them."

"I know. I watched you tonight." Picking up her left hand, Morgan grazed his thumb over her bare third finger. "This is what concerns me."

The pain in his voice went straight to her heart. "Alix invited the media. I didn't want them asking about the ring."

His gaze flickered briefly to her neck. There was no gold chain. "You did it to protect me," he said flatly.

"Yes," she quickly agreed. "It's already October. You'll have to file to run for the city council position soon. Media attention will follow. But don't worry. In New York we can still be together."

He glanced out the tinted window. "You see me and you don't."

"Morgan, I don't understand."

Slowly he turned to her. "You see me so clearly in your mind, but not in your heart."

Before she could answer, the limo came to a halt. Neither said anything on the elevator ride to the sixteenth floor or the short walk to her apartment. Opening the door, she invited him in. "Can I get you anything?"

"What I want you aren't willing to give."

Tossing her clutch on the antique console table in the wide foyer, Phoenix wound her arms around Morgan's neck. "Wanna bet?"

"You're wrong. Again. I want more than a few hours. I want it all. I won't settle for less." He unwound her arms from around his neck. "When you see me with both your mind and your heart, you know where to find me. Good night, Phoenix, and congratulations. You have everything you wanted."

The door closed, leaving her shaken to the core because she knew he wasn't coming back.

Phoenix didn't even attempt going to bed. Instead she'd changed clothes and gone to the studio she had created in one of the three bedrooms and worked all night and into the early morning on a figure of a man, his back against a tree, his long legs crossed, and a wisp of a smile on his lips. *Morgan.*

His image was so strong that she had felt compelled to do the piece although she knew she'd never sell it, just as she'd never sell the bust. They were all she had left of him.

Her hands clenched. Why couldn't he understand that she was offering all she could?

You see me and you don't.

Coming off the stool, she went to stand by the window. Why did he have to be so noble? She bowed her head. Because that's the way he was. Uncompromising. He wasn't the kind of man to settle.

She couldn't change him, but perhaps she could make him understand. Quickly she went to the phone and called his cell phone and got voice mail. Hanging up, she dialed Information. She paced as she was connected to the Plaza Hotel. "Morgan Grayson, please."

"I'm sorry, miss. Morgan Grayson just checked out."

"Sierra or Ruth Grayson then."

"I'll connect you to their room. Have a pleasant day."

"Hello."

Relief swept through Phoenix when she heard Sierra's voice. "Sierra, I need to talk to Morgan. It's important."

"He and the rest have already left."

Phoenix's hand on the phone clenched. Not only did the Grayson family come to support her, but Daniel Falcon, his wife, Madelyn, and Daniel's parents as well. Morgan's doing. He was such a caring man, but such a stubborn one as well.

"Pierce and I are taking an evening flight. I wanted to get in some shopping, and Pierce is being Pierce," Sierra said with mild annoyance in her voice.

Phoenix paced. If Morgan was in the air his cell phone would be off. "What time will they land?"

"They're in Daniel's private jet and I'm not sure of the flight plan. No matter. I can get you a seat on the commercial flight out with us," Sierra told her. "We can pick you up on the way to the airport."

"I can't go back. I just need to speak to Morgan. Make him understand."

There was a long pause. "Then you're wasting his time and yours. Despite how this irritated the hell out of me at first, Morgan's in love with you. After seeing *Defender,* I know you love him, too."

"It can't work."

"It will. If you really knew Morgan, you'd know that once committed he's there all the way. Other women know that, even if you don't, and you can bet they're going to be trying to catch him on the rebound at the bachelor auction in two weeks," Sierra said. "Alecia Stephens has the hots for Morgan and enough money to outbid every other woman in the room."

"She can't have him!" Phoenix said, outraged.

"Then you had better come and prove it to that brazen woman, because that's exactly what she plans."

"I can't come." Morgan wasn't the only stubborn Grayson.

"Then I guess Quick Hands Alecia gets Morgan. Good-bye, Phoenix."

"Good-bye." Phoenix hung up the phone unable to get the picture of the faceless woman trying to seduce Morgan out of her mind.

Arms folded, Morgan slouched in the chair on the stage. The other chairs were empty. He was the last sacrifice of the evening.

"This is your last chance, ladies, to bid for a bachelor and help the Women's League in the process," Amanda Poole said. "Morgan Grayson, prominent lawyer and community leader."

The hotel ballroom erupted into joyous screams. Morgan wrinkled his mouth. He supposed he should try to look a little enthused, but he couldn't manage it. He hadn't found much to be happy about since he'd left New York two weeks ago.

Phoenix was still there and, as he had predicted and known, she was immensely popular. On one of the many interviews she'd given she'd explained the similarities of her work to Andre's by saying she'd assisted him when he'd been ill, and she'd apologized profusely for not coming forward sooner.

With Alix's backing and that of her well-connected friends, Phoenix's explanation had been accepted without question. Andre's disappearance gave credibility to her statement. In fact, as Alix pointed out when she was interviewed, those who had the collaborative works were in possession of very rare and valuable pieces, since only thirty-one existed in the world. Speculation was running high in the art world as to where the bronzes from the Seattle and New York show had disappeared to.

Morgan had them and all the other pieces, including *Everlasting*, which he kept in his bedroom. The broker who had handled the purchases for Morgan with the private collectors had called a few days ago to say some of the sellers now regretted their hasty decision and wanted to repurchase the bronzes. Not a chance. Morgan was keeping every one. Just like he planned on keeping the woman.

He'd give Phoenix another week and then he was going after her. Maybe he'd tempt her to come back so she could decide if she wanted to keep or sell the bronzes from Duval's aborted openings. If that didn't work, he'd follow his uncle John Henry's method and kidnap her.

"Two hundred dollars!"

"Two-fifty!"

"That's the spirit, ladies," Ruth said from beside Amanda. "Remember, this is for a good cause."

"Three hundred!"

Morgan slouched lower. He'd offered to write out a check to the Women's League, but his mother wouldn't hear of it. He'd been listed as a bachelor months ago.

"Five hundred."

He recognized that voice. Alecia. He'd be fighting her hands off all evening. The only hands he wanted on him were small, delicate, and—

"One thousand dollars."

Morgan shot up in his chair. Standing in the middle of the aisle was Phoenix in the most provocative little white dress he'd ever seen.

"Fifteen hundred!" shouted Alecia.

"Two thousand," was Phoenix's quick comeback, accompanied by a glare at the other woman.

Bounding up from his chair, Morgan politely took the microphone from Amanda just as Alecia called out, "Twenty-five hundred!"

With a glint in her eyes, Sierra moved toward Alecia. He almost felt sorry for the other woman if she opened her mouth again.

"Four thousand," Phoenix said, and started toward Morgan.

A startled yelp came from the direction where Alecia was sitting. She plopped back into her chair.

"Not acceptable," Morgan said into the microphone. His eyes never left Phoenix's face.

Phoenix sighed. "I love you."

Groans sounded all over the room.

"I love you, too, but that's not enough."

Shaking her head, Phoenix walked closer to the stage. "I've been miserable without you."

"Same here." He put his hands on the podium when he wanted to put them on her.

She shook her head. "I'm not neat. I'll drive you crazy."

"He's driving the rest of us crazy since he came back from New York," Sierra shouted as she stood next to a very pained-looking Alecia.

"Come on, Phoenix. You know what I want." Handing the microphone back to Amanda, Morgan came off the stage and started toward Phoenix.

"I can get lost in the studio for hours."

Grinning, he placed his hands on her small waist. "I think I can find a way to remedy that."

"You won't get an argument from me," Phoenix said, her arms sliding around his neck. "There isn't much you can't do."

"Keep going." It was so quiet you could hear a pin drop as people strained to hear each word.

"I finally understand who you are in my head and heart. The man I'll love forever and trust with my heart and everything that I am or hope to be. The defender. You'll go down fighting for those you love. I'm blessed to be in that number." Phoenix glanced around the ballroom. "Sorry, ladies, he's off the market and all mine." Facing Morgan, she held up her hand. The diamond and emerald ring glittered beneath the bright lights. "I accept your proposal. I'll marry you."

"Sold for a lifetime." Ruth grabbed the gavel from Amanda and banged it on the podium.

Epilogue

The official letter arrived from Austin the day after Morgan and Phoenix left for their honeymoon in Florence, Italy. Ruth, who was taking care of their house while they were gone, smiled as she walked inside from the bricked mailbox on the sidewalk.

She'd call the newlyweds later. With the time difference being seven hours, it was three in the morning where they were. But there was one phone call Ruth could make right now.

In the kitchen she picked up the receiver and dialed. The phone was answered on the fifth ring.

"Hello."

Ruth smiled on hearing the sleepiness in her sister-in-law's voice. "Wake up, Felicia; we have more work to do."

"It came." All sleepiness left Felicia's voice. "Her record is clear."

"Yes." Ruth sipped her coffee. She'd learned early in life to always complete one project to her satisfaction before taking on another. "Morgan has filed to run for city councilman. Phoenix's record has been wiped clean. She's in demand all over the country, and has shows scheduled a year out on weekends so Morgan can travel with her. They're so happy. She's probably the first woman in history to receive a thoroughbred as one of her wedding presents. I checked on Crimson and Lady yesterday."

"We did it again." Laughter floated through the phone. "I thought she would be perfect when I met her at Duval's show here."

"You were right. Just as you were about Catherine." Ruth smiled. It was nice when things worked out. "Now it's Brandon's turn, and you know he'll be the most difficult."

"But not for us."

Ruth laughed. "Or her."

"You have her picked already?" Felicia asked, excitement in her voice.

"Yes. Let me tell you about her."

Felicia listened, then said, "I may have to come down to see the fireworks. This is going to be priceless."

Ruth laughed again. "Oh, yes, it will. Brandon is next."